Becoming Tara

Tammy Fournier

www.urbanbooks.net

Urban Books, LLC
78 East Industry Court
Deer Park, NY 11729

ISBN 13: 978-1-60162-281-5
ISBN 10: 1-60162-281-3

First Printing September 2010
Printed in the United States of America

10 9 8 7 6 5 4 3 2 1

Distributed by Kensington Publishing Corp.
Submit Wholesale Orders to:
Kensington Publishing Corp.
C/O Penguin Group (USA) Inc.
Attention: Order Processing
405 Murray Hill Parkway
East Rutherford, NJ 07073-2316
Phone: 1-800-526-0275
Fax: 1-800-227-9604

Becoming Tara

A Novel

By

Tammy Fournier

Dedication

This book is dedicated to the heroes I've lost along the way—those who have inspired me to know that I can live life out loud on my own terms. To my late brother Reginald Dewayne Morgan, I love you and I will always fight for beautiful minds like yours to fly free. I wish I would have spent more time with you before you left us. To my darling late cousin Duncan Eric Nesbitt, my little brother, you've left a legacy of four hand-some, proud black men. I see a part of you in each one of them and you did an outstanding job raising them. I miss you both terribly. I am comforted in knowing that you both are up in heaven smiling down on me, encouraging me to fly. I'm still holding it down for our Buckeyes every Saturday in the fall. O-H-I-O! Give Mommy a hug for me, Morgan. Rick, don't you ask Mama Gracie too many questions your first week with her. We all miss all of you every second of every day. Will one of you please ask Aunt Bootsie for her dinner-roll recipe? The family gatherings will live on, I promise you. Each day I carry you all in my heart. I pray I become the woman you all have empowered me to be. May the peace of God guard our hearts until we are all together again.

*Those things which you have both learned
and received and heard and seen in me do,
and the God of Peace shall be with you.*
—*Philippians 4:7*

ACKNOWLDEGMENTS

As I continue traveling through life's journey, I remain blessed and humbled by God's faithfulness. He just keeps on proving himself to me, and I am empowered by his love. My desire is to become the manifestation of his character, as he uses me for his service. I finally get it: we are blessed each day to be used in service one to another, guiding each other to a higher calling, where there is perfect peace. The best way I can explain it is to say that it is like the peace you feel watching a baby takes its first steps, or the smell of fresh flowers on a spring day, watching the waves on the beach crashing against the shore, Christmas morning at Grandma's (Mama Gracie's) house. . . I could go on but I think you feel me. I spent a lifetime searching for purpose and meaning, and it came in the form of service to my God, my community, my family, and this world, and finally I am complete.

One of life's greatest gifts is true friends: the ones that guide you, comfort you, and tell you what you need to hear, not what you want to hear. They're always there when you need them most. Keith McCormish, Sharon Ware, Lenny Hall, Kim Hairston, Donna Hayden, Sharon Gordon, Weslee Pullen, and Brandy West, I thank you for being my friends and I value your wise counsel.

To my warriors on the battlefield alongside me, don't believe the hype. We are winning our young people back one inspiring mind at a time. Craig Mann, Diana Lee, Shirleen

Acknowledgments

Anderson, my sister Kimberly Castaneda, my brother Pastor Michael Nesbitt, Tei Street, Heidi Yoakom, Nancy Brody, Janet George, Dawn Tyler Lee, Tracy Maxwell Heard, Tamela Collins, W, Shawn Gibbs, and Jerry Saunders: You may never know all the lives that we have touched, but God knows and we will receive a just reward.

Young people across this nation are making commitments to get in the game of life and to make a difference in their own communities. They are empowered by the fact that one man can change the world. We have to thank President Barack Obama for his living example. A few of these game-changers have graced me with their presence working side by side with me in our neighborhoods. Every time I'm with them I believe I can fly. Thank you to my future CEO's: Ashley Price, Sam Briggs, Jason Tyson, Jazimine Lewis, Kate Russell, Rebecca Hairston, and my mentee Malakia Williams. I love you all with my whole heart.

There is no greater joy than getting up every day becoming who you were created to be. I am honored to be of service to these amazing organizations: Revival Development Corporation, the Girl Scouts Heartland Council, Franklin Pre-Release Center, Marion Correctional, Bonds Beyond Bars, *Urban Trendsetters* news magazine, Juvenile Justice Planning Committee Initiative, Franklin Pre-Release Citizen Advisory Board, the Central Ohio Pre-entry Collaborative, the Franklin County Reentry Taskforce, OSU Youth Violence Board, and the United Way of Central Ohio Neighborhood Partnership Center. I am forever humbled by your trust and support.

And to my beautiful family and precious children and grandchildren. I love you and worship God for having you all in my life. To my editor and only daughter Ashley Danielle Price and her sweet friend Sam Briggs, thanks. I love you two wild and crazy, free-spirited young dreamers.

Acknowledgments

To my son Lamarz Deone Price. You are a great man and I am proud of the dad you are. You have a genius son, my Jaden, and a good wife, Donavan. Young love is at its best with you two wonderful parents.

And my eldest, Larry Donnell Price, Jr. You are my sunshine, my only sunshine. I love you and you are a good father. You are so much like your father in so many ways. You are raising three beautiful children. Emmanual, Heaven, and Precious, my Maggie: Nana loves y'all.

Prologue

Lovin' You

Tara's head gently tossed from left to right as the smell of garlic and seafood tickled her nose. She pulled the crisp, white and cobalt-blue bedsheets up over her smooth, chocolate-colored shoulders, feeling so relaxed and peaceful resting in the comfort of her home that she ignored the smell that filled the air. Tara and Julio had been holed-up in their new home for three whole weeks. The young couple couldn't have cared less about leaving their private little paradise. Tara opened her eyes slowly and she immediately focused in on the empty pillow lying neatly next to hers. Her brown eyes began adjusting to the dimly-lit room as she rose from the bed.

The room was neat and clean. She smiled as she smoothed out her long, dark-brown hair and made her way across the room. Tara was a sexy, fine-ass sister. Even without make up she stopped traffic. Julio had obviously gotten up before her and cleaned their bedroom. She knew her man well; whenever he did housework he had something serious on his mind. Tara tiptoed onto the cold, black-and-white tiles on the bathroom floor and quickly moved to the plush rug lying beneath the twin sinks. Quickly, she brushed her teeth, washed her face, and headed downstairs to her sweet baby.

Julio moved around the kitchen very seriously. He had just finished mopping the floor and all he had left to do was to add the vegetables to his fish stew. Julio's papi made fish stew for him all the time when he was a little boy in the Dominican Republic. Every time he ordered what he thought was fish stew at restaurants in Columbus, he was always disappointed, so he decided to make his own. How fuckin' hard could it be? Julio was a real man and a true gangster. He had that sexy, Latin-lover look that made women weak in the knees whenever he walked by. Hookers were always throwing their panties at him, but he was hopelessly devoted to Tara. He promised her, on the day he asked her to be his wife, that he would start backing out of the game, but the streets weren't trying to let him go so easily. It was looking more and more like he was going to have to take his happiness by force.

Although they had been married for a few months, Julio felt like he had just stood in front of the confident, young preacher, who looked like Lionel Richie's little brother, and promised to honor and cherish his beautiful wife until death parted them. It seemed as if the words of the preacher were burned into his soul, and on that day he knew they would be together forever. In the instant Bishop Hairston said, "By the power vested in me, I now pronounce you man and wife," their fates were fused together.

"How you going to leave your baby all alone?" Tara whined, sliding up behind her beloved Julio and softly kissing his bronze-colored neck.

"Hey, mami. Sleeping Beauty finally woke up, huh?" Julio teased, enjoying the gentle kisses of his lover.

Tara molded her body close to the back of her lover and enjoyed his warmth for a long while before she released him. "It's hard to sleep with all this going on," Tara said, making her way over to the stove. Julio was her life; their love comforted her and gave her great peace. In him she found rest. Her life had always been a hustle. She had learned the hustle from her hustling family. Tara was born in the game. She was the heir to street legends, and she reigned like the queen she knew she was destined to be.

"You don't get to see the masterpiece until it's done," Julio said. He delicately grabbed her by the arm and led her away from the kitchen onto the back patio. It was a warm, sunny morning. The heat of the day wrapped itself around the young couple. Tara felt completely safe as Julio sat down in the wicker patio chair and pulled her onto his lap. "I'm making lunch for us. You get to taste *my* cooking. You're going to love it. I'm making my father's fish stew," Julio boasted, rubbing Tara's shoulders as she lay gently in his arms. He could hold her like that forever.

"Fish stew? I never had fish stew. Hell, I never heard of fish stew," Tara laughed, turning up her nose and frowning. Julio smiled at how cute she looked sitting there before him like an innocent child who was being forced to eat vegetables.

"Just try it, it's good. I promise you'll like it. I used to eat it all the time in Monte Cristi when I was a kid. My papi used to make it for me. It was my favorite. The only other place I've had it was at this little Cuban joint in Queens. I'll have to take you there someday. Plus they have the best rum punch." Julio explained as Tara got up from his lap and stretched out on the matching lounge chair next to him.

"How long until we can eat? I'm starving," she asked, rubbing her belly through her Victoria's Secret black and pink T-shirt with matching boy shorts.

The handsome couple was the picture of happiness, enjoying a lazy summer morning on their furnished patio deck. Julio's golden, tanned skin complemented Tara's dark complexion as he sat next to her in his drawstring, silk pajama bottoms. The pair looked like models posing for the cover of some tropical magazine.

Tara gently ran her hands across the soft hair on the back of his thigh as she relaxed.

"You might want to eat something now. The stew won't be ready for a while longer. Want me to bring you some cereal and juice for now?" Julio asked his baby, enjoying the feeling of her hand on his skin. He rose from the chair reluctantly, wanting to stay in the moment but needing to check the stew and add the vegetables.

He could spend every waking moment with Tara. She was his life and he loved her desperately. Julio knew what they had was special. It was rare to find someone who understood a gangster like him, but Tara was cut from the same cloth. She was the daughter of legends: her father was one of the biggest pimps in the game and her mother was one of the Midwest's most infamous boosters.

Julio knew how lucky he was to be with her and he cherished their love. He was willing to do anything to protect it.

"Yes, baby," Tara began placing her order. "Please bring me some cereal, juice, and some toast."

"Yes, ma'am. Coming right up," Julio sang, playfully mimicking a waiter with an attitude. As he entered the kitchen, he could hear Tara humming peacefully just outside the door. He carefully added the mixed vegetables to the rapidly boiling pot of chopped fish on the stove. Then he turned down the heat and stirred the stew in rhythmic, precise circles.

His thoughts were on the conversation he'd just had with his attorney, James Watson, who was a seasoned criminal attorney with a reputation for getting dope boys the best plea deals possible. A niggah knew he stood a chance if Watson was reppin' his case. The only problem was that Julio had been getting deals for years. He got popped over on the eastside a few months back by some punk-ass rookies in the Columbus police department. The soft rookies were so scared of a gangster during their search and seizure that they fucked up their own case and half of the evidence had to be thrown out. If his record wasn't so long he probably could have walked, but the reality was that he was going to have to lay it down for a minute.

Julio was a vet to doing time. He could do it with his eyes closed. In the joint, it was survival of the fittest and he was a heavyweight. He'd survived on the streets in Queens with true soldiers. His only worry was if his marriage would survive the time and space apart from his beloved Tara.

Julio placed the heavy stainless-steel lid on the oversized pot and exited the kitchen. The morning sun blinded him as he reached for his sunglasses resting safety on the top of his head. His low cut, silky black hair framed his face perfectly as he studied his wife who was curled up, fast asleep on the lounge chair. He hated the feeling that swept across his soul. He couldn't shake the feeling that there was danger some-where around the corner for the two of them. Each time he imagined a life without Tara, his heart ached. It pained him to think of being without her. His plan was to spend the rest of his life with her. He knew his love could stand the test of time, but could hers?

"Who are you staring at?" Tara questioned, opening her eyes and stretching her body out on the lounge chair.

"I'm staring at you, sexy," Julio shot back, joining her on the chair and placing her manicured feet in his lap.

Tara sensed something worrying her man, but she wanted to allow him the space to share what was on his mind in his own time. He sat tensely at her feet and all she wanted to do was comfort him. Whatever was on his mind, it was serious. Julio was a smooth operator and most people never saw him sweat, but Tara knew him. She had a gift for sizing a person up from the gate. Her skills kept her making the right moves always. Hell, she'd sat at the feet of hood icons.

"What's up, baby? You look real cute, all serious sitting there," Tara questioned, sitting up and joining him on the edge of the chair. They sat there staring into each others' eyes for what seemed like an eternity. Slowly, tears began running down Tara's face. It pained her to see him that way. Julio watched as the warm tears fell from his baby's face and landed gently on his hairy arms. Neither one of them spoke; their hearts spoke to each other as Julio wiped Tara's tears from her face.

When Julio finally broke the silence, his voiced startled the both of them. "Tara, I need you to be honest with me, okay? Check this, I'm probably going to have to lay it down for a minute and do some time. And I need you to let me know if you can hold it down for a niggah." Julio looked away, bracing himself for her answer. He wasn't new to this; a sister was known for bouncing on a brother when he was out of the rotation. His heart told him that their love would stand the separation, but he couldn't shake the feeling that he was going to lose her to something he couldn't control.

Tara thought long and hard about her answer before she spoke. She loved this man and she wanted to spend her life with him. She was used to telling men whatever they wanted to hear, but she knew she couldn't play that game with Julio—he'd see right through it. Game recognized game and the two were masters. She knew their love demanded her honesty.

"Baby, I love you with my whole heart," she said. "Your love has set me free. I finally know what real love feels like for the first time. And I never want to hurt you. I promise you I will love you for the rest of my life. That's bank. I've never had to do no shit like hold it down for my man on lockdown. I don't know what that's like, but I know your love is a part of me. As long as there is breath in my body, I'll fight to find my way back to you." Tara turned toward him and kissed his lips.

Julio breathed in her breath with each wet kiss. Her words calmed him and he believed them. The love they shared ran deep, and he knew it was real each time she was in his arms. They were connected on a higher level and that was why he made her his wife. He was tired of the negative energy he'd experienced in his past. Now he was with his sexy wife in their lovely home and life was good.

Tara's eyes quickly dried as Julio slipped his hand inside of her shorts. She lay back on the lounge chair and her legs fell freely to her side, allowing him access to what he craved. He was addicted to her; he wanted her desperately.

Her pink and green panties, intertwined in her shorts, landed in a heap on the patio floor, as Julio buried his head between her legs. He kissed her thighs hungrily, as if they were made just for him, before making his way to his main course. Tara moaned with pleasure, enjoying his touch. She wasn't really sure if the cherry-blossom trees blocked their patio from the view of their college-student neighbors. But the danger of their public sex excited her.

Julio was a beast in the sheets. He knew just how to make her body scream. The fire between her legs grew wilder. Before she could control the flames, she came. Julio felt her orgasm pulsating through her body. She cried out his name as he quickly ripped off his pants and climbed on top of her. He cried out once his rock-hard dick found its home. He was where he belonged and he never wanted to leave. Julio kissed her soft lips as he rode her. The look in her eyes told him all he needed to know. She loved him and that shit turned him on. He looked into her eyes as he whispered in her ear, "I'm going to love you for life. You're the reason I live." When he excitedly came deep inside her, they both were at peace.

Chapter One

Months passed and the young couple lived out their fairytale dream life together. It was as if the streets understood a gangster needed some downtime. The pair was naturally comfortable with each other. From the day they met they were inseparable. Julio could not get enough of his beloved Tara. Wherever he was, at any given moment, his bride was always with him. Their love was all-consuming. They craved each other constantly. For the first few months of their marriage, things had been falling into place swell. Julio's strategic, five-year plan for retiring from the game was falling into place rapidly. He arrived in Columbus focused, with one goal in mind: stacking paper. The all-American Midwestern city was ideal. It was a college town bursting with potential. The college kids kept a motherfucker with a steady flow of customers. The liberal, hopeful, bright-eyed young people stayed high and Julio stayed paid.

The Ohio State University was located in the heart of town. It was surrounded by some of the richest communities in the country. An added bonus was the fact that the state's capitol was within walking distance of the university. Columbus, Ohio, was just a friendly, happy place to kick back and enjoy the scenery.

High Street stretched from one end of the city to the other. Julio enjoyed cruising down the busy street enjoying the sights and sounds of the day. Watching people go about their daily lives with purpose calmed him. He always paid close attention to the white women, especially the ones who seemed to be carefree, walking about their daily lives, not a worry in the world. Sometimes he'd watch as they joined some lucky bastard for some personal appointment or meeting. He always studied their faces. He could always read a person's face, even as a child. The truth was in the eyes; they never lied to you. All he ever needed in order to stay one step ahead of the next niggah was to read what his eyes were saying—or, better yet, not saying.

Fall was settling in across the city. The kids were back in school. The Ohio State Buckeyes were 10-0 and they had just beaten Michigan in a decisive, impressive win that afternoon in the college stadium known as the Shoe. The rivalry game was important to everyone in town. True Buckeye fans anticipated a win every year, and it was rare that they were disappointed. They expected to win every time the team took the field. People in Columbus loved their team. When Ohio State won, the entire city partied until the wheels fell off. The Buckeyes were headed to the national championship and the whole town was going crazy. Niggahs was getting high and celebrating in every neighborhood.

Everybody in Columbus was in a good mood. Through the open windows on his ride, Julio could hear people yelling "O-H-I-O" to each other in passing. The unofficial Buckeye greeting was known to all. It could get a conversation going in a New York minute. The hard-ass gangster loved that shit. The first week he arrived in Columbus, a red-haired cute-ass white girl yelled that shit at him and he almost pissed his pants.

The cutie damn near kissed his ass right in the middle of a small Iranian corner store in the Short North. She'd been watching the last five minutes of a nail-biter. The Buckeyes' star running back had just ran a kick-off return all the way back for over a hundred yards to win the game. The stadium and the whole city erupted at the same time. It was a typical Saturday afternoon in the fall in Columbus.

"Life is good," Julio said to himself, smiling, and looked over at his lovely wife. Tara sat lazily in her cushioned leather seat, her head bounced in time to the beat of the music playing on the car stereo. The sun shined through the window and its rays lit up her face. She looked like a goddess sitting there beside him as she put her favorite sticky lip gloss on her full lips.

"What you looking at, sexy? You don't want none of this," Tara purred, licking her lips as she closed the visor over the dashboard.

Julio reached over and slid his hand between her thick thighs. He felt her hips rise to meet his touch. He loved that shit. His baby was always ready. She knew how to please him. A confident woman was a turn-on for a gangster. He was used to being in charge, making all the decisions, but he enjoyed kicking back and letting Tara call the shots sometimes.

"Hey, why are you turning this way?" Tara questioned, watching Julio pull the car off of the main street. She wanted to go downtown to pick up some stockings at the mall then run over to German Village and stop at the Thurman Café to grab something to eat. She already knew what she wanted and she was anxious to get a hot fish sandwich in front of herself.

"Don't worry. I'm going to get you to your fish sandwich soon. I have to run by Candy's house and drop her some ends for Francisca. It won't take long. After that you can run the show, all right?" Julio waited for her answer out of respect for her thoughts—not because he would be swayed by her reaction.

"That's fine, baby, just hurry up, please. I'm really hungry and you know niggahs going to be acting crazy in the hood and shit. I bet the traffic is slow as hell down Main Street," Tara warned, sitting back in her seat to prepare for the drama. It was the weekend and an OSU football game day too. People had been drinking before, during, and after the game. Boys in the hood loved their Buckeyes. It would be thick in the streets.

Just as Tara expected, the hood was alive with activity. Black folks celebrated their team's victory with the rest of the city. Groups of people were hanging outside of storefronts just to hang out and enjoy the fellowship. The OSU game was topic of most conversations. Average people from all over town sounded like commentators as they recalled the plays.

Each time their car stopped at a traffic light Tara could hear bits and pieces of the lively conversations. By the time they reached Main and Wilson, traffic had come to a complete stop. Cars were bumper to bumper up and down the street on both sides.

"What the fuck this niggah lookin' at?" Julio questioned, staring out of Tara's window into the car idling beside them. A trickedout, old-school Chevy with tinted windows was hemmed up beside them. The driver's window was halfway down. Julio could see the top of the heads of about four or five young bucks inside the car. They all starred thirstily into his window at Tara. The driver undressed her with his eyes. He licked his thick, ashy lips and grinned. Julio reached under his seat, pulled out his gun so the driver could see it and placed it in his lap. The look on his face said it all.

The driver of the Chevy pulled his car as close to the bumper of the car in front of him as possible and quickly turned down the next side street. Tara quietly placed her hand over her man's hand to calm his quick temper.

Tara was used to the flirting of other men. She enjoyed the constant attention, but it drove her husband crazy. He took it as a sign of disrespect when he was with his woman. It was considered a call to battle in his culture.

The traffic began to move again slowly. Julio regretted his decision to go to the hood the minute he turned onto Main Street. It had been a good day. He was with his wife and he didn't need the problems of the streets. Not today. Not to mention he was alone with his girl. He never went to the battlefield without his soldiers for backup. You had to roll deep in the streets. It was a war zone and you had to stay ready for battle.The excitement of the football game had him slipping.

When he finally reached Wilson Avenue, he let out a sigh of relief because he wanted to get in and out of Candy's house quickly. The residential street was just as alive as the main streets. Brothers and sisters were everywhere, up and down the street. Kids ran around in the street and in and out of yards freely. Meanwhile, teenagers hugged the corners, flirting with each other and talking shit.

Julio pulled his car in front of Candy's house and put the car in park. "I'm just going to drop this money off and then we're going to eat. Okay, baby?" Julio told Tara, leaning over the seat. He kissed her sweet lips before she could say a word. She kissed him back passionately. When he was caught up in the moment completely, she pushed him away.

"Now hurry up before I miss you too much," Tara teased, pushing her baby away from her. Julio laughed playfully and leapt from his Range Rover. His girl had a way of making everything all right. Just minutes ago, he was ready to lay a motherfucker down. Now all he was thinking about was waxing that ass when he got her home. Julio walked up to Candy's front door and walked in without knocking.

Tara turned the music on the CD player up. The smooth, silk sounds of Jodeci blasted from the speakers and filled the car. *"Last night, I wrote a short letter and it went this waaaay,"*

Tara sang along with the music and dreamed of the things she planned to do to her lover once they got home. She couldn't wait to be back in bed with him.

Suddenly, noise could be heard above the music in the car. Tara looked up to see two girls come from the back of one of the large Victorian-style houses on the corner. Both of the girls were dressed to kill. Tara could hear them talking about some club they were going to where the drinks were watered down but two for one. "Fuck the drinks. All I want is some good dick!" the taller girl yelled into the air as they got into their car. Tara watched as their taillights disappeared down the street.

When Tara turned to the stereo to skip to another track, she knocked over her purse and its contents spilled out onto the floor of the car. She bent over and started picking up her belongings and putting them back inside her purse. Then she noticed her wallet. Tara quickly opened it and searched inside for her pick-me-up.

The folded-up dollar bill was all the way at the bottom of Tara's purse when she finally found it. She carefully unfolded the crisp dollar bill and the crystal-like power sparkled back up at her. She could have sworn she heard it call her name.

With her fingernail, she lifted the powder from the dollar bill and quickly sniffed the drug into her nostril. She repeated the action again before refolding the dollar bill. Before she could put it back into her wallet, it seemed to call her again.

The second time, she unfolded just a small corner of the dollar bill. She snorted a little more of the powder, licked the tip of her finger, and dipped her it into the powder. Tara then rubbed the wet cocaine across her teeth and licked her lips.

The rush paralyzed her for a minute. She laughed to herself as the pure, Peruvian flake cocaine drained down her throat. She was high as hell. The music, along with the drug, lifted her and took her to another place. She loved this new toy Julio hipped her to. It made her feel alive and oh-so-sexy. "Come on, Julio," she muttered, looking at the door to Candy's house. "What the hell is taking him so long?"

She didn't even want to go eat anymore. All she wanted to do was go home and climb into bed with her baby. The street had gotten quieter in the last few minutes. She could still hear a few loud voices in the distance but not as many as when they first arrived.

Something shiny glistened from the floor of the car up at her. Tara bent down to see what it was. Just then, loud shouting could be heard coming from Candy's porch. Julio and Candy were on the porch, having a heated argument. Tara could not make out what they were saying but their body language spoke volumes. Every time Julio walked away to leave the heated exchange, Candy jumped in front of him.

Candy was Julio's baby's mama. She was a thick, light-skinned scrapper, and wherever she went bitches respected the work Candy put in on the street. She was known for being a valued solider on anybody's team. The neighborhood dope boys loved and respected Candy. She knew a little something about all things pertaining to hustling in the city of Columbus. Candy could literally tell you where every trap house was on the eastside.

When Julio first arrived in the city he was quickly introduced to Candy. It wasn't long before the two were trusted business partners. But Julio soon discovered the man-eater had other plans for their relationship. He made the mistake of getting between the sheets with her. After that, taking over and stacking paper went out the window once Candy embarked on a course to bag the kingpin for herself. She was convinced her plans were working until Tara arrived on the scene. All Candy's hard work was derailed once Tara got all up in the mix.

Julio was blindsided by Candy's rage when he arrived to drop off money for his daughter. He knew she had issues with his relationship with Tara, but the way he saw it, Tara was off limits to her. He never discussed any part of their lives with Candy. He took excellent care of their daughter Franni and he made sure they had everything they needed. Candy wanted for nothing.

The timing of his visit was all wrong. During Candy's Michigan game party, a chickenhead from up north announced to everyone that Julio and Tara had gotten married. The chicken- head knew the news would get the party going for sure. Candy didn't disappoint either. She flew into a rage. Candy was in full swing when Julio pulled the front door open, surprising the already frightened guests.

At first, Julio tried to explain his reasons for not telling Candy the news sooner, but the more he tried to explain the more angry Candy became. He finally gave up and left. He wasn't prepared for Candy to follow him outside.

Domestic violence was not in Julio's DNA and Candy knew it, so she pushed back hard against all of Julio's attempts to defuse the heated exchange.

"Candy, yo' ass is trippin like crazy. I came through because you led me to believe you needed some punk-ass money right this very minute. I shoulda known it was just another one of your fucking games. I been trying not to hurt your feelings with shit I know you don't want to face, but this shit is going to stop today. Since you want to know every fuckin' thing, here it goes. Tara is the love of my life, okay? We are going to be together forever, whether you like it or not. I will be a damn good father to my daughter always. We do not have any other business other than Franni. Now back the fuck up *now!*" Julio yelled out the last part of his statement for the entire world to hear. He was done with the madness. The weary gangster stepped from the porch leaving Candy standing alone with her anger.

Tara sat in the car glued to the show on the front porch. She was prepared for the argument to spill out into the street. At one point she almost got out of the car and joined Julio on the porch but she was sure he did not want her to get involved in the struggles between him and the mother of his child.

As a woman, Tara understood Candy's anger. She would have probably done the same thing if the shoe was on the other foot. Julio was a catch. The whole city knew that. Nobody expected Candy to just roll over without a fight. Tara cursed Julio's decision to come to the hood. For weeks she'd been getting weird feelings every time she rode through the ghetto. She felt as if the streets were sitting back waiting to swallow her whole. No matter how hard she tried she could not shake that feeling.

"That crazy-ass bitch ain't going to be happy until I catch a case. Please, don't even say nothing, Tara. Not one thing, please," Julio snapped angrily at Tara, slamming the car door. He threw the car into drive and burned rubber pulling from the curb.

"Oh, hell no. Don't even try blaming that shit on me. I wasn't the one who decided to come by the circus on the way to dinner. You did," Tara shot back, mad as hell.

Dinner plans flew out the window with the air that blew through Tara's long black hair. You could cut the tension with a knife as the lovers sat side by side in silence in the small space. What was really fucked up was they both were hungry as a motherfucker.

"I fuckin' told you to open this damn door, girl. Yo' ass always trippin'!" Julio yelled through the closed bedroom door at his wife. The young couple had been arguing all night long. The fight started earlier in the evening at the club. "What the fuck is wrong with you, Tara? How the fuck you gonna take off your fuckin' wedding rings and leave them on the bar like that shit ain't nothing?" Julio demanded to know for the third time that night. He was mad as hell at his hot-headed wife. He knew when he met her that very first night that she was a baby gangster. He just didn't know until recently just how big a gangster his boo really was. She had no problem going toe-to-toe with her love struck husband.

"How the fuck you gonna let a bitch be all up in your face like that shit ain't nothing?" Tara shouted through the heavy bedroom door. She was mad as hell too. She was sick of being disrespected by all the chickenheads that were always all up in her man's grill. Grant it, Julio was a fine-ass motherfucker and all, but he was *her* fine-ass motherfucker. She had to constantly let a bitch know to back off.

The thirsty bitches were always up in her man's face. This was a blatant sign off disrespect in Tara's eyes. She refused to be disrespected by anybody especially not by some nobody bitches. She wanted the hoes to know she didn't play.

Looking at herself in the mirror, Tara shook her head. She couldn't figure out why she was always letting her temper get the best of her. She wanted everything her way and she always had to be right. She knew deep inside that Julio loved her with all his heart, but the constant drug use had her thinking crazy thoughts. When she was thinking sanely, she knew beyond a doubt how much Julio was in love with her.

Theirs was a once-in-a-lifetime love. They came into each others' lives at the perfect time. He completed her and she adored him for it. When he touched her, time stood still. Nothing mattered. They were the only two people on the planet. There were days when she lost track of time just being with him. He was her everything—all she ever wanted.

I love him so much, Tara thought, pacing around the spacious master bathroom. She was tired of fighting with her baby. She wanted to make up. Walking slowly to the wooden bathroom door, she listened for her lover. No sounds came from the other side of the door. She listened longer and she could hear faint salsa music playing in the distance. The upbeat, happy music calmed her as she started to dance in front of the full-length mirror on the back of the bedroom door.

Julio had moved from the door. She figured he had finally realized how wrong he was for letting that little chickenhead be all up in his face when she arrived at the club earlier in the evening. All she wanted now was to put their silly fight behind her and call it a night. If things went her way she would crawl into bed with her lover and make sweet love to him until the sun came up.

A warm, calming feeling swept across her soul as her body longed for his touch. She physically shook at the thought of his hands on her skin. She needed to be with him immediately. Her body craved him and she began moving around the room with a purpose.

Before heading downstairs, she washed her face, brushed her hair, reached into her makeup dish on the rose-colored marble counter and retrieved her **M•A•C** glass lip gloss. Tara applied the shiny lip gloss to her lips and checked her hair before exiting the bathroom.

Julio paced around his sunken living room. His Italian leather shoes disappeared into the carpet with each determined step. He was salty. Tara's ass was too much. She had him so mad he was ready to break some heads. This shit had gone way too far.

Suddenly, Julio felt a presence in the room. He turned

around to see Tara approaching him. Before he could open his mouth to speak, she jumped up and smacked him. Julio pulled back his hand to smack her back when his telephone rang. The two froze in place and stared into each others' eyes. They both instantly realized they had taken the argument too far. Julio snapped from the dark place he'd allowed his anger to take him as his phone rang a second time. He was heated with himself for being two seconds away for smacking her back. He couldn't believe he'd let the madness of the streets follow them home.

Julio turned away from Tara and picked up the phone. "Hello? Carlito? Where the fuck are you? You said you'd be here in half an hour," Julio said. The tone of his voice made it obvious that he had no patience left.

"I'm pulling up now. Had to drop in on a bitch real quick," Carlito replied. "What's goin' on? You sound like shit."

"Hurry up," Julio said and abruptly hung up the phone.

Carlito was an old-school, *Scarface*-loving Hispanic hustler with way too much swagger. The young primo stayed in trouble about a bitch. Lately, Julio had to remind him far too often who was boss. Carlito was loyal but he made foolish mistakes over girls all the time.

"Where are you going?" she questioned, standing barefoot before him and staring up into his eyes. She knew he was leaving to clear his head, but she didn't want him to go, so she stalled by asking a question. She hoped he would just let the shit slide and come back upstairs with her. She was so sorry.

Once again, her anger had gotten in the way of her heart. Her man looked sexy as hell standing there. She wanted nothing more than to hold him, kiss him, and tell him she was sorry for all the madness.

Her eyes begged him to stay and he wanted to give in to her but he had to teach her a lesson the hard way. *Her cute ass is getting out of hand*, he thought to himself as he walked out of the house without saying another word. It pained him to close the door on his queen, but he was also a king. If he was going to reign with dignity and respect, then he would have to rule with the utmost authority, both in the streets and at home. As the weary kingpin stepped off his clean, neat front porch, he thought he heard her calling out his name. A cold chill swept across his body as he walked away from the house and got into Carlito's car.

Carlito held a lit blunt up to Julio. He took it without looking and hit it hard. He then leaned back in the comfortable passenger's seat and relaxed for a moment, glad to be away from ground zero. His beautiful home faded in the distance as his mind remembered the cold chill from before. He pushed the thought out of his mind and thought of his wife again.

"You forget an anniversary or something?" Carlito laughed, trying to lighten the mood. He could tell things were heated with Tara and Julio the moment he entered the car.

Julio passed the blunt back to Carlito. "She's trippin'. I had to get the fuck outta there," Julio said, and then he reached into his pocket, removed his pager, and quickly checked it. "Man, do you know she smacked me? That shit stung like a motherfucker too. Little mami packing a mean right hook. I think my shit gonna be swollen tomorrow," Julio said, looking in the mirror on the sun visor and rubbing his cheek for emphasis.

As Carlito relit the fading flame of the joint, his cellular phone rang. "*Hola?*" Carlito answered.

Roberto spoke smoothly into the line. "*Hola*, Carlito. *Que pasa?*"

"You know how it is. Same shit, different day."

"*Sí, sí.* Where you at?"

"On my way. I had to roll up to the suburbs and pick up Julio." Julio looked up at Carlito again.

"Julio? Man, why you got Julio wit' you?" Roberto asked with a little nervousness in his tone.

"Julio and Tara goin' through some shit. He had me get him up out of there."

"So, you droppin' him off somewhere or he rollin' with you?" Roberto questioned.

Passing back to Julio, who was now rechecking his pager, Carlito said, "Nah, man, we headed that way now. See you in a few. Peace." He hung up the cell phone.

"What was that shit about?" Julio said, sitting up in his seat.

"Roberto just got back from up top with my shit. Told me earlier he wants some product. Got his money straight so he payin' up front this time," Carlito said before speeding through an intersection.

"Whatever," Julio muttered. He didn't care where they were going, as long as he was out of the house and able to think clearly again.

Tara fell to the floor and burst into tears. She lay there wishing she knew when to put the brakes on with her temper. She was always backing herself into a corner because she never wanted to back down. She'd learned that shit from her parents and running in the streets. You had to win by any means necessary. Keep fighting was the rules she'd been taught. Why couldn't she just trust his love?

Tara lifted herself from the floor and dragged herself up the stairs after laying there for over an hour. She cried all the way up to her bedroom. She looked around the room for her purse, grabbed it from the dresser, and fished out her phone. She hoped he'd called her to say he was coming home.

There were no missed calls. The house phone hadn't rung either, so Tara crawled in bed and tried going to sleep. She wasn't so lucky. After two hours of tossing and turning, she reached for the remote control and began searching the channels. Thinking of Julio, she fought back her tears.

Chapter Two

Carlito's car pulled into the far end of the Swifty Mart convenience store. The headlights shut off but the engine kept running. Watching the Escalade, Black lowered his sun visor and killed his headlights. A few seconds later, he watched Julio get out of the passenger's side and go into the convenience store. As Julio pushed through the store's front door, Roberto pulled into the parking lot and parked next to the Escalade. Roberto got out of his car, walked to the passenger's side of Carlito's ride, and jumped in.

Inside of the Swifty Mart, Julio stalked the freezer aisle looking for his girl's favorite drink. Even though Tara could get under his skin, she was the Bonnie to his Clyde. He knew she had a temper when he met her. It would take more than some bull shit arguing to change his feelings. He walked over to the wine coolers section but the doors were blocked by a pair of chickenheads. One was wearing cut off Daisy Dukes, a brightly colored halter top and a gold chain. The other reeked of hairspray and her tits were spilling out of her shirt, exposing a tattoo of a rose. When Julio approached, the girls looked him up and down and smiled.

"What's up, papi?" the first purred, showing that she was missing one of her front teeth. Julio ignored them and went straight for the door handle. The taller of the two girls stepped out of the way and continued to watch his every move. "A sista would love to get wit' a playa like you. I can give a brother something he can feel."

The other girl giggled flirtatiously. Julio reached into the freezer, pulled out two cases of Jack Daniel's coolers, and shut the door. He turned to the girls, said, "I'm straight on that. I got a wife," and started toward the checkout counter. The girls watched him pass then went on with their conversation.

Out in the Escalade, Carlito and Roberto made small talk while Roberto put an envelope of Benjamins into the glove compartment. Carlito reached under his seat, retrieved a small duffel bag, and tossed it onto Roberto's lap. "We're straight now?"

"Yeah," Carlito nodded. "Hit me up if you need to holla at me later." Looking over at Roberto, Carlito noticed Roberto's expression change, even in the dark. Just as Carlito sensed uneasiness in Roberto's look, a swarm of officers surrounded the car, including the DEA, FBI, Immigration, and Columbus police. Roberto jumped out of the car. "Motherfucker," Carlito shouted and hit the steering wheel.

At the cash register of the Swifty Mart, Julio dropped a twenty onto the counter. He looked over the impulse items, grabbed a pack of gum, and laid it by the coolers. He'd been getting high all day and smoking all night and he planned on having Carlito drop him off back at home right after he had a few words with his boy. He didn't like the fact that he'd been brought to his little business meeting with Roberto.

He hadn't seen Roberto in a minute. Motherfuckers had been looking for him for weeks. Everybody knew that Carlito was fucking Roberto's woman. Everybody except Roberto. It was just a matter of time before the shit was going to hit the fan. The Latin lovers had built a dynasty together and now they were throwing it all away for some pussy. The crazy shit about the whole thing was the tender-ass freak they both were chasing wasn't serious about either one of them. The strawberry was simply gold-digging and the two gangsters couldn't even see it because they were thinking with their dicks.

The hot-ass trick had even thrown her panties at Julio a few times on some freaky shit, but he wasn't on that shit. Plus he knew Tara wasn't having it. He'd thought about a wild-ass freak party with the three of them but that was before he'd fallen in love. His marriage and his wedding vows meant way too much for him to bring all the madness of his bachelor days into his marriage. All he wanted was to get back home to his baby. He'd left her hurting and he needed to comfort her. It pained him to know she was home missing him. He would make up for everything once he was home. He needed to get back to her. He could feel her body calling him.

"Shit," he heard someone behind him say. He turned around and saw that the man standing behind him was looking outside toward the parking lot. Julio followed his gaze and saw a posse of cops covering Carlito's car. Four suits were running toward the front doors of the store. Julio took a deep breath, stood his ground, and waited for the apprehension. He slowly turned around as the undercover agent pointed his weapon in Julio's face.

Across town, Tara woke from her sleep with the television still on. Hours had passed. She quickly checked her phone. There still were no calls from Julio, and she was beginning to worry. Her gut told her something was terribly wrong. She called his phone back to back for over an hour and he didn't answered. Something was really wrong. It was more than just the heated argument they'd had earlier. This was something much more. She felt as if the distance between them was growing larger with each passing second. Julio was out there somewhere and she felt strongly that he was in danger. He needed her. It was as if, somewhere in the distance, she could her him calling out her name.

Chapter Three

Julio was arrested that night and held without bail on federal drug-trafficking charges. If a person didn't know better, you would have thought they were arresting America's Most Wanted. Law enforcement showed up in full force. The DEA, U.S. Immigration, and Columbus's finest all played a role in taking down the infamous Dominican kingpins. For months they paraded the trio of drug dealers before judges and magistrates in every jurisdiction in the State of Ohio. The kingpins were charged with drug conspiracy, which carried life sentences if they were convicted. The side-show stretched on for over a year, and the stress of it all took a heavy toll on Tara. The sadness and loss of it all became her new world. The emotional roller coast she lived on began destroying her life. Her pain drove all her decisions,

During the first few months, her lifelong friend Karen rode the roller coaster with her. The minute Tara found out that Julio was arrested, Karen rushed to her dear friend's side. Karen was a warrior in her own right. She had known Tara most of her life. The two friends trusted each other and had each other's back. Karen practically had to spoonfeed Tara during those first few weeks.

Before long the friends were back to their old tricks. Boosting stolen clothes from the best stores in town was their claim to fame. They settled back into it with natural ease. The only problem was their growing addiction to crack cocaine. Between the drugs and Tara's sadness over Julio, the two quickly drifted apart.

For a while Tara was able to keep up her weekly visits to Julio at the county jail in downtown Columbus, but the controlling sheriffs decided out of the blue to move all of the federal prisoners out. They were packed up and transported to the Pickaway County jail, an hour away. The sparkly-clean jail was newly built, with lots of room for the heavily guarded drug dealers. The longer they were held in local confinement the bigger flight risk they became in Columbus. The city didn't house federal prisoners in a federal facility; that was left to the county.

Due to Julio's many connections, attempts were made for him to be released on bond on several occasions but every time he was given a bond another jurisdiction blocked his release.

Tara spent so much time running back and forth to court, jail visits, and to attorney appointments, that it literally sickened her. Everybody wanted a piece of Julio. The feds wanted him to pay for his crimes against the U.S. government, and his attorneys wanted their piece as well. Everytime she turned around they were asking her for money for one thing or another. She was dropping thousands of dollars on them like it was nothing. Of course, nobody in the crooked government ever asked where Tara got the money to pay their outrageous fees. All that mattered was that they got their money.

The visits were the worst. Tara hated everything about them. She suffered through them as long as she could. They were killing her. In order to get through them, she'd get high as hell the night before. Once she was high enough, she'd cry all night from the pain of losing her darling Julio. By morning she would be in a panic because she had not been to sleep and she looked like hell. This would cause her to spend hours trying to look her best before she left for the hour-long drive out to cow town. The drive ran straight through the heart of small-town USA in Ohio. Tara always felt uncomfortable driving through the country. The white people she encountered always stared at her as if she was an alien whenever she had to stop for anything. She worried that if ever something happened on her trip, she would never be heard from again.

When Julio was arrested, the business-smart drug dealer and his bride managed to have a nice bank-roll stashed for their retirement from the game, but at the rate the people who keep him from her had their hand in her face for large sums, Tara was slowly going broke.

With much regret, she began boosting clothes every day to pay lawyer fees and to support her growing drug addiction. By the time she graduated to crack cocaine she was happy as hell. The drug was cheap and she stayed high longer. She never thought much about the addiction part. She was grateful for the drug because it eased the pain of it all. Her new home was the Cross Country Inn on Dublin-Granville Road. It provided a safe, private place where she could be alone with her pain.

Her life consisted of crying over Julio, going to see Julio, surviving for Julio, and getting high as a motherfucking kite over Julio, every single, solitary day. She was a professional Julio worshiper. She worshiped all things him. Her nights were drug-induced one-woman parties in his memory. As the months slipped by, her love for the man got intertwined with her love for her precious crack. Her crack was easily accessible, it held her close every night and it never judged her.

The rock became her everything and soon her love for Julio got put in a box on a shelf in the secret parts of Tara's heart. That love hurt too much and she could no longer face it or him. The last time she'd gone to visit him he hurt her to her core.

After waiting in the usual long-ass line at the county jail, she finally made it to the visiting room. She was confident she looked fine as hell. She knew once Julio saw her he would forget he was mad at her for not coming to visit. She hoped he didn't start bitching about shit. Niggahs in the street was filling his head with all kinds of nonsense. She wasn't trying to hear that he-said-she said bullshit. She just wanted to talk about them and their shit. He had to know it was hard out there for a sister. She was doing all she knew how to do to keep it together. Everybody was mad at her. She was prepared for some questions from him. She just hoped he didn't push shit too far.

Julio watched her step from the elevator. He studied her up and down. She hoped her appearance didn't confirm what he already knew. She was smoking; his wife was a crackhead. She was half her normal size and she couldn't even look him in the eye.

That day her Julio felt a piece of his heart break. He felt helpless. He could control everything in the streets, but he couldn't control this. All his boys told him that she was smoking, but he didn't want to believe them.

Every time he questioned her about her smoking crack, she would beat him to getting mad. She would cuss him out and hang up on him, knowing damn well that it would take forever for him to call back. He would wait in the phone lines for hours trying to reach her.

And, worst of all, word on the street was she was kickin' it with a couple of young gangsters. Julio couldn't tolerate that kind of disrespect. She was his fucking wife. He gave her his name. She was treating that shit like it didn't mean nothing. He was so mad that day. His sexy brown eyes turned black and hollow as he chastised her.

All she wanted to do was see his face, hear him say that it

was going to be okay, tell her how much he loved her. Instead she got his wrath. His looks crushed her that sad, sad day. She slowly walked to the small booth and picked up the phone on the wall. She wanted to die; the look in Julio's eyes said everything. She wanted to run from the room and never return.

The hurt in his eyes demanded that she stay. How did she begin to explain to him that she loved him deeply and being without him was killing her? How could she make him understand that being high kept her from being consumed by the pain of him being gone?

"Hi, baby," she spoke quietly into the phone. If only she could burst him free from behind the confining wall. He was just on the other side of the wall. If only, for a split second she could penetrate the damn wall and run into his arms.

"So, you finally found time to come see about a niggah?" Julio spat, staring her up and down as if the mere sight of her disgusted him.

She tried to fight back the tears that filled her eyes. "I'm sorry I haven't been about to see you. It's been hard out here for me. I miss you so much," she tried to explain.

"Fuck that, Tara, it's been hard in here for me. The only thing I asked you to do was take care of yourself. Do you know what worrying about you is doing to me in here? Do you? I got to depend on other bitches to hold a niggah down. What that shit look like when I got a wife? Huh? A wife. Not no bitch. I got a real wife!" he shouted at her as if he could not stand the sight of her.

The deputy got up, walked to the holding cell, and looked in. He could tell that the couple was having a serious conversation, so he left them alone with their problems.

"Julio, I know I hurt you. I'm sorry. I thought I could do this shit. I wanted to be strong for you," she cried, looking at him sincerely, hoping to reach him.

"Tara, you need to get yourself some help. I've see women sell themselves, even their children, for that shit. You can't control it. Tara, do you see yourself? Everybody can tell you smoking," Julio pleaded with her. She felt his pain with every word he spoke; the words cut her to her core. She struggled to choke back her tears during his tongue-lashing. He was so angry he couldn't speak for a moment. She tried to read his expression, but his look was so cold. She didn't recognize this man. He wasn't the man she knew. This man hated her. She was sure of that fact.

"All you want to talk about is smoking," she shouted, annoyed. She hated all the questions and she squirmed in the small visiting booth.

"Yo' ass still going for bad, ain't you?" he shot back. He was so angry with her for treating this shit like it was nothing.

"I don't want a crackhead for a wife. When you decide you love me more than that shit, you holla at me. Until then I'm cool on the visits. I got somebody that don't mind visiting a niggah," he spat, then banged on the bars to signal the deputy he was ready to return to his cell.

Tara watched through teary eyes as Julio walked from the room and never looked back. She was sure he would turn around at some point, but he did not. She took a few minutes to dry her eyes and straighten herself before she prepared to leave the jail. Tara pushed the button for the elevator and it seemed to take forever. The ride down to the lobby seemed like an eternity. She wanted to get the hell out of there. She needed to get back to the hotel as soon as possible and smoke. That was her only escape from the madness of reality. A crackhead doesn't care if they are a crackhead when they are high on crack. The yellowish cracked-up pieces of rock cocaine were the only things that could ease her pain right now. She cursed herself for going to visit him and doing this to herself.

She knew she had disappointed him and her family too badly to expect anything but the anger. She couldn't deal with their disappointment any longer. She was never doing this shit to herself again.

When the steel doors to the elevator opened, she came face-to-face with Candy and Julio's daughter.

Candy stared Tara up and down. Tara still scared Candy just a little bit. Candy used the opportunity to parade her baby's mama status to the fullest.

"Word on the street was yo' ass was a crackhead, but I didn't believe that shit. Damn, you done fucked up now. Julio ain't gon' never claim a crackhead for his woman. I knew it was just a matter of time before you was history," Candy spat.

"You ghetto, stupid project chick. I will always be in his life. The niggah ain't gon' never be done with me. Oh, and did you forget I got his last name, you nothing bitch?" Tara shot back.

"I don't know why I'm even wasting my time talking to a crackhead. Fuck you."

Enraged, Tara leaped at the back of Candy's head, but she was grabbed from behind and led swiftly from the waiting room.

"Get your fuckin' hands off me! Get your fuckin' hands off me!" she yelled, spinning around to see who grabbed her. She stopped and stared into the sexy green eyes of Scott Mitchell.

"Calm down, baby girl. I'm just trying to keep you from catching a case at the jail," Scott whispered. He quickly escorted her out of the building and to his car. Once they were inside his truck she began to cry.

Scott pulled a fat one from the ashtray and lit it. He sucked in the smoke deeply and handed it to her. He watched her hands shake as she put the joint to her lips.

Scott put his keys in the ignition and started the truck. He pulled from the parking lot of the county jail and headed for the freeway.

"Thanks for looking out for a sister," she offered once she calmed down and the jail was out of sight. The motherfucker looked fine as hell, leaned back in his fine-ass whip. Gangster-ass Scott was a sight for sore eyes that cold, lonely day. It was as if somebody somewhere said, "Damn. Give a sister a break."

"How many times you done looked out for a brother? You got that coming, boo. Good thing I was out here putting some money on my boy's books or a honey might have been laying it down," Scott said, reaching for her hand and holding it gently.

"Shit been crazy, Scott." She leaned back in the passenger seat and allowed it to hold her. She did all she could to fight back the salty tears that were filling up in her tear ducts. She wanted to fall into her friend's arms and just rest there for a while.

"I know, let's just forget about it and chill. You need to clear your head," he said, getting off the exit ramp to his house.

She sat back in the warm leather seat and thought about everything that just happened. Julio was done with her; she knew that bitch Candy would be laying in wait to move in. Why didn't he understand the pain was more than she could take? She needed her drugs. They were the only thing that eased the heartache.

She glanced out the window as the car pulled into a carport in a large apartment complex. The apartments were brick with brightly painted green shutters. Everything looked clean and fresh. It calmed her.

"Where are we?" she asked, sitting up and looking at Scott.

"You need to relax. This is my spot, and you can crash here as long as you need to, no questions asked," he told her in a reassuring voice. His warm, soothing words wrapped themselves around her and rocked her gently.

"Thanks. I really appreciate you looking out for me," she said, following him from the car into the apartment.

Scott's spot was surprisingly well decorated. She never took him to be the decorating type. The place was comfortable and masculine. The living room was inviting with brown and sea-green furniture. She was instantly drawn to a large bookshelf that took up one whole wall. All the books were by black authors and there was shelf after shelf of books about the civil rights movement and slavery. She ran her fingers over the titles until she found one that caught her eye. It was *Convicted in the Womb* by Carl Upchurch

"That's a good one. I read it twice." Scott stood close behind her, peeking over her shoulder. She could smell the scent of his cologne. It tickled her nose."I didn't know you liked to read," she said, moving nervously away from him. She could feel his body heat and it made her uncomfortable.

"Like to read? Shit, I love to read. I read all that shit. You got to school yourself or the motherfuckers will get over on you. Here, let me show you around. Bring your book," Scott instructed, taking her by the hand and leading her upstairs.

His place was really nice. She was surprised by the warmth each room held. Once they reached the top of the stairs, a second side of him was revealed. The entire hallway was filled with African art.

"Wow, this is beautiful. Where did you get all these wonderful pieces of artwork?" she questioned, moving from piece to piece, examining each one carefully.

He sat down on the small hand-carved church pew that sat in the corner near the bathroom and enjoyed Tara's excitement over his collection.

"I've been collecting pieces for the last few years. I found this bench in an old second-hand store on Parsons Avenue. From the moment I saw it, I felt connected to it. It was like it

was a part of me. I been trying to trace its history and that's
led me to all these other pieces. A collector in the Short North
told me it looked like some of Elijah Pierce's work," he shared
with a serious look on his face.

She studied him while he spoke. The thug she knew was
different. He was more mature than she remembered. He still
had his swagger but there was a man where a thug used to be.
She joined him on the bench and listened to the excitement
in his voice. He told her the story behind each of the pieces
of art.

"I never would have thought my Harley-driving thug would
be an art lover and a reader. Are you sure this is your place?"
Tara joked, getting up and peeking in one of the closed doors.

"It's my place, all right. I got a stack of bills with my name
on them downstairs to prove it. A boy got to grow into a man
sometime. It just took me a little longer," he laughed, opening up the door Tara was peeking in all the way. "This is the
master bedroom. The king lives in here."

The bedroom was huge. A king-sized bed filled most of the
room. African art accented everything and books littered the
floor and both dressers. A full balcony could be seen through
the sliding glass doors that took up much of the wall to the
left of the bed.

"Your place is nice, Scott," she said with a sudden yawn.

"Come on, boo, let me show you the spare room. It's a cool
spot with its own shower. You can freshen up and get some
rest. You're straight here. We can talk about all the crazy shit
that's been going down tomorrow."

The pair left his room and entered the guest room. The
second bedroom was a lot smaller than the master suite but
just as nice. A plush terry-cloth bathrobe and slippers lay on
the bed.

"All the bathroom stuff you need is in the closet next to the tub. Get some rest; we'll talk in the morning." He kissed her gently on her forehead and left, closing the door behind him.

She stood there stuck for a long time before collapsing on the bed. She laid there for what seemed like hours. She was mentally and physically drained. Her mind raced from Julio to Candy to Scott and back again.

She squeezed her eyes shut tightly, wishing the pain would go away so she could rest.

She wrapped the terry bathrobe around herself and then rolled up inside the comforter. She felt so cold and empty; her body ached from all the pain. Staring up at the ceiling, she could hear Scott in the next room turn on the shower.

Scott was the last person she expected to see that day. He rushed in like a breath of fresh air. She could only imagine what would have happened if he hadn't been at the county jail at the same time. The niggah was still fine as hell. He was doing good for himself. She could kick it with him for awhile. She didn't care how he was living like a square up in his cozy apartment. He was a dope boy through and through. He'd just mellowed out with his hustle.

The time she spent with him before Julio was all good. He was always a loving giver when they were together. She liked that about him. Not to mention the sex was good.

She rose from the bed; the room was dark. She felt her way to the light switch on the wall and turned on the light. Tara caught a glimpse of herself in the mirror on the dresser. She looked awful. Her eyes were puffy and swollen and her hair was a mess. It stood straight up on her head. She looked like a clown; she couldn't help but laugh at herself.

As she stared in the mirror the taste of cocaine entered her brain. It flooded her body within seconds and she instantly began looking for her purse. Before her feet moved toward it, she remembered there were no drugs inside. She'd left her small stash with Karen before going to the county jail. That shit was as good as gone by now and she knew it.

Fuck, what am I going to do? she thought, pacing the floor.

The sound of the water being turned off in the next room interrupted her thoughts. She knew he wouldn't want to get it for her so she thought hard about what she was going to say to him. Each time she thought she had rehearsed her speech to perfection, she changed it. By four in the morning, she was so tired of thinking that she gave up.

She wasn't ready for all the drama that would come with asking Scott for dope, so she quietly called Karen on her cell phone. The two of them had recently hooked up and were hanging out again. It took her a minute to convince Karen to pick her up. She didn't even know where she was for sure.

"Girl, I'm just going to check one of his bills on the table downstairs for the address and then I'm bouncing. I remember passing a main street when we turned into the complex. I'll meet you up there. Once I get outside I'll call you and let you know where I am," she instructed Karen.

"Yo' ass will ask a bitch anything. Damn, Tara, it's four in the morning. You better be glad I just came in my damn self. Call me back the minute you get outside. I'll be on my way," Karen ordered, hanging up the phone.

She crept from the bedroom and tiptoed through the hallway. She could hear music playing loudly from inside Scott's room. She paused outside his door and listened for the sound of any movement. All she heard was rap music and she thought she heard faint snoring mixed in with the rap beat.

Her next moves were thought out carefully. She skillfully slipped from the hallway and down the stairs. Once she reached the bottom she could see a lot easier. The light from the front porch flooded the foyer. On the table next to the door sat his mail.

She crept to the table and removed the letter on top. The crisp white envelope read SWITCH BACK TO GEICO TODAY AND SAVE BIG, in neon orange letters. Under the bold letters were his name and address.

She stuffed the envelope in her pocket and moved to the front door. Please, please don't let him have an alarm system turned on. She thought hard about their arrival to his place. She didn't remember seeing him set an alarm when they entered earlier. She took a deep breath, turned the lock, and then tried the gold doorknob. Turning the knob slowly, she pulled the front door open. She froze and waited for the sound of an alarm. No sound came, so she slipped from the house.

Chapter Four

Her body was so tired from the all-night smoking sessions on the streets. Her ritual was the same daily. She'd get up around four in the afternoon and dress in one of the few outfits she had with her and then head to the nearest mall to hit a quick lick. She would be in and out of the mall within a couple of hours. She knew good shit and it didn't take her long to pick up some fast movers and be out and then push the pieces on the street.

It was a nice day so she'd gotten up early and decided to take some of her leftover pieces back to the store for cash. She didn't need to steal another thing until she moved some of the inventory she had on hand.

Her customers weren't shopping like they use to so she had a lot of leftover stragglers stacked up on the door in her motel room. Her plan was to take back her leftovers, get some quick cash, and then treat herself to a nice dinner before she got high the rest of the night. She decided to go way to the eastside to make sure she wouldn't run into anyone she knew. Her crew were mostly north end shoppers, so she felt she could get in and out with having to see anybody she knew.

She was so ashamed the minute she got there of all people she could run see she run into, Scott was right outside the Foot Locker as she made her way through the mall.

He was dressed to kill as always and his sexy green eyes still pierced her soul. He still had a way of making her panties wet. She wiggled from side to side in front of him like a little schoolgirl—damn, this niggah was so fine. She undressed him with her eyes.

"Yo', Tara! Tara, slow up, baby girl. Is that you?" Scott yelled, catching up with her.

"Scott, what yo' sexy ass doing on the eastside? You know you a north end niggah," Tara teased as the former lovers hugged.

"And you know this, but the eastside was the only ones with a thirteen in the new Jordans and I had to swoop me up a fresh pair. You know how we do," he said, patting his black-and-white Foot Locker bag.

"Where you running off to, baby girl? Can a brother get a minute?" he questioned, pulling her to a nearby bench. He wanted to question her about the night she ran out on him. He wanted her to know he understood where she was in her life right now. She looked so sweet and innocent standing before her, he just wanted to hold her.

"I was on my way to handle some business," Tara explained, as she pushed the return receipts and cash deep into her jean pocket. Lazarus had just paid her six lovely twenties on two silk blouses she returned. Damn, she was glad she'd taken the extra time to make sure her appearance was right before she started her day.

She still took the time to look her best even though she was spending more and more time smoking crack. She rarely left her motel room unless it was to hit a lick at some mall or make a crack run. She knew the people who really knew her personally would be able to tell she was smoking that shit.

Crack had become her lover and her friend. As long as she could feel the rush of the drug in her body, she didn't have to feel the pain of Julio being gone.

Tomorrow would mark a year he'd been in jail. He was

now being held at the Pickaway County Jail in Circleville, Ohio, awaiting trial with the feds.

All she wanted to do was turn the hundred-dollar bill in her pocket into her precious drug and post up in her room at the Cross Country Inn and get blowed and not think about anything else in life.

"What you been up to? Where yo' fine ass being hiding?" Scott questioned as his cell phone started vibrating. He pulled his cell phone from his pocket, annoyed, and quickly checked the number.

"Here, Tara, take this number and get at me tonight. You hear me? I mean tonight. Don't let me have to hunt yo' ass down, you know I will. Yo' ass done walked back in a niggah's life and I plan on spending some time with you," he said, kissing her and handing her a professional-looking business card that read Souljah's Recording Studio as he quickly got up to leave.

Tara watched him exit the mall and thought how fine he was and how bad she needed to just forget all the sad stuff. She looked at the number he gave her and stuffed it in her pocket with the money.

Tara called him that night and the two of them ended the night locked in a kiss on his king-sized bed. The kiss freed her mind for awhile. When he kissed her she felt something. She hadn't felt anything with anybody in a long time. His kisses moved her.

"Tara, let me make love to you, real love—not that knockin' boots shit. Will you let me do that?"

"I need you to do that," Tara answered.

Scott was so gentle with her, the worries of the world slipped away. He wanted desperately to save her from herself. He lovingly undressed her completely; he then began kissing her naked body. He sucked at her left nipple before moving lower. She slowly parted her legs to allow him to please her more. What he really wanted was to be inside her. He climbed on top of her.

Tara lay beneath him, enjoying the pleasure he gave her body. He made love to her mind and her body. He stared into her eyes the whole time. Within minutes the two of them came.

"Tara, I was young and dumb when I met you. A brother was trying to find his way in the streets and you gave a niggah the time of day. I don't know what you been through and I don't want to know, but I need you to know that I'm here for you now. I won't go nowhere," Scott told her.

Chapter Five

The plastic seats of the antique bus squeaked annoyingly as the gray-haired deputy sheriff struggled to safely drive down the narrow country highway. The bus was the oldest in the county's fleet. It was a miracle that the bus still made the hour-long trip out to the farm. The poor bus was overcrowded as usual, each seat holding three inmates. The seats directly behind the deputy held two inmates and an officer.

The deputy was always amazed by how quiet the ride out to the farm was on each and every trip. The Ohio Reformatory for Women in Marysville, known as "the farm," was a place to be taken seriously and the women aboard the bus knew it. Each woman sat quietly in her seat trying to imagine what lay ahead. The farm incarcerated all female inmates in the State of Ohio. Everyone, from murderers to career prostitutes, did their time in Marysville on the farm. The prison was located in the middle of nowhere out in Ohio farm country. The rumor was that the inmates actually maintained a productive crop of fruits and vegetables years ago. Now the inmates were used in factories inside of the prison to mass-produce everything from dime-store trinkets to clothing sold in chain stores across the country. Each inmate worked in one form or another and the women were paid pennies a day for their exhausting labor.

Tara awoke from her daydream and reality quickly set back in. She had been on the raggedy bus for far too long and the fear of the unknown was starting to play tricks on her

head. She would have to put Julio out her mind for now.
She couldn't allow herself to get caught up in the pain of
their loss. The shit hurt too much, and that pain had cost
her freedom. Their love was the once-in-a-lifetime kind, but
that fantasy was over. Julio was gone due to circumstances the
two of them could not control and the pain of that made her
weak. But Tara could not afford to be weak. She would have
to forget about Julio if she was going to survive her three-year
sentence of incarceration. She didn't know how she was going
to do it, but she knew she couldn't do it crying over their lost
love. She manned up and made the decision to do whatever it
took to get through the joint.

Handcuffed to a red-haired, pregnant teenager, Tara sat
thinking of what the future held for her. Each girl sat silently,
side by side, deep in thought as well. Tara's mind raced from
thought to thought. Each time she focused in on one subject
another came to mind. She glanced around the bus, trying
to focus on something other than the thoughts racing in her
head. As she searched the faces of the other women, Tara recognized the sobering look of the unknown in the eyes of each
woman. Tara was on her way to do three years on the farm.
She still found it hard to wrap her mind around that shit. Her
addiction to Julio led to her addiction to crack cocaine, and
that monster took her out but hadn't taken her life.

"Baby, you can do the time or let the time do you. Layin'
down ain't easy but it ain't got to be so hard either." Tara
could hear her mother's voice in her head as the old bus shook
noisily down the road. Each woman on the bus understood
the same things Tara did— things were getting ready to get serious real quick. A bitch was getting ready to start jockin' for
position. Prison was built on a foundation of respect. From
the gate, you had to demand respect. Although she knew her
homies from her hood would hold her down, Tara had nev-

er been incarcerated in a state prison before. She knew she would have to deal with a lot of different women from across the state, and that shit was going to be work. Bitches were always flexin', trying to be seen. Avoiding a confrontation was going to be next to impossible.

Tara sat in her seat, repositioning her hips for the tenth time, as her heavy, state-issued green pants stuck to her thick thighs. All the while, Tara kept her eyes on a light-skinned, thick gay girl, who had been staring her down the whole bus ride.

"You think we almost there?" the scared redhead whispered to Tara as she rubbed her stiff knees. Tara almost forgot about the young girl seated next to her. She turned to look at her for only the second time since boarding the bus back at the county jail, and could see that the white girl was almost frozen in fear as she spoke nervously.

"Yeah, I think we are. I saw a sign for Marysville a few minutes ago," Tara shared with the young girl seated next to her. It was obvious that the girl was frightened to death. If somebody real didn't take this fresh bait under their wing, she was a goner.

"This your first time? Where you from?" Tara questioned all at once, hoping to lighten the mood. The girl looked like Sissy Spacek in the horror classic *Carrie*, with dirty hair and pimples all over her face. She rubbed her hands together nervously the second time she spoke, as if she was not allowed to use her voice in front of strangers.

"I never been locked up a day in my life, until now. I ain't really been more then a few miles from my town before now. When I was little we all rode to the state fair but that was years ago." Linda shared with the black girl who was the first person to show genuine interest in her in a long time.

Linda Loudermilk was a corn-fed white girl from Circleville,

Ohio. She was the oldest child of eleven raised by a single, young mother. At fourteen, Linda had her first baby and was living with a paint-sniffing seventeen-year-old runaway who beat her for breakfast, lunch, and dinner. The shit got old and Linda popped nine caps into the abusive bastard's back while he was staggering off her from raping her for the third time that night.

The old bus swerved off the highway and turned onto what looked like a smaller highway. At the very first intersection, the bus made a sharp left turn and the infamous Ohio Reformatory for Women came into view. The historic prison compound was made up of eight mini-plantations and one main, brick administration building. The bus slowly pulled up to the guard station and two armed sergeants in uniforms appeared with their weapons drawn. One of the authority figures climbed the metal stairs onto the bus with a clipboard in hand and began counting the women. No one spoke, as if their words would seal their fates. The stern officers moved silently, as if they were on a top-secret mission.

The scary-looking sergeant exited the bus, spat slimy black snuff from his tight, thin lips, wiped his mouth with his shirt sleeve, and waved the bus on. The metal gates slid open noisily to let the bus enter the compound. The administration building loomed in the distance.

"Damn, I be glad when we get in this bitch. I'm sick of being all close to all these soft-ass, amateur hoes," the light-skinned gay girl shot in the air before spitting on the floor.

"Don't start your fuckin' shit, Moore. I'll keep all y'all stinkin' heathens on this bus until I get ready to let y'all off, you hear me?" threatened the overworked veteran bus driver.

***

"That institutionalized, miserable bitch always earth-disturbing," the inmate directly behind Tara whispered to the inmate seated next to her, waking Tara from her daydream. "Make sure you stay clear of bitches like that when you get inside the walls. They dangerous," she added before getting quiet when the bus pulled to a stop in front of what looked like a horse stable with glass windows all around it. Suddenly, a starchy-clean, plus-sized white woman with jet-black hair entered the bus and started shouting instructions to the anxious ladies.

Before Tara realized what was going on, the women were being herded off of the bus in small groups and sent in different directions. Heading into her second interrogation room, she realized that Linda Loudermilk was gone. Tara sighed and hoped for the best for the young victim.

"What's up, baby girl? What you doin' in this hellhole?" Tara turned to stare smack-dab in the face of Toby, an old friend of her mother and another inmate. She hugged Toby quickly, hoping not to draw attention to the family friend.

"I caught a case and got sentenced to three years," Tara replied to the old veteran.

"Well, you keep yo' nose down and fly under the radar and you can get through this bitch with ease. Most of these wannabes is all game, but you got a few with heart. I'll spread the word that a soldier is on the compound. If you have any trouble, let me know. I got you," Toby schooled the young worrier. Tara came from royalty on the streets. Her family had put in work to earn that respect on the street and in the joint. It was an honor for Toby to look out for her old friend M&M's baby girl. The farm was known for breaking a bitch.

"Place your shoes on the bottom shelf and stand firmly on the scale," Toby directed, changing her tone. "One hundred and twenty-two pounds." She made a notation on the clipboard in her hand. "You may move to your next station," Toby emotionlessly told Tara as the next victim entered the room. Tara did what she was told as if on a conveyor belt being pulled to her next invasion of her personal space. At each stop along her journey she felt like a faceless, soulless piece of meat.

Chapter Six

The women's eyes on both tiers of the admissions dorm sprung open as the correction officer's voice rang through the cells. "Rise and shine, ladies. It's your first full day of hell. Get your asses up, chickies," CO Hall called out his first direct order of the morning. The sound of the women scrambling to get dressed could be heard by all.

Tara exited her small, two-man cell slowly. Her state-issued tennis shoes squeaked as the cheap rubber stuck to the perfectly buffed floor. She descended the metal stairs and joined the other women in the orientation room.

Sixty "chickies" were in Tara's admissions group. CO Hall was in his element, playing the puppet master. Hall was a professional at breaking-in the new arrivals. His sole purpose was to put the fear of God and people with uniforms into the inmates. He was proud of the fact that he was known for making an inmate in each new group piss her pants. He loved doing that shit.

The women studied his every movement. The top of his bald head shined like a crystal ball at the front of the sterilized room. He was a short, stocky white man in a dingy gray shirt with his silver nameplate pinned sloppily on his shirt. He was overweight and the thin material of his shirt stretched painfully across his fat belly. "You girls are stuck here with me for the next six weeks. You are either going to hate me or want to kill me when your time sentenced to me is up. I ain't takin' no shit from any of you lawbreakers. You ain't at no freakin' hotel, so don't expect nothing but three hots and yo' freakin' cot. Ya got it?" CO Hall proclaimed to the inmates. "I said, you got it?" CO Hall barked at his prey.

"Yes, sir, uh-huh," the women mumbled in unison to the controlling little man standing threateningly before them.

"Now let's start with the housekeeping rules around here. You little nasty inmates better get one thing straight today. I better not walk past your doors and look in your room and see no nasty mess. Let me catch you touching yo' self and there's goin to be problems," Hall warned. He then pulled on his belt and adjusted his nasty dick in his worn-out, stained black pants. A ghoulish grin spread across his fat face.

Tara became distracted as the rust-colored red door behind Hall opened, allowing Linda Loudermilk and a female officer to enter the room. Linda was quickly seated in the front row by the female officer while Hall continued talking. Everything seemed to be happening in slow motion.

Tara watched as Hall removed a sanitary napkin from his pocket and began to unwrap it as he continued lecturing them. The female officer seemed to be whispering something to Linda Loudermilk while her shoulders rose and fell. The other women stared at the bizarre scene at the front of the room, stuck on stupid, as the CO handled the sanitary napkin as if he had been using them personally for years. "I want you paying attention to me. I'm only going to teach this to you once so you better get it. This is how you wrap these nasty things up once you done with them." CO Hall then pulled a state-issued roll of toilet paper out of nowhere and began wrapping up the pad. He wrapped the paper around the width of the pad several times before flipping it and swiftly wrapped up the length. The women sat there mesmerized, trying to wrap their minds around what their eyes were seeing. *Is this clown serious?* Tara thought to herself, feeling like she was in the *Twilight Zone.*

"You roll the sucker up real tight and then you make damn sure it lands in the trash can." Hall proudly threw his masterpiece across the room and it landed perfectly in the gray bin against the wall.

A loud bell rang in the orientation hall and the female officer anxiously stood up. "Hello, girls. My name is CO Spencer and I will be taking you to central food services for all your meals. You will also be assigned to me for all your screenings over the next few days. Once you have completed your mental health and physical evaluations you will each receive one phone call for the week. Numbers 32017 through 32085, join me at the red door, please. The rest of you will be assigned with CO Hall for your admissions intake," CO Spencer instructed. The women noisily began trying to figure out their assignment based on the numbers on their ID badges hanging from their green shirts.

Tara quickly figured out that she was included in the group joining CO Spencer at the door. The young female officer was a refreshing contrast to the overbearing CO Hall. Tara was happy to be leaving the *Twilight Zone.* The unlucky Hall victims walked in disgust in the direction of the puppet master.

"Hey, Tara," Linda Loudermilk sang softly, joining Tara in the line at the door. "I sure am glad you're in this group."

"Girl, you okay? Where you been?" Tara wondered, studying Linda's puffy red face.

"I'm okay. It was kind of hard for me to get used to this place, and I had a few nightmares last night. They took me to a psych evaluation late last night," Linda confessed. It was obvious the girl had been crying all night. Her hair was matted and it stuck to the side of her face in an odd pattern.

"Girl, there's a comb in the care package they gave you yesterday. Yo' ass ain't gon' be all stuck under me looking like a victim all the time. Ain't none of us having a picnic in this madhouse, but it is what it is. We gon' have to make lemonade out this shit," Tara explained the situation to the young girl as Spencer opened the door to the big, scary new world on the other side of the heavy, metal door.

Chapter Seven

Scott eased his classic Lincoln Continental onto the block, allowing the bass in his gangster rap music to penetrate the soul of the hood. The sounds mixed seamlessly with the swagger of Courtright Road, which was alive with hustlers, their customers, and black folks going about their daily lives. Easthaven was the candy shop; young folks from all sides of town respected the set. It was a daily circus up in that bitch. Passersby watched the commerce in amazement but, for the residents of Easthaven, it was just another day surviving in the neighborhood. You could get whatever you needed up on Courtright, at the corner.

Scott pulled up in his pride and joy, black on black with vintage interior, Lincoln with the kissing doors. He pulled to a stop in front of his favorite barbershop on the eastside. Scott was an Old G folk with a legendary reputation. The cutie-pie with the light eyes stopped traffic everywhere he went. Niggahs wanted to get at the legend on one level or another and hoes just wanted to get with a thoroughbred. His muscle, Spoon, rode shotgun with his sawed-off shotgun in his pant leg. The hard-ass banger took no prisoners; he was a warrior from the womb. The pretty boy and executioner made an odd pair.

The pair hopped from the car with a bounce in their steps and a twinkle in their eyes. "What's up, Gator?" Scott questioned the seventy-two-year-old shoe-shine entrepreneur. Gator ran his business from the front of Soldier Boy's Barbershop year-round. He smiled proudly back at the young gangsters.

"Top of the morning to you young bucks. It's a great day to be aboveground," Gator paused to acknowledge them as they passed. Scott watched the tall, thin professional masterfully spit-shined the shoes of a pimp in a sky-blue suit and navy blue, lizard-skin Italian leather kicks.

"Wow-we," the pimp sang, paying the old businessman. "You the motherfuckin' best, Gator. You the motherfuckin' best."

Scott and Spoon entered the barbershop and all eyes were on them. "Yo', yo', yo', what's poppin', playa?" Speedy, the shop owner, questioned his best customers as they entered his establishment.

"What it do?'" Scott shot back, greeting his boy. Spoon nodded in Speedy's direction and posted up in the back corner.

The shop was on blast. All eight barbers' chairs were filled and the three manicure girls at the back of the shop had customers waiting patiently for their turn. Even the waiting room was full of customers. A young buck with a briefcase full of burned CDs moved through the crowded shop hustling his merchandise. "I got five for twenty on all the latest shit," the young buck informed no one in particular while walking slowly through the room in his XXL white T-shirt and baggy jeans.

"Let me get that new joint by Jay-Z," an older brother yelled from his barber chair where he was getting his braids re-twisted by the shop's gay stylist.

Speedy quickly finished up his customer and motioned for Scott to hop into the chair. The other waiting customers complained quietly among themselves.

"What you been into, Do Dirty?" Speedy called the old G

by his gangbangin' name, which was legendary in the Hood. Do Dirty was known for knocking a niggah out with one punch. On cool summer days, in the ash-colored dirt yards on blocks in the inner city, young kids in the projects practiced the Do Dirty right hook on the regular.

"Shit, just tryin' to stay out the way. Man, I miss my boo Tara like crazy. Shit fucked up. She had to lay it down for a minute. I was feelin' like I was startin' to reach her on that crack shit before she got popped. That beast is takin' out some pros. A niggah fucked around and caught some real feeling for that dime piece," Scott offered, staring into space, remembering another time. Tara had been on his mind all day. He hadn't heard from her in weeks. He had one of his chickenheads call down to the county and she found out that Tara was moved to Marysville. He'd sent the chickenhead to Tara's mom M&M's place to drop off some paper for her books, wanting to do whatever he could to help her time go smoother. There were so many other things he wished he could do for her.

Scott knew when she ran back up in his life he was her rebound niggah, but he didn't mind playin' the role. She had always been his everything from the beginning, when they both were young and dumb. Scott was a thug who grew into a true gangsta. He'd paid his dues on every set, and he earned his respect the hard way, putting in work. He earned the name Do Dirty on the streets the old-fashioned way. He and Tara met for the first time when he was still finding his way. He didn't realize what he had back then. He let her get away, and he'd been chasing her ever since.

Damn, a gangsta was stuck, Scott thought to himself as Speedy faded him up, respecting a man alone with his thoughts. Speedy knew both Tara and Dirty from way back. It was like the timing of them was always off. Every time they came in and out of each others' lives they were always in different places. Their love for each other could never catch its rhythm. They vibed with the bass always a little too loud, never finding the sway of the beat.

Scott willed her safe until he could see her again, and then safely tucked the thought of her away deep inside his heart. "Man, Speedy, hook a brother up right. I got some honeys to chase tonight," he announced, changing the mood.

"And you know this," Speedy chimed in, glad his friend was back from memory lane.

The barbershop doors swung open as two college hotties from up at Wright State entered. It was all eyes on them immediately. Niggahs started kickin' game as the young hotties strutted their stuff for the ballers in the room.

"Man, you know you can't handle that," Scott teased Speedy as the two friends watched the hotties prance around the room. He paid his partner for his cut, tipped him nicely, then signaled Spoon and the two gangstas exited the shop, just as a silver four-door Camry pulled from the curb. Scott caught the eye of the Camry's clean-cut driver. Before he could get the words out, Spoon turned to him and said, "feds."

Chapter Eight

The bright, morning sun blinded the inmates as they exited the admissions door. They were greeted by a masculine-looking female CO who looked through the women as she spoke. "I want one single file, tight line all the way to central food services. Let me catch one of you talking at anytime and your ass is mine. You are in CFS to eat and that's it. You start that socializing and your little asses are toast. I better not see as much as a nod of your head to anyone in general population, you hear me?" the he-man female correctional officer shouted as the inmates streamed from the exit and snaked through the yard in silence.

There were people hustling and bustling about their daily routines in the yard. If you didn't know better you could have sworn you were on some college campus in the Midwest. Women moved around the grounds as if they all had some important task to perform. There were women of all shapes and colors, in different colored cotton short-sleeve button-front pink, green and orange shirts with khaki pull-up pants. Each color represented a designated security status. Naturally, inmates put their own flavor on the uniforms and rocked them proudly. The women in admissions wore all khaki, as their security status had not yet been determined.

Tara's eyes instantly focused on a Puerto Rican gay girl who looked hauntingly like her beloved Julio. Her hair was cut close to her head and slicked back in wavy curls. She had spit cresses in her pants and she wore a brand-new pair of Timbs with the white cuffs. A pack of Marlboros were rolled up in the sleeve of her pink shirt. "Hey mami. What's ya name?" The latina sang in Tara's direction.

Tara was in awe watching the hard-ass cutie stand there holding a rake and kickin' straight game. She was almost temped to shout, "My name is Tara and you can get all my milk money."

The ladies were paraded through the yard like fresh meat. Everyone in general population waited anxiously for the parade from admissions with the new girls. It was the chance to see who was new on the compound. The veteran inmates used the time to call in favors. If a bitch was lucky she could come up on everything from cigarettes to a motherfuckin' perm if she played her hand right. The only drawback to getting your hustle on was that you could wind up in the hole if you weren't careful.

Tara saw several people she recognized from one set or another, but she could not recall any names. She was so busy taking in everything around her that she ran smack into the back of Moore, the thick gay chick from the bus ride from the county. "Damn, clumsy bitch, watch the fuck where you go," she spat in Tara's direction.

"I got your bitch. Whenever you feel like you want to make a move, make a move," Tara shot back, standing her ground.

"What's all that noise in my line? I know y'all don't *eveeeen* think you can try me," CO he-man shouted from the back of the line.

"Rissa, hold it down, you just got out the hole yesterday. Don't go doin' nothing to get sent back. I missed you. I ain't trying to lose you when I just got you back," Rissa's petite, Jada Pinkett-looking girlfriend purred, rubbing her women's back. The two women fell back to fight another day.

The group entered the squeaky-clean, empty cafeteria. They followed the instructions of CO Spencer, who ushered them through the food line with precision. The only other people in CFS were the inmate food-service workers. Each inmate followed the lead of the inmate workers in front of them.

When Tara reached the beverage station, she was pleased to see a face she recognized from home. It was Angel, Julio's partner Carlito's little freak from back in the day. "Tara, how you doin', girl? When you get here?" Angel questioned the street royalty. The last time she saw Tara she was reigning with the Dominican kingpin Julio. It was rare to see street legends in the joint anymore. The farm was full of petty thieves and crackheads now. Angel felt privileged to be able to say she rolled on their set.

"I'm good, Angel," Tara whispered, trying not to get caught talking. It was good seeing a familiar face. Angel immediately started telling the white girl at the beverage station with her all about Tara and Julio and their reign in the hood.

The other girls in the line overheard the conversation, including Rissa. Her hatred for Tara grew deeper with each moment as she studied Tara from a distance. "Oh, so the bitch think she special, walking around here with her nose in the air playing Captain Save a Ho. I'm gonna show her how we get down in my hood," Rissa vowed, slamming her tray down on the metal table as she positioned herself on the narrow bench.

Marissa Moore was from the wrong side of the tracks. Everyday someone reminded her of that her whole life. She was constantly having to prove she belonged in the room. She stopped trying to fit in; instead, she just took what she wanted by force. If a bitch knew what was good for them they'd better give her fifty feet.

***

Tara sat perfectly still on the narrow bunk bed, locked away in her concrete tomb. The tiny cell was so small she could stand in the center of the room and touch both sides of the wall with her arms stretched out. A metal slab held her thin, worn-out mattress. The metal slab was bolted to the concrete wall with its twin bolted to the wall three feet above. There were no windows to the outside world or no clock. Time was determined by the turning on and off of the lights.

The bed was wedged perfectly in the right-hand corner of the room. On the opposite side of the room, in the left corner, was a metal shelf with two large, open storage spaces at the top and two metal drawers at the bottom. The only item in the drawers was a King James Bible.

Each inmate was issued three pairs of khaki pants, two khaki shirts, one pair of navy blue slip-on tennis shoes, three pairs of state-issued panties, three bras and four pairs of 100 percent cotton white socks. Tara neatly folded her new state-issued wardrobe and placed the items in the top metal drawer. She'd lucked out and been placed in the cell alone so far. She hoped her luck held out because she was not in the mood to be all up close and personal in the tiny space with another inmate right now.

At the foot of her bunk was a four-foot-tall, concrete privacy wall that separated the bed from the stainless-steel toilet and matching sink. Above the sink was some sort of plastic mirror that showed a distorted reflection of her face.

The most overbearing thing in the room was the huge, red rusty steel door. At the top of the door was a large, glass window with bars on the outside. At all times of the day and night, Correctional Officers could be seen peering through the huge window at her every move. Tara felt like some type of science experiment sitting there inside of the tiny cell. All there was for her to do was think and constantly reflect on all the madness that was her life now. How in the hell had it come to this?

She'd spent her time in the county jail trying to find those answers. Prayer gave her the strength to get through the days without Julio. His love left a hole in her heart and she'd used crack cocaine to fill that hole for well over a year. That decision turned a veteran booster into a petty thief and barely functioning crackhead.

The day Julio was arrested by the feds signaled the beginning of her rock-bottom. Her enjoyment of narcotics began well before her addiction to crack. Her man was a drug dealer; he kept them stocked in the best Peruvian flake cocaine. They had indulged in the recreational drug often, so it was only natural when Tara didn't see her addiction coming. Initially, she thought she could control the drug, but she didn't understand the power of the little white rocks.

Now, trapped behind a heavy steel door, sat so much wasted potential. Bishop Hairston told her that day on the phone back at the county jail, "Your life is not beyond repair." His words were imbedded in her mind. She wanted to repair the damage, but how did she start? It was so much easier just to escape with drugs. Unfortunately, there was no escaping the concrete walls and the mess of her life.

CO Hall kicked the steel door with his foot violently. "Three-two-oh-two-six, you get one phone call today. I'll be back to get you and you better be ready or lose your call," Hall yelled through the door. He could be heard shouting the same order at a door down the range.

As Tara leapt from the bunk her heart leapt with her. She would finally get to make contact with the real world. She hoped it still existed.

***

Scott entered the foyer of his condominium and tossed his keys into the bowl on the table by the door. He quickly tapped his code into the keypad to his alarm system while slipping off his shoes. His phone vibrated loudly in his pants pocket. "Speak," Scott yelled into the phone on his way to the kitchen.

"Word, soldier, I know yo' ass ain't trying to hear this, but that westside niggah Nate got some fat ends he trying to spend with a brother. Shit, way he talking, niggah can make some kick back paper and just chill for a minute," Spoon shouted on the other end of the cell phone.

"Damn, Spoon. I just got in the fuckin' door. Do a niggah ever get to rest?" Scott questioned, reaching for the orange juice on the top shelf of the empty side-by-side refrigerator. He took a gulp of the thick orange liquid and returned the gallon jug to the shelf. "Niggah, can't you take care of the order without me?" Scott asked, hoping to post up at his spot for awhile.

"I ain't sure yet, soldier. I'm waiting on that niggah to call me back and let me know what he need." Spoon offered to keep his boy on standby so he could make some easy paper. He called his friend by the name he called him way back in grade school. Scott was always putting in work on one chump or another. The cock-strong pretty boy stayed in a rumble. Soldier kept his guns drawn, ready for battle, and niggahs respected that. He was a warrior through and through.

The friends were old G's from the infamous Chicago street gang the Folks. Bangin' wasn't the same anymore on the streets. Now there were too many babies in the shit, making shit up as they went along. The young bucks were fuckin' it up for everybody. Too many people were dying over a little bit of money. You didn't experience soldiers like Scott much anymore; just imitators and thirsty motherfuckers.

"Shit, Spoon. If it wasn't you, I'd say fuck that shit, let the niggah wait until tomorrow. You better be glad you my boy, man. I still ain't fixin' to stop and roll for that bitch-ass niggah Nate, though. You give me a call when you know what that niggah want. I need to grab a shower. I'll get at you later," Scott instructed his friend before hanging up.

Scott's home was well decorated and very comfortable. He had a thing for African art; his love for it was apparent throughout his home. The pieces seemed to speak to him from some faraway place. Whenever he bought a piece, he held it for a long time before he made the decision to add it to his collection.

He climbed the stairs two at a time, leaping at them with force and great speed. In the distance, the sound of a ringing house phone could be heard. He had the line for one reason only; it was his lifeline to Tara. "Hello? Hello?" The gangsta quickly disappeared and all that stood in the room was a man missing the woman he loved deeply without ever being able to tell her so.

"Hey, Scott," Tara's soft voice sang over the phone. "It sure is good to hear your voice."

"It's so good to hear your voice too. Damn, I been worried about you. I found out they rode you to the farm, but that's all I knew for about a week now. You keep a niggah sweatin' yo' ass, girl. But for real, how you been?" Scott asked, anxiously wanting to know everything. He stretched his body across his king-sized bed and got comfortable, wrapping himself in her voice.

"I'm making it. Trying to stay out the way and get through this madness. You never warned me about how crazy this shit is. Everybody jockeying for position, trying to get theirs. Don't get me started on these insane COs in here," Tara complained, glad to share the nightmare with someone who understood her fate.

She'd called her mom first, but nobody was home. M&M was no doubt somewhere chasing paper. Tara would have to call her with her one call next week.

She valued her friendship with Scott. He was a true friend. Their relationship went way back. They'd tried a couple of times to be more than just good friends, but that never seemed to work out. Scott was her road dog. They understood each other.

"Man, right. Them motherfuckers be trippin', don't they? Everybody got they chest stuck out trying to go hard. Half them niggahs ain't ever seen no real battlefields. If they only knew, huh," Scott shared, understanding the bullshit Tara faced daily.

"But seriously, how you holding up? Do you need anything? I hope you know I got you. As long as you in there, I got you," Scott spoke seriously into the phone, wishing he could trade places with her.

"Thanks, Scott. You're a good friend. You always have been. I know I'm lucky to have someone real in my corner. I'm good in here; I'm just going with the flow. It's good to hear from the outside, for sure," Tara explained to her close friend. He was her rock, always there for her—a true homie, lover, friend.

She valued his male energy. He always kept it real with her, at least most of the time. Tara was sure that Scott was catching serious feelings for her right before she got popped, but whenever she questioned him about it, he denied it. They'd gotten physical right away. He was a natural fit, and he helped to fill a huge void left by Julio. She selfishly allowed him to be a distraction from the pain. But she knew now that was a bad decision and prayed he wasn't holding on to a dream of them.

Tara was devoted to the love she shared with Julio. It was a once-in-a-lifetime love. His five year federal sentence for intent to distribute cocaine, along with her addiction to crack cocaine, cost the young lovers everything. She wasn't even really sure he still wanted to be with her. Tara did not know what the future held for their love, but what she did know for sure was that she didn't wish the pain of lost love on anyone, especially her close friend Scott.

"Listen up. Go hard on them bitches at all times. A bitch get in yo' face, back 'em up with yo' mouthpiece. Then you can smell their fear. Tara, you're a veteran. You know how the game go. You got to demand your respect from the jump-off. I'm mad serious, Tara. You can't show no fear 'cause the sharks smell that shit a mile away. Don't ever underestimate the power of the haters, either. They need watching the most," Scott schooled Tara long-distance, hoping to equip her for the battle ahead.

"I hear you, Scott. I can handle the hookers. It's the fear of the unknown that's the hard part. Everyday it's some new shit. You got strange motherfuckers controlling your every move. That shit drives me crazy. I don't know how long I can take these bitches all up in my face on petty, dumb-ass shit all the time. I can't stand a petty motherfucker," Tara explained, reliving the last few days in her head.

Tara was so caught up in her conversation that she didn't hear the CO give the three- minute warning, signaling that the call would be ending shortly. "Hello? Scott, are you still there?" Tara yelled into the black, antique receiver to the phone that was bolted to the concrete wall. The line had gone dead.

"Your call is over, inmate. Time to go, let's move it," The female rookie CO ordered Tara from her seat at the single metal desk in the room filled with telephones and small stools. The five other women rose reluctantly and started moving toward the rusty red metal door that confined them.

Tara sat perfectly still, holding the phone as she stared a hole into the rookie CO.

"Three-two-oh-two-six, I'm giving you a direct order to hang up that phone and join the line at the door," the nervous officer announced in her toughest voice as she quickly pushed the panic button. Tara hung up the phone and moved to the red door, realizing she couldn't win this fight.

The red door flung open and three WWF-size wrestlers entered the small room. "Everything okay, Jackson?" Officer Smackdown questioned, strolling around the room, staring the women down with his hand on his gun.

"We're good in here. You can send in the next group," CO Jackson explained. Jackson was a peaceful young woman who had taken this job reluctantly, vowing to treat the women like human beings. The inmates were escorted back to their cells quietly. No one spoke or looked in the direction of their WWF smackdown jailers.

"Tara, Tara. Are you there, Tara?" Scott yelled into the phone, hoping he'd hear her voice rejoin the line. He sat there for a long while with the receiver in his hand, angry at the world for dealing them these cards.

He missed her so much and blamed himself for not protecting her. He was so busy chasing paper that he didn't slow down long enough to see she was in pain and needed him until it was too late. He'd never let that happen again.

If he was ever going to have a real shot at her, he'd have to start becoming a man she could count on; a man who would be there for her. That shit would take work. Hell, he didn't even know where to begin.

Chapter Nine

Tara entered the small cell reluctantly, her anger consuming her. She wanted to scream, but she refused to allow her jailers that satisfaction. She would not give them the pleasure of thinking they could break her with their controlling ways. She walked slowly to her bunk and sat down. The room seemed to close in on her. She could have sworn she saw the walls pulsating as if they would conquer her and eat her whole.

She quickly rose from the bed and began pacing around the small cell. "Stop it, Tara. You are stronger than this place and these crazy people," she told herself while looking in the small mirror above the metal sink at her reflection. Staring back at her was the weak girl who had gotten her into this mess in the first place. The weak girl who allowed lost love and drugs to control her every thought and action.

She was the daughter of hood legends. Her mother did three years with her eyes closed, and her father was a thoroughbred pimp who'd never done a day of time. Tara refused to let this punk-ass time break her; she'd have to man up. She was only on her second week in the bitch—she had a long time to go. She could stress out all the way through it or roll with it.

Her thoughts were abruptly interrupted by a woman screaming at the top of her lungs. The screams were quickly followed by the sound of COs running. Tara ran to the door and pressed the side of her face to the glass window. She could hear women yelling and arguing, but she could not make out their words. The yelling was mixed with male voices shouting direct orders.

Tara placed her ear tightly to the glass, hoping to make out what all the shouting was about. She could faintly hear the sound of a female voice screaming obscenities, mixed with crying and officers yelling what sounded like, "Bitches, get down on the ground now!" Tara continued listening as a large group of COs rushed past her window in full SWAT assault gear. The yelling ceased almost instantly; the silence was disturbing. Tara stared through the small window. All she could see was the concrete wall directly in front of her that led to the stairway to the top range where she was being housed.

The sound of rattling keys, crying, and the squeaking of leather shoes could be heard in the distance. The sound grew louder and louder until it was deafening, then suddenly a large group of people passed in front of Tara's window. The snapshot moment revealed a young black girl who looked like she had been beaten within an inch of her life. Her face was bruised and bloody, and her right eye was black-and-blue and completely swollen shut.

As quickly as the first group passed, a second group followed. The COs aggressively rushed a manly, gay inmate past the window. The gay girl was yelling, "You better give me fifty feet from that tramp or I swear the next time you gon' need a body bag for that ho." The butch inmate continued to yell out her threats all the way down the hall. The sound of other women yelling threats back could be heard up and down the range.

The buzz of the loudspeaker interrupted the yelling as a female correction officer came over the PA system. "Attention, inmates. Attention, inmates. Dinner will be delayed indefinitely until order is returned to this housing unit. All inmates are ordered to return to your bunk and prepare for count time. Once again, this is a direct order. Those choosing to disobey this order will be dealt with severely," the invisible correction officer advised.

Tara returned to her bunk and sat down. It wasn't long before one of the SWAT team members, still dressed in full riot gear, walked swiftly by the window, peered in, counted Tara and kept it pushing. It was as if he looked straight through her, like she was merely a number on the small count sheet in his hand.

It seemed like an eternity before the whistle was blown, signaling the count had been cleared. Only after the whistle was blown were women allowed to move about their small cells. Tara rose from her bunk and straightened her state-issued hook-up. "Damn, what happened to the silk and the satin?" she thought, looking at herself in the strange, plastic mirror stuck to the wall.

No makeup was available to her in admissions. The inmates weren't allowed personal items until their status was classified. You were given the bare minimum during your time there. So all she could do was concentrate on her hair after she brushed her teeth. She combed her hair back into a neat ponytail.

The thick, state-issued hair grease made her hair lay flat to her head but the hairstyle gave her a calm, in-control look. The old Tara smiled back at her reflection. She could feel her swagger rushing through her body and she was instantly at peace.

The loud release of the lock from the steel door signaled that it was time to eat. Tara filed from her tiny room with pep in her step. She was glad to be free from the confinement of her cell. She rushed to the stairs and headed down.

"Aw, hell no! I know that ain't you, Tara," Rosie yelled up at her, parking herself at the landing.

"Hey, Rosie, girl. It's good to see a homie," Tara sang, glad to see familiar face.

Rosie was a known prostitute with a reputation for always keeping it real. She didn't take shit from nobody. On the street or in the joint, she demanded respect and got it. She would smash a bitch if she dared step to her. She was also known for running in and out of the joint. She was on her fourth penitentiary number. Rosie could do time standing on her head. She had learned years ago how to adapt to her environment. Usually, she just played wifey to some horny CO and just skated through her time from the gate.

She was a beautiful, biracial girl with dyed blond hair who walked with the bounce of someone who was on a mission. You knew you were headed for an adventure whenever you kicked it with Rosie.

"Shit, Tara, we gettin' ready to take this bitch over. 'Bout time some gangstas was up in this bitch. Yo', Shorty, you know Tara?" Rosie questioned a butch Puerto Rican girl who joined them at the back of the line. Shorty was hard; she gave Tara a chin check "hello" and lined up with them at the door.

"I sure am glad to be out the motherfuckin' hole. I got sent to that bitch my second week for smoking in the shower. Shit, I smuggled two cigarettes all the way from the workhouse. I was determined to smoke them bitches. I would've got away with that shit too if my punk-ass roommate wouldn't have snitched on a hooker," Rosie laughed, joking all the way to CFS. "What's up, Graves? Where you been? I haven't seen you since I got here," Rosie asked the CO at the entrance to central food services.

"'What's up, Graves?' I should be saying what the hell you doin' here again, Rosie? That's the question, right?" CO Graves questioned the familiar inmate with so much potential.

"I know, Graves. I be tryin', man. They always fuckin' with a bitch. They love hemming a sister up. What's a girl to do? Hell, I needed a vacation from the madness," Rosie justified her actions to the corrections officer she respected. As the group headed inside the cafeteria, the smell of tomato sauce and garlic filled the air.

Chili and grilled cheese sandwiches were on the menu and the ladies waited in line patiently for the meal they all enjoyed. Tara waited in line with the rest of her group. She glanced around the room, which was nearly full of hungry inmates. Across the crowded cafeteria was CO Hall, who could be seen arrogantly hassling a food-service worker for giving away extra sandwiches. Hall nastily snatched an extra sandwich from the plate of a powerless inmate and violently threw the uneaten sandwich into the trash can. "What a miserable motherfucker," Tara thought, shaking her head at the control freak.

Behind the counter of the food-service line stood a handsome CO who stared in her direction. "Rosie, who's the cutiepie officer on the line? I haven't seen him before. His ass is fine," Tara complimented his good looks as the two stared at each other a little too long.

"That's Jefferson. His ass is hot as hell, but he won't give you the time of day. Trust me, I've tried with that one. Nothing, girl. Nothing," Rosie shared, reaching for her glass of watered-down iced tea from the line.

The girls quickly found seats together in the crowded cafeteria before the officers separated their group. The table was full, causing the women to sit closely together. Every time the overweight girl next to Tara lifted her arms to eat, her huge forearm nudged Tara in the chest.

Tara hoped she would be finished fast so she could enjoy her meal. This was the last meal of the day; she hoped to enjoy it and get full. The women weren't allowed to purchase extra food items from commissary until they were out of admissions. They often smuggled food back from CFS to eat later in the night. The extra food was considered contraband and inmates were given a ticket for extra duty if they were caught with it. Of course, that didn't stop hungry women from smuggling contraband from CFS every chance they got. Believe it or not, there were actually two officers posted at the exit whose sole job was to pat inmates down as they exited the cafeteria in search of contraband food.

Tara sat there wondering what kind of world was this, that you could catch a case for being hungry. Her mind drifted suddenly as she unintentionally locked eyes with CO Jefferson. The pair held their intimate exchange for a long moment before Tara turned away and joined the conversation around the table.

"Girl, they talkin' about letting us out of admissions early because the joint is so overcrowded. I hope I'm not assigned to Hale dorm. That motherfucker is a hellhole. A bitch will go crazy down there all summer long. It gets to be about a hundred degrees at night in that fuckin' basement," Rosie complained, drinking the last of her cold iced tea.

"Hell, yeah," Shorty added with a look of disgust on her face. "I ain't even trying to go to that bitch either." Shorty was on her second number. She'd done her whole first bit in Hale dorm. It wasn't nothing nice. You could go crazy in the prehistoric basement of the old administration building.

There were rumors that several women had hung themselves in the spooky basement. Inmates were known for freaking out in Hale and being sent to isolation indefinitely. The women shared the horror stories of the dorm like a Friday the Thirteenth campfire tale. There was even mention of ghosts and everything. First-timers sat listening in fear, silently hoping not to get sent to Hale dorm.

Tara didn't want any part of Hale if she could help it either. "So, what's the best dorm, Rosie?" Tara asked curiously, wanting to learn about her environment quickly. She took full advantage of her friend's knowledge of the joint and listened to the vet's every word.

"Well, if you ratin' the best, laid-back opportunity then you talking Elizabeth Cottage. It's an old building but it's the nicest setup. The only problem is that it's the drug-treatment housing unit. You gotta be ready to deal with your issues if you go there. You have to convince them to even let you in the program. The next best thing is the camp. It's a small setup outside the compound, along with boot camp for first-timers," Rosie explained to her homie.

"Let's go, inmates. Chow time is over. Empty those plates. Other people have to eat today, ladies," CO Graves instructed Rosie's group of young girls as they slowly rose from the table and emptied their dinner trays. Graves studied the group closely as they passed before her. She always hated to see the ladies return again and again.

Each time she saw one of them locked up once more, her heart went out to them. Graves had been employed at the Ohio Reformatory for over fifteen years. She saw more and more of the same women again and again. There was little reform in the work they did inside the prison anymore. It was just housing bodies and preventing the inmates from killing each other. Each day on the farm was a challenge for the veteran officer.

The group of girls floated out the door, glad to be in the beautiful sunshine. CO Graves said a quick prayer as the girls disappeared into the crowd in the yard. It was a hot summer day and nearly the entire population was in the yard enjoying the weather.

In the center of the compound was a large yard. To the front of the yard was a baseball diamond and to the back half was a full basketball court. A running track circled the field. The inmates weren't permitted to actually run, so they just walked swiftly around the track as fast as they were permitted.

Tara studied the girls in the stands surrounding the baseball field. Several of them were hugged up, very obviously in relationship-like conversations. She was shocked to see one interracial couple rubbing each other's backs with their hands under each other's shirt.

"Run, China! Run, girl," most of the girls in the stands began screaming as Tara and the other inmates from admissions snaked past the field.

A sexy, Melissa Etheridge–looking gay girl ran all three bases and slid home in lightning speed. The stands erupted and even the girls in the admissions line and the COs in charge of the line cheered.

Chapter Ten

Tara stood at the door anxiously waiting for the CO to come and release her for her weekly phone call. She silently prayed that her mother would be home when she called. It would be nice to hear the familiar voices of her family members. Things between them had gotten really strained while she was out there chasing her next high.

She respected her parents too much to allow them to see her weakness. Her mother was a true soldier; she demanded you come hard at all times. Tara was ashamed that she had allowed the drugs to separate her from her family. The self-imposed isolation fueled her addiction. Before she realized how much time had really passed, it had been months since she'd seen her mother.

"Hello? Tara, baby? Is that you, baby?" M&M sang into the phone while she watered the flowers in her flower bed in front of her picture window. Her pink and orange sundress complemented her brown skin. She paced up and down the sidewalk along the flower bed.

"Hi, Mommy, it's me. How you been doin', Mommy?" Tara asked, wrapping herself in her mother's loving voice. She could hear her mother calling her dad to the phone as she spoke.

"Slim, get out here. Tara's on the phone. Hurry up, you know she ain't got long to talk. Hurry. Baby girl, how you doing? Did you get the money we sent you? Can you get a box yet?" M&M shot all her questions to her daughter like a speed round on a game show. Tara's nephew Tee burst through, the door glad to hear from her.

"I haven't gotten out of admissions yet. They said we should be getting out sometime this week. Once I'm out you can send my box. They gave me a money slip for the hundred dollars you sent but I can't spend it yet," Tara informed her mother from the small, metal telephone booth in the concrete room filled with inmate phones and metal stools bolted to the floor. The room was ash gray; the color gave the room a boring vibe. Tara closed her eyes and dreamed of home as she spoke into the receiver.

The smooth sound of her father's voice joined the line. "Hey, hey, baby girl. You all right in there, right?" her father questioned, wishing his daughter some other fate.

"I'm good, Daddy. I'm just rolling with the punches. I got this," Tara said offering her father assurance of her well-being. She didn't want her parents worrying about her, so she lightened the mood. "What's Tee been up to?" she asked.

"He's right here. I'm going to put him on. Hold on, Tara, here he is now," Slim yelled into the phone, mindful of time.

"What's poppin', Aunt Tara?" Tee asked his favorite aunt. He respected a sister doin' time. He'd been lucky not to have had to lay it down himself. He respected anybody that was forced to raise up out the rotation for a while. His aunt was a gangsta, and he hoped the time would give her a chance to get clean from her addiction.

"I saw your boy Scott the other day up on the avenue. He asked about you. That niggah got it bad for your ass, Auntie. I swear I saw a tear in his eye when he drove off," Tee teased his aunt about her old boo.

"Here, give me the phone, Tee. I need to tell Tara about Julio before her time is up," M&M yelled, snatching the phone from her grandson. The two men sat down on the cushioned lounge chairs on the front porch and listened to the fast-paced conversation between mother and daughter. "I spoke to Julio last week. He's in Manchester, Kentucky, at the fed joint down there. All he did was talk about you, Tara. That child is truly hurt behind what happened to y'all. He blames himself for your drug use. You both have some forgiving and healing to do. He is so mad; he feels you disrespected y'all wedding vows for drugs."

"I know he feels that way, Ma. I don't know how to change the way he feels. I have to work on me first before I can deal with us. I love him too much to hurt him again. I won't do that," Tara shared honestly with her mother, who paced back and forth up and down the sidewalk in front of her home listening to her baby girl.

Before she was even close to being ready to end the call home, the CO gave the signal to hang up. Tara rushed and got in her last few words before the line went dead. "Mom, tell Julio I love him and that I'm okay. Get his address so I can write him. I love y'all. I'll call next week," Tara breathed into the phone hurriedly before the line went dead. She sat there for a long moment, holding the phone and willing her love to her family and to her beloved Julio.

Her mother hung up the cordless phone and joined her man on the porch. They sat there silently, both thinking about their child. Tara was so strong-willed; she did everything to the fullest. She always came hard; wherever she was, she took the fuck over the hard way. Their fear was that she was locked away with the state's hardest motherfuckers. She would have to stay on her game.

"I got the word out on the street that my baby's behind the walls. I should get a report soon from the inside. Motherfuckers better give my little girl her props or there's going to be hell to pay. That's bank," Slim schooled his grand-son calmly from the porch.

Slim handled everything with brute force, but M&M at-tacked things differently. She had already begun calling in favors from the outside to make sure Tara was set up com-fortably on the inside. M&M knew firsthand that doing time was much easier when you had everything you needed. She'd already gotten her baby everything she could have in her first box. The box was stuffed full and waiting by the door to be shipped once the okay was given from the institution.

M&M had packed more boxes than she cared to count. "Who wants to ride to Johnson's for some butter pecan ice cream?" she announced, wanting to change the mood. She could tell by the look on Slim's face that he was worried about their baby girl. Tara was the first of their children to get hemmed up doing time.

Nobody wanted the system to control their babies, but the couple had chosen the streets long ago and doing time was a cost to doing their kind of business. The game played hard sometime; if you studied hard enough you got the chance to play. The two street legends rose from their seats on the porch with Tee in tow, each anxious to turn the page on the mood they were in. Life was a bitch sometimes; you just had to keep rolling with it.

Tara was grateful for the chance to speak with her family. The sound of their voices was comforting to her. The separa-tion from the people she loved most was the worst part of all she was going through. She was so powerless over so many things. All she could do was hope that things would work out for all of them.

Her mother's words echoed in her head: "Julio is so hurt."

Hell, she was hurt and disillusioned by all that had happened to both of them. Their love never slowed down long enough to see that their lifestyle was a threat to their happiness.

She wished he understood her pain, but he only saw it as weakness or her not holding him down. If only he understood that the loss of him was more than she could handle, so she allowed sex and drugs to comfort her on the streets. She refused to be weak to the drugs, or sex, or even to the love of Julio.

Once she was back inside her cell, Tara began thinking about the prayer groups she used to have back at the workhouse. The madness of this whole new crazy world caused her to crave some sort of peace. She recalled the peace she felt in the prayer groups and Bible studies. Remembering the King James Bible in the drawer next to the door, she hungrily reached for it.

Tara got comfortable on the bunk, randomly turned to a page in the book and began reading. The words spoke to her spirit. They spoke of peace and love and gratitude. She searched the top of the page for the page number she was reading, wanting to remember it. The top of the page read Philippians, Chapter IV and she was reading from verse 19. She read the chapter again and again, each time feeling more relaxed. Before long, Tara was fast asleep on the bunk with the Bible on her chest.

Chapter Eleven

Tara stood by the rusty red door awaiting the click of the lock. She was leaving her hell-hole suite for the unknown. She'd been given her housing assignment and she was anxious to see what phase two of her journey through Marysville held.

The sound she'd been waiting for came and Tara sprang from her confinement. She glanced back at the small tomb and exhaled freely, glad to be done with it. As the other women poured from their hellholes two at a time, Tara wondered how she'd been lucky enough to spend her time in admissions in a cell by herself.

She'd done a lot of soul-searching and crying all alone. The crying washed away some of the pain and the wounds of her loss didn't hurt so much daily. Some days she even laughed until her side hurt.

The last five weeks had been an adventure and a trip. She'd gained some-ride-or-die friendships with Shorty and Rosie. The trio was thick as thieves; when you saw one, you saw the other two. The farm was in for a ride with this cast of characters. Wherever the trio went they were the center of attention. And as fate would have it, all three were headed to the camp located just outside the main compound. It was called the camp because the state-run boot camp for first-time female offenders was located on the grounds as well. The idea was to keep the first-timers separated from the other hardened population as much as possible, when the place was first buiLieutenant That policy was followed to the letter by the prison administration.

Low level offenders were mixed in with first-timers due to the overcrowding in the Department of Corrections across the state, both in the men's prisons and in the women's. The explosion of incarceration across the country in the last few years was bankrupting many states, including the State of Ohio. It was literally like you woke up one morning and everybody in your hood knew somebody in the joint. Prisons were raising black folks at an alarming rate. African Americans were disproportionately sentenced to lockup everyday in overcrowded courtrooms and shipped off to never-never land with little regard for the damage it was doing to black families.

In order to incarcerate all the women shipped to the farm weekly some rules had to be overlooked often. It was a miracle the women survived the day-to-day madness that went on behind the walls of the institution. No one stopped to look anymore at the damaging effects of mixing low-level offenders with first-timers. Prison was a training ground, the predators were ever-learning, and their prey got their basic training.

It was hard for the department to give the women the things they really needed; all their time was spent processing women in and out of the penitentiary. As fast as they came in they were poured back into their depressed community with very little training. The overcrowding was a strain on the system and a bonus to the veteran inmates. It allowed them to reign in their own little circles and cliques. Within these groups the dominators used their individual power to control large groups within the prison. Tara was a ruler and it wouldn't take her long before she would be sitting pretty posted up at the camp.

Her genetic makeup dictated that she began studying her

surroundings—she would need a strategic plan of attack to survive her new environment. She would go out fighting before she allowed the joint to get the best of her.

A few years ago, the institution placed oversized, army-like barracks on the land next to the boot camp due to drug-case overcrowding. Most of the women at the camp needed treatment, not confinement. The barracks were their own self-contained prison for low-status inmates needing one kind of resource or another that the system overlooked. That was until the general population grew so large over the last few years that the decision was made to house medium security and nonviolent inmates on the camp in order to address the overcrowding problem. Now you had fresh meat mixed with hungry lions at the camp.

The two buildings were connected by a small administration building that held classrooms, processing stations, and a smaller central food service cafeteria that the two units shared. The compound was a lot nicer than the farm because it was so new; things were more modern and up-to-date.

The latest inmates released from admissions to the camp strolled through the yard carrying their belongings, glad to be leaving. The around-the-clock supervision was draining on all of the women. You couldn't turn without some control freak breathing down your throat, telling you what you should be doing or thinking.

The women in general population yelled and waved at people they knew as the women wound through the yard toward the gate. In some ways, it felt like some special freedom, as if a new promised land was on the other side of the gate.

Tara strolled with her group toward the enormous gate with razor-sharp barbed wire wrapped through the top. When the front of the line got within ten feet of the entrance of the camp, the gate slid apart allowing the women passage through the opening. The women funneled through and then the gate quickly closed behind the chain gang headed for their new land.

The women were led into a holding room once they arrived, where they were each called up to a desk in an office cubicle and asked their first and last name, and birth date along with their institution number. They were then given a brand-new, state-issued ID that they were instructed to leave clipped on the right-hand side of their uniforms or personal clothing at all times. The only acceptable time to be without your state ID was in your sleeping area or while taking showers.

The group was led down a long, clean hallway, past a culinary school–style cafeteria. The spotless tables sparkled in the light as the women passed. The long hallway poured into an oversized, open break area. The room was built in a circle; to the left of the circle was a hallway that led to the boot camp compound. To the right of the circle was a hallway leading to the sleeping quarters for the camp.

At the front of the room was a double-wide desk where two COs sat. Directly in front of the desk was a set of doorways that led to the showers, outside, supply closets, laundry, and break rooms. The room was built in a complete circle. The guards never had to leave their stations at the oversize desk, if they chose not to do so. Most times during the lazy veteran COs shift they did just that, they just sat there. They spent their days talking, women moved about freely, coming and going at their leisure. Nobody seemed to be in a hurry. Tara watched as a group of girls tossed a ball back and forth and headed outside, laughing and joking all the way. "Hey, Shorty, baby. What's poppin', cutie-pie?" one of the girls in the group questioned as she passed.

"Ain't nothin' shakin', Goldie baby. Same-old, same-old," Shorty shot back.

The women were told to take a seat at the tables in the break room. Three inmates wearing crispy white Nike tennis shoes and perfectly wrapped French rolls joined the COs at the desk. The dark-skinned inmate with the ghetto booty reached in front of the male officer and retrieved a clipboard from the desk drawer. Her breast lingered a few seconds too long in his face and the officer licked his lips, enjoying the moment. The male officer favored a young Al Pacino but with way too long hair; every time he spoke he pushed his jet-black hair from his eyes. He rocked back on two legs in his chair while he watched Tonita's ass bounce from the room. He would have to take the tender little hot thing to the laundry room when she was done with the new arrivals. "He was going to have to get his self a few things while they were back in the laundry room." the young CO thought as his manhood pressed against his thin cotton uniform pants. "Damn that girl keep his shit hard." Hoping she would be done soon.

His overweight shift partner mistook the bulge in his pants for her, she just knew her sexy pookie bear couldn't resist her daily stories about all the sex she'd had the night before with whoever, she knew he wanted her, she just didn't know when he was ever going to make the first move. Damn, he's so shy, she thought, wishing he'd touch her.

The inmate in charge began reading institution numbers and last names from the clipboard. The women rose as their names and numbers were read. "You women follow Davis. She'll show you to your bunks," the inmate in charge instructed the first group standing at the front of the room.

A few rounds later, only a group of twelve women remained, including Tara. The chick in charge instructed the remaining women to join her at the front of the room. The inmates obeyed their leader. "Hi, y'all, my name is Tonita and I'm going to take you to your sleeping area. Follow me, please," Tonita directed, leading the way down the hallway on the right of the room. The long hallway opened up to the largest bedroom Tara had ever seen.

As far as the eye could see were bunk beds neatly lined up end to end. In-between the aisles of bunk beds were locker boxes and metal dressers in sets of four. The arrangement of the bunks made housing units within the massive space, with housing units of two at the intersecting aisle in the center and at both ends.

Ground-level windows lined both sides of the massive room. The room was surprisingly quiet for its size and the amount of people housed inside. Tara noticed, as she passed the bunks, that the women were softly speaking among themselves, respecting the peacefulness of the room.

The chick in charge expertly dropped women off along their stroll down the last aisle of the barracks. As they approached the back of the room, Tara began feeling a cool, refreshing breeze. She could hear the humming of a large motor in the distance.

At the end of the aisle, at the left corner, was where Tonita stopped with her last drop-off. "I got the word that you wasn't just anybody, so I hooked a sister up. Remember that shit when the time come," Tonita said, licking her lips. She pressed her fat ass into Tara's crotch on her way back down the hall, her hips bouncing from side to side all the way down the long aisleway.

"That hooker throw that used-up pussy every chance she get. She don't never get tired of working them hips," a voice spoke with disgust from under the bottom bunk. A Woodstock-looking, carefree white girl stuck her head out from under the bunk and continued speaking as she set up on the bed. She then reached for her cigarettes on the locker box beside the bed. "My name is Pammy. Welcome home. Sorry 'bout my outburst but that girl gives us truly gay girls a bad name."

Pammy got up from the bunk, stretched and shook out her long, dark-brown hair. She rolled a pack of Marlboros into the sleeve of her state shirt and checked her watch.

"My name is Tara. Thanks for the welcome. Which one of these lockboxes is mine?" Tara asked her roommate, wanting to get settled in.

"The one up against the wall is yours," Pammy explained to her new "bunkie."

"Tara? Tara, girl, where yo' ass at up in here?" Rosie yelled from the other side of the room in the center aisle. Tara climbed onto her top bunk. She could see her friend in the distance, standing up on her top bunk, yelling into the air.

"*Ssshh,*" could be heard coming from several bunks. "Ssshh yourself, bitches. Try and make me be quiet if you can, bitches," Rosie shot back into the air.

"Girl, get your ass down from there before you break your neck with your crazy ass. I'll see you outside in a minute," Tara yelled back to her friend. She climbed down from the bunk and prepared to head outside.

"It's almost count time. The count whistle is going to blow any minute now," Pammy shared, hoping her new roommate wasn't planning on being this noisy all the time. Pammy liked things quiet in her little space.

"Sorry about all the noise. My girl's glad to be free from admissions. You know how that is, right?" Tara apologized, not wanting to start off on the wrong foot with her new roommate.

The four o'clock count whistle blew loudly on the compound. The women in the barracks climbed onto their bunks. Women streamed in from outside and the room came alive. Every shape, size, color, and race entered the huge room.

From the top of the bunk, Tara could see the entire housing unit. All four corners were visible to her. She recognized several faces from either back home or the workhouse—she wasn't sure which. One face she recognized right away was Rissa. Tara's self-proclaimed enemy entered the room like she owned it. Several girls cleared a path as she passed by with her entourage. The earth-disturbing group continued rowdily down one of the long aisles. Tara wondered if it was legal for a place this size to have only one entrance. "Damn, a bitch could get trapped back in this bitch," she made a mental note to herself; it could definitely work in her favor later.

Rissa's bunk was at the opposite end of the room. Tara was glad she didn't have to be too close to the chick at night. It was going to be hard enough with the hater at the camp with her. She was going to have to watch her back for sure with Rissa nearby.

The cool breeze from the industrial-size fan blew across Tara's bunk. She laid perfectly still as the second count whistle blew, signaling the women to get silent and still on their bunks. Two COs entered the room and started the count on opposite ends of the room.

Across the back wall of the housing unit was a row of bunks. In the bunk in the corner at the bottom sat a sandy-blond–haired white girl whose eyes caught Tara's and the two women smiled at each other. Blondie's smile was warm and comforting. Tara enjoyed the exchange for a long while before she turned away.

Tara walked slowly from the phones. She'd tried one last time to reach Scott before giving up for the day. She hadn't heard from him since she was in admissions. He was always hard to nail down, but it had been a minute since they talked. She hoped he was safe.

Word on the street was that a lot of soldiers were getting popped or leaving here way too soon. She prayed the street would keep her friend safe; the unknown was a killer. She still hadn't received any mail from the outside world or from Julio. The thought of him made her body ache. She wasn't even really aware of how she wound up back at her bunk, but she was glad to be there.

Warm tears ran down her face as she climbed onto her bed. The emptiness of being without the people she loved hurt like hell. She laid on the top bunk staring out the window. "Hey, Tara, you want to play some kickball with us? We need an extra player," Pammy asked, rushing in to change her shoes.

"I'm good, Pammy. I think I'm going to take a nap before lunch," Tara explained, rolling over so Pammy couldn't see the tears on her face. Pammy finished changing her shoes and left as quickly as she came.

Tara laid there for a long time, crying silently. Her shoulders rose and fell with each sob. When her hips began to hurt from the thin, state-issued mattress, she turned over onto her other side. The bright light from the window caused her to open her eyes. Far away in the distance she could see birds flying free across the sky.

"Why don't you come outside and enjoy the weather? It's supposed to rain tomorrow and we'll be stuck inside all day," the sandy-blond girl from the bunk in the corner asked Tara. She stood at the end of Tara's bunk and stared up at her. "My name is Sherri. What's yours?" she asked like they were at happy hour.

Sherri was very cute and friendly. Tara welcomed the company, and she wanted to learn more about this girl who always seemed to be staring at her from across the room.

Sherri waited patiently while Tara put on her shoes. Sherri was surprised that she had agreed to leave her pity party.

The two new friends exited the shiny red door into the yard. The pair vibed instantly. Sherri talked with a raspy voice that was hypnotizing. She ended every sentence with, "You know what I'm saying?" that made Tara constantly answer back, "No, I don't know what you're saying." This made the pair laugh every time.

Sherri shared with Tara that she was on her second year out at the camp. She told Tara how she was doing time for forgery, which was really cashing bad checks to support her drug addiction. Sherri was a recently divorced mother of two who got married way too soon. Her newfound freedom introduced her to crack cocaine and the rest was history.

Stolen check writing, or "paper hangin'" as Sherri called it, became her profession. She quit her job and became self-employed in a matter of months after she first tried almighty crack. "The drug ruled my every thought and action," Sherri shared as the two made their third lap around the walk-jog exercise track that circled the entire rec yard. As they began the next lap, Tara noticed a familiar person seated on one of the benches to the side of the track.

Snuggled up on one of the green and blue metal park benches was Linda Loudermilk and an inmate who was clearly her man. Linda sat with her thin, sunburned legs crossed tightly at the knees. She wore a state-issued skirt and her state socks were rolled down to her ankles. The coupled stared into each other's eyes like they were on a private island alone somewhere in the Caribbean. Linda looked tan and happy sitting in the yard enjoying the sunshine.

Located just outside the shiny red door was a bank of red, metal picnic tables that the inmates used to play cards and board games during yard time. Rissa was sitting at one of the tables in a heated exchange. "I'm gonna split that bitch's wig. Watch what the fuck I'm sayin', man. Watch what the fuck

I'm sayin'," Rissa spat, slamming her cards onto the table and getting up.

One of Rissa's crew swiftly pulled her back down by her shirt. "Come on, Rissa, you overreacting. They just talkin'. Besides, you and Sherri been broke up for over six months now," Rissa's partner reasoned, hoping to calm her hotheaded leader down. Shante liked being in the crew with the power. The job came with so many benefits. Whatever they wanted they got, and they fucked on the regular. Shante wasn't going to lose her golden ticket, not to the hole or a bitch.

"I can't stand that fake-ass Tara bitch. She think she some kind of royalty or something. Every time I turn around bitches bendin' over backwards for the bitch. I heard Tonita's ass pulling strings to get that bitch's bed assignment changed when Ms. Queen Bee got here, like she special or something. Let that ho sleep in the yard. Fuck her!" Rissa shouted her venomous words in Tara's direction.

Tara lapped the track once more, unaware that all eyes were on her. Sherri was one of the baddest chicks on the compound. All the players wanted a piece of Sherri. Tara was just glad to talk to someone who understood her story. To her the two were similar in their loss. Sherri missed her children like crazy and she was afraid she might not get a chance to be with them as a family again. Tara missed her husband like crazy and she was afraid she would never get the chance to make up for all the pain she'd caused him.

In the distance, up against the wall, Tara could see Rosie, Shorty, and several other inmates engaged in some sort of exchange. She caught a glimpse of Rosie tucking a carton of cigarettes inside her pants. The pack separated quickly, and Rosie skipped inside with her loot.

Chapter Twelve

Julio sat down in the mahogany chair and pulled his seat close to the large, matching desk. Both windows in his spacious dorm room were wide open. The fresh air blew through the screen, relaxing him. This was his third attempt at starting the letter. He didn't know where to start. Finally he decided to just write.

Tara,

I know you know that I am mad as hell with you. I've been so mad for so long that I'm tired of the madness for today. Today has been one of those days where I've felt depressed all day, just heated about the past. They say it's not good to think about the past because it's all gone. That's what the mother-fuckers tell me when I go off in this bitch, but you can't help thinking about the past sometimes. Thinking of the past when things were so beautiful and today they so ugly and full of changes. Who was to say this was going to happen to you or to me, your big problems, or the distance between us. Out of this time I have learned some hard lessons about life and love. Love is a beautiful thing to have in life, but it can be so painful, especially when there is love between two people that is a very strong love. Then for some reason beyond our control one day everything changes. One takes one path and one goes another way. Who would know that in such a short time there could be so much love and then so much suffering? Who was to say that the love after being so strong was going to vanish where no one could see it, going and coming, change after change. This has been a very painful journey for me, only I can speak to the pain I feel locked away behind these walls. But life has to go on and I ain't never ran from a damn thing and I damn sure won't start running now.

I don't know, maybe a niggah get lucky and that "happier-ever-after" shit really mean something or some shit like that. Maybe the love might come back like it used to be. Now that's some fairy-tale shit, huh. These motherfuckers in here be trying to get you to believe that shit for real. I be wanting to tell them that I almost had that shit for real, then I remember the almost part, damn. They say some things happen for the best. I keep trying to understand the best of this shit, I try to figure that shit out but it just makes me crazy. Tomorrow never comes in this bitch, things just remains the same with no changes. I am glad I still have the beautiful memories of the life we had, that's why I stay mad constantly. Sometimes I will them to come back, but my wishes never come to reality. I just hope the pain stops. I can't control it and that drives me crazy.

Damn you, Tara. We had it all. I thought that mattered to you but you just threw it all away. How could you let that fuckin' rock be more important than us, than me? You put that shit before everything. That shit keeps me mad. Did I not cross your mind when you were out there chasing that shit? Didn't you think about us? Do you know how it made me feel to get reports my girl was out there with another niggah? Did you think about that shit at all Tara, did you? Shit so bad now, I don't even allow a motherfucker to let your name drop out they mouth before I lay a niggah down. I been to the hole so much up in here that they got me seeing the psych doctor. That motherfucker crazy too, he always talking all soft and looking at me like I'm his science experiment. You'd think he'd never seen a true gangsta before. I talked to your mother; she shocked the hell out of me by telling me that you still loved me, that shit fucked me up. I told her I did not know of your kind of love. I don't think you were ready for my kind of love. I don't think you have experienced real love before me. Love is not just about things and places. Do you know what love is about, do you? Ask yourself that question, Tara. "Did I really love Julio or want him forever?" There is no one in this world who will ever love you as much as I did, my love was a real love and you walked on it. Maybe it's my fault, maybe I gave you too much too soon. Maybe I was around you too much, or maybe I let you know too much how much I loved you. I fell in love with you after being with you for a little while. You were the perfect girl, the one for me. I was around all the time checking you out. Before I really knew what happen I was in love. I fell hard for your beautiful smile, your body, and your sexy eyes. I always just wanted to make you happy and see you smile. Each day I wanted to fill your heart with my love. My plan when I stood before the minister and said "I do" was to have you by my side for a lifetime. We were inseparable; you were right by my side, always me and you. I did what I thought a husband was supposed to do for his wifey. You was my queen, I tried to make you comfortable in every way.

We had our moments, you was always so jealous. I always wished you could see inside my heart. I trusted you with that shit and you smashed it. I feel like a soft-ass motherfucker. I'm supposed to be a thoroughbred and I let some pussy knock me to my knees, what kind of gangsta shit is that? You were the only mami for me; I was satisfied with our life and with my wife. I'm not going to lie, pussy was thrown at me daily, but I never cheated on you Tara, never. You can ask any niggah or bitch out there, ask them. I coulda fucked everyday if I wanted to, but I always returned home to you, most times I came home *with flowers. See what I'm saying, you had me on all that lame-ass shit, Tara, you really chumped a niggah off. I know you can't say the same thing on that faithful piece and that shit burns me the fuck up, man. So now you know why I'm so mad, I'm mad at everybody and everything, I must say though, it feels good to say this shit to you. I have been needing to say all this for a long time. We both have nothing but time, to do a lot of soul-searching. I promise you one thing; I will never allow myself to be hurt this way again, not ever. I knew the moment I saw you that you was going to be a heartbreaker. Hey, but for real, real, keep your head up. Motherfuckers are a trip, watch your back on them bitches up in there, these niggahs petty as hell out here now. They keep a motherfucker putting in over-time. If they don't know who you are, then you let them know.*

Julio

Chapter Thirteen

Scott sat at the back of the bus with his hands in his lap and his head down. He stared at the floor, his body language daring anyone to speak to him. His black-crocheted Kufi Muslim head gear was pulled tightly down around his head. He was handcuffed to an old-school hustler who had other things on his mind too.

The busload of state prisoners was headed north on State Route 23 to Mansfield Correctional Institution for medium-security male state prisoners. Scott was so angry at himself for being here again, on a bus headed for another state plantation. It was as if he was set on a collision course for the motherfucking joint.

He had a plan; he'd been studying and working his plan for months. He was so close. He had enough paper stacked to jump completely out the game. His two soul food restaurants were pulling in mad cash and he was ready to open up a spot on the westside.

It was just pure greed on his part for being in this predicament. He had skillfully avoided the feds on some serious drug cases. He still couldn't believe the petty motherfuckers were laying him down on some punk-ass weapons shit. A motherfucker needed a gun in his neighborhood. Where he came from, you reached for your gun with your shoes every morning.

Scott was trying not to go crazy on these soft-ass bitches.

His best bet was staying on some Muslim, positive shit or else he was going to have a hard twenty-seven months to do.

Motherfuckers were given him his props so far, but he was a street legend in his hometown. Everybody on the local level knew what time it was, but it would be a different story once he got to the joint.

Regardless of how much respect he had riding in, thirsty young bucks were always looking to make a name for themselves. Scott loved making believers out of his eager students. He was anxious for class to begin; doing time was entertainment for him.

He knew from the jump that his Folk homies had him but he wasn't really on all that madness. This time he wanted something different.

He thought long and hard about all the plans he had for Tara. He wanted so badly to give her the life she deserved: a life without fear. Way back when they were just kids he saw fear in her eyes. It was only when she was vulnerable, when she had her guard down, that he got to see it. He knew her well and he knew she needed him now.

"What's up, Do Dirty, man. I'm glad we ridin' with a true G, man. It's good to see ya," a young soldier called back four rows to holler at a true playa. Niggahs all around the bus started pointing and looking back to see if it was really the infamous street legend.

"That probably ain't even no Do Dirty either. I heard that motherfucker dead. Stupid niggahs believe anything they hear. That professor-looking pretty boy ain't hardly no Do Dirty," Ant sang, sucking his teeth and looking back over the plastic green seats on the bus. He studied the face of the other passenger a little longer before looking away.

He was sure the pretty boy wasn't Do Dirty, but he wasn't sure the professor-looking, house niggah wasn't an easy mark, either. Something told short north Ant that the professor had heart.

Damn, a motherfucker would have to recognize me already. A brother really just wanted to lay low. Shit couldn't ever just be easy. Can't a niggah catch a break sometime? Scott thought, looking around the bus. Niggahs were whispering and pointing already. He was hoping he could skate through this time, maybe take some classes and chill. He didn't want to get caught up on no bullshit. His bangin' days were over, but he was obligated to hold down his crew if shit hit the fan.

He needed to get his mind right and prepare to do his time. Scott knew he would have to come out of all the lost time a better, wiser man. He always got close but he never got the opportunity to cross the finish line.

The bus jerked to a quick stop. Scott looked up from the ground and realized that they had reached their destination: prison; the joint; the big house; the motherfucking belly of the beast. *Let the games begin,* he thought, exiting the bus in full swagger. Some things just came naturally.

"Mitchell? Aw, hell no, not you, Mitchell. I don't want no mess out of you. We got a new warden and he ain't on none of your shit, boy, you hear me?" The intake CO recognized him immediately and was glad he was assigned to intake. The CO knew Mitchell from his rookie days. The young thug was nothing but trouble.

"Damn, punk-ass motherfucker. The least you could do is say 'welcome home', shit," Scott spat, flexing in the old correctional officer's face. The poor, scared CO almost pissed his pants. "Don't start out disrespecting me. I got my Kufi on and you going to respect me or else. Tell that to the warden while you telling shit," Scott continued as a crowd started to gather.

Six more correctional officers entered the room out of nowhere. The room got silent. It had been a long ride and a very hot day. No one was ready to go to battle over petty shit, so they all fell back. Most of the inmates were veterans to the process; they were processed through in record time.

Scott was already in the medical line before he knew it. If they were lucky they'd be in their cells by dinnertime and they wouldn't be forced to eat cold bologna sandwiches. Maybe they'd catch a break if no drama jumped off.

"Enter, inmate," the CO at the desk yelled to the door, never looking up. Scott entered the room and recognized the officer at the desk immediately. They had a history and he planned to use that to his advantage.

"Shit, this tired-ass job is starting to look up. A bitch thought she was going to have to go through the summer without some good-ass dick. Come over here with your fine ass and let me see your dick, Mitchell," Officer Ward ordered the inmate as she unbuttoned the top three buttons on her shirt.

Scott walked to her like the person in charge. He pulled her up from her chair while grabbing her breasts. He pulled her plump right breast from its confinement and sucked at its brown, hard nipple like a newborn baby. Ward moaned from the pleasure of his forceful touch and her eyes rolled back in her head.

Scott roughly pushed her back into a cheap, plastic chair on wheels. The strength of his push caused her to slide across the room and hit the wall. "Slow down, baby. You know you can get some of this. Slow your wild ass down," Scott told her, adjusting his dick and returning to the other side of the desk.

Damn, that's a fine piece of meat. I can't wait to get me some of that, Ward thought, watching his every move from her seat. They had been lovers in Mansfield previously. The dick was so good it almost cost her job. She was so dick sick back then that inmates were starting to call her Mrs. Do Dirty. Luckily, she was cool with her captain and able to explain that shit away. She would have to be a lot more careful this time around. It would be hard but the dick was worth it.

Ward quickly processed his paperwork and moved his inmate record file to the top of the pile in the next room. She watched from the doorway as the next CO called him to the next metal desk. He looked so sexy standing there with all his thuggish tattoos and his Mr. Universe body, her panties got wet just thinking about him inside her.

She stood in the doorway watching him through the entire process. They all were ahead of schedule today, so he wasn't at the desk long before he was sent to the next room. The identification room was the last stop. Inmates were issued their institutional picture ID and their bed assignments before they were paraded over to admissions.

Scott towed the line through the halls of the prehistoric penitentiary. Everything was old and gray. The place was very clean, and everything had a fresh coat of gray paint. There were very few windows, so it was extremely dark and depressing. The place made you instantly sleepy as soon as you entered the hallways.

Scott was the first to be dropped off at his range, thanks to his girl Ward. He entered his housing cell. It took a minute for his eyes to adjust to the darkness of the room. Once his eyes were focused, he locked eyes with the young soldier from the bus.

"Dirty, man, it's an honor to get to be in the room with you, man. Damn, wait 'til my boy Diamond find this shit out." The young soldier jumped up from the bottom bunk and bounced around the room shadowboxing.

Scott put his few items on the floor beside the bunk. "Simmer down, partner. You awful geeked up, ain't you?"

The young soldier checked himself and sat back down on

the bed. "My bad, Dirty, my bad. Hey, my name's Rayshawn but everybody calls me Ray Ray, man. You want to take the top or the bottom?" Ray Ray offered, getting out of the way in the tiny space.

"I'll take the top. All the decisions are made from the top, and don't you ever forget that, dog," Scott taught, jumping up on his bunk to prepare for count time.

He would have to get a cell mate that was motherfucking starstruck and shit. The little G sat on his bunk in amazement. He was acting like he had just seen his maker. Young people need some more heroes.

Officer Ward damn near served the pussy up on a platter for a brother. If his memory served him right, she was a fatal attraction that a brother could get to do anything as long as he gave her the dick on the regular.

He was going to have to pull some strings to get moved through receiving. Scott didn't plan to spend six weeks locked back in the hellhole they were currently locked in. He would need to call in his first favor with Ward A.S.A.P. If he was sentenced to this circus, he might as well enjoy the show.

Chapter Fourteen

Tara stared at the bold, black letters on the white paper. The words were intimidating: GED HIGH SCHOOL EQUIVALENCE TEST. The words stared back at her, daring her to touch the clean, white paper and turn the page.

She glanced around the room at the other students. Only four of them had started the pop quiz. Five inmates had their heads down sleeping and four hoochie mamas were all up in the cute teacher's face asking him unnecessary questions.

Tara looked at the big classroom clock for the tenth time; only a minute had passed since the last time she looked at the thing. She had another hour and a half to go in the mandatory GED class. It was mandated by the state that all high school dropouts be enrolled in school. Everyone else was given a state job. Inmates earned twenty dollars a month for their labor.

"You ladies need to take your seats and start your tests. It is a timed exam and you are using up your time foolishly," the cutie told the inmates but they just flirted with each other when the young teacher got up from the desk and walked away. He walked around the room in a big circle twice and then turned and started down Tara's aisle. He stopped when he got to her desk and bent down. "You haven't even opened the packet. How are you going to get through this class if you don't start the darn thing?" He then stood back up, winked at her, and started back down the aisle. The white boy had swagger. No wonder the hoochies couldn't stay in their seats.

Tara opened the intimidating packet and began working on the material. She was surprised how easily she floated through the writing and language arts sections of the test. It took her a little longer to finish the social studies portion. All that remained were the dreaded math and science sections. Math had always been Tara's weakest subject and she knew very little about science.

"You have thirty minutes left, ladies. Please use your time wisely. I would suggest you complete the sections you are most comfortable with now. This will help increase your score if your answers are correct. Don't waste time trying to figure out answers you don't know. Come back to those if you have time," young cutie explained to the nervous ladies while he paced the room.

The classroom was located across the hall from the cafeteria. The noise made by the kitchen staff could be heard throughout the classroom. Tara tried to focus on the papers in front of her and not on the distractions around her. Completing the test was now her goal. Sailing through most of the sections gave her a sense of pride and it boosted her confidence in her ability to get her GED. If anyone had asked her, she'd swear up and down that she didn't give a fuck about getting her GED, but deep inside it was very important to her.

Most of the science questions were multiple-choice story problems. Tara answered the ones that she knew and gave her best guess to the rest. She closed her test packet with three minutes remaining on the clock, proud of what she'd been able to accomplish.

The young teacher collected the few completed tests. He was happy for the ladies who were able to block out all the distractions to get their tests done. It was a miracle he was able to assist some of the women in obtaining their GED. Many of them weren't mentally ready to focus on applying themselves in the classroom.

The moment the class was released, Tara headed straight for the game room because she knew her crew would be there. The game room was the spot; it was where everybody kicked it and exchanged information. Plus, you could catch a decent game of bid whiz if you were lucky.

The game room was on blast when she arrived. One of the inmates had their music up way too loud and the bass from the earphones was pumpin'. Inmates were coupled off all around the room. The line at the microwave oven was seven deep with people trying to cook their lunch before count time. A lot of the inmates refused to eat at central food services and cooked everything they ate while doing time. Meanwhile, a group of inmates were working diligently on a thousand-piece puzzle at a table close to a set of large picture windows facing the boot camp across the compound. At the front of the room, a thirty-six inch Samsung television was bolted to the ceiling with neat rows of chairs arranged in front of it. Inmates who were soap opera faithful seemed to always be glued to the tube.

"What's up, Tara? You been held hostage in that punk-ass school all day. Damn, that shit is crazy. You want in on the next game? We been whooping they asses all day. I know they ready for a new belt," Rosie sang to her homie as she joined them.

"Hell ya, I got next. I'm ready to get some shit started, cuz," Tara shot back, sitting down at the metal recreation table, glad to be free from the pressure of her class.

"That's what's up. And while you getting comfortable, ain't there something you want to tell a playa about you and that fine-ass Sherri?" Rosie asked the question that was on everyone's mind. The clique had been discussing the subject all morning. If the nosy-ass bitches wanted to be all up in her girl's business, Rosie planned on putting the shit on blast.

She knew her girl well enough to know that there wasn't any shame in her game. If Tara was fucking around she'd let the shit be known.

Tara was fine as hell. She had connections and much swagger, so hustlers and hoes alike wanted to know if she fucked around. Most of the women did; they were either suckin' or getting sucked. That was the normal up in the joint. Everybody was fuckin' to pass the time and keep from going crazy.

"Hey, bunkie. Sherri wanted me to let you know that she's fixing some kind of casserole and some other shit for lunch and she wants you to eat some with us," Tara's cool bunk partner shared, walking up to the table and making herself comfortable.

Everyone stopped what they were doing and waited for Tara's response. You could hear a pin drop. "Damn! I'm going to need all y'all to get some fuckin' business. Y'all all up in mine. Pammy, I'll holla at you later." Tara dismissed Pammy before she even knew what happened.

Tara had way too much game than to ever let the amateurs at the table know what the fuck she was doing. She didn't roll like that. Everything about the place was way too open. Tara knew not to let everybody up in her mix. At an early age, her daddy taught her that everybody wasn't her fuckin' friend; most were just motherfuckers she knew. Rosie and Shorty had proven to be down with her, but the other inmates around the table were new faces.

"My bad, cuz. These bitches is all up in yo' grill and shit. Damn, y'all nosy, sitting up in here like y'all watching the *Young and the Restless* or some shit. Come on, cuz, let's bounce. I'm tired of being all stuck up inside," Rosie shared, getting up from the table. Shorty rose with her and headed out the door with the two friends as if her name had been called.

Tara was comfortable with Shorty. She started talking the

minute they were in the yard. The women instinctively made their way to the walk-jog and began circling the track. "Go on and ask. I know you're dying to ask about me and Sherri, so go ahead, ask," Tara instructed Rosie, lightening the mood between the girls.

"Hell, if Rosie ain't gonna ask the fuckin' question, I will. What's up with you and your girl Sherri? Are y'all kickin' it or what?" Shorty asked Tara straight up.

"Y'all so nosy. Sherri is my friend. We are just friends, that's it and that's all. I like her. She's cool and easy to talk to. That's it. I know both you freaks are hoping that I've crossed over to the dark side. I'm sorry to disappoint everyone," Tara announced to her friends as they walked the yard. She was being as honest as she chose to be with her friends. She trusted the two girls at her side. They'd all grown close over the past few weeks. They were real, rare ride-or-die soldiers.

There were far too many imitators—motherfuckers pretending to be down and crowning themselves king. Kings and legends are made, tested on the battlefield. Unfortunately, you ran into fewer and fewer true gangsters. Shit was changing. There was no honor or heart in the game anymore.

The joint was full of perpetrators and amateurs. Tara had little experience dealing with the breed. She was grateful to have her girls down with her. She knew they had her back. The two of them understood what it meant to be down. That's why it pained her to withhold a bit of the truth from them. She wasn't ready to tell them that sometimes when Sherri talked to her about her goals and her dreams for a different kind of life it inspired her. Tara was drawn to Sherri. She was like a refuge from the storm of prison. When the two of them talked, she felt a sense of peace. Her conversations were always centered on change and hope for a different kind of life.

Chapter Fifteen

All inmates were required to be on their bunks and still at count time. Count time was very serious business and the interruption of the count was considered a serious offense. Women weren't permitted to leave their bunk until count was cleared. Correction officers didn't play about count time. Every inmate sentenced to the prison was accounted four times a day. An inmate could easily face a trip to the hole for disrupting the count.

Tara sat perfectly still on her top bunk, enjoying the tuna casserole that Sherri made for lunch. Her new friend had outdone herself. Tara was blown away by how good the casserole tasted. She could even taste some onion and celery in the dish. She didn't even want to know how Sherri and her girls got the veggies. She was just glad to be down.

Tara attacked the homemade microwave meal with much passion. She looked across the room hoping to catch Sherri's attention and thank her. To Tara's surprise, Sherri was stretched out across her bunk staring straight at her and smiling. The smile caught Tara off guard and she quickly turned away to look in a different direction. Across the room, Rosie waved at her friend while doing a silly dance on her bunk. The CO turned in Rosie's direction and she made herself instantly still on her bunk.

Tara laughed at her friend and continued eating her food. She held the bowl up in the air and showed the inside to Rosie, teasing her with the meal. She'd nearly killed the casserole already. Rosie motioned for Tara to give her some, but Tara mouthed back, "Come and get it," holding the bowl in the air.

Rosie mouthed back, "Here I come," while standing up partway on her top bunk. She glanced around the room to see where the COs were and then she jumped down from the bunk. Tara watched nervously as Rosie weaved in and out of the bunks, skillfully making her way back to Tara. Several other inmates watched Rosie along with Tara, amazed by her heart and silliness.

Rosie's supporters cheered her on as she made her way back to Tara's bunk. The excitement caused the whole room to get involved in her antics while the clueless COs finished the count and exited the room. Rosie crawled along the concrete floor the rest of the way to her girl's bunk, feeding off the energy her fans gave her. When she got within a few feet of Tara, she did a handstand and walked upside down to the bed.

"What would you do for a Klondike Bar," Rosie asked, snatching the bowl from her friend with a smile.

"What the fuck ever it takes, obviously. Do you, sister," Tara laughed. Rosie crept to the edge of the aisle and looked down it, checking the whereabouts of the COs. She repeated the same lookout down the back aisle as well. After studying her escape route carefully, she started back up the aisle.

Tara watched, hoping she didn't get caught. "Wish me luck," Rosie called over her shoulder before creeping back down the aisle, weaving in between the bunks. The other inmates began guiding her escape route, directing her on which turns to take.

Tara was relieved when Rosie got close to her bunk. The girl was a fool who always kept Tara laughing. You could count on her to lighten the mood and keep it real with a sister. There wasn't anything fake or petty about Rosie. She was a veteran to doing time. People respected that in her. The girl knew the hustle of prison inside and out. She kept her hustle on, already pimpin' the system to her advantage.

The day she arrived, two gay girls chose her and attached themselves to her hip. The pair constantly competed to see who would win her over. Rosie used the strawberries to her benefit daily. "Strawberry" was the name given to girls who only started fuckin' around with women after coming to the joint. Marysville was full of strawberries anxiously waiting to be turned out by vets like Rosie.

There wasn't much to do in the joint, so relationships between inmates were the way everybody passed the time. The drama that came with the relationships was crazy, though. On any given day, a bitch was gunning for you over another bitch. The shit was crazy and Tara wanted no part of the nonsense. She saw how the women got caught up. It was easy to allow another woman to help you pass the time. Unfortunately, there were mostly predators out there trying to take advantage of an easy mark. Tara knew firsthand what it felt like to be hurt by love. She didn't wish the pain on her worst enemy.

Tara was pleased to see Rosie approaching her bunk, but the excitement over her escapades was getting out of control. The women were so excited by the entertainment that they forgot all about count time. Their noise reached the COs desk out front. Just as Rosie prepared to climb back onto her bunk from the back side of the bed, she was confronted by the first-shift CO Everyone in the dorm froze along with Rosie. A collective gasp was heard throughout the room. It was all bad for Rosie.

Chapter Sixteen

Kohr Place was jumping with cars lined up, bumper to bumper, up and down the street. People were everywhere; young and old folks were gathered in groups along the street sharing stories. Mama Gracie's house was ground zero. Everybody gathered there whenever the family came together for any occasion.

Unfortunately, the occasion that brought everyone together on this day was the family gathering after the burial services of Tara's third cousin Belinda. She was the oldest daughter of Granddaddy's baby brother. It was particularly sad because Belinda had been a handsome, young, beautiful lady full of potential. She came from educated parents who gave her every advantage in life. Belinda went to the best schools and got an Ivy League college education. All the women wantd to be like her and the men wanted to be with her. Unfortunately, she started messing around with recreational drugs at a young age, and by the time she got to college she had graduated to the hard stuff. The drugs proved to be way too much for Belinda and it took her from her family way too soon.

Belinda was older than Tara and she hadn't known her very well. She was real cool with her mom, though. Most of Tara's relatives who played around in the fast line wound up connected to her mom. This always placed M&M between a rock and a hard place with the by-the-book members of the family. She was constantly blamed for turning one family member or another out, which was rarely the case. Most of them were already deep in the streets well before they landed at M&M's door.

Tara sat on the sunny porch of her grandparents' house and enjoyed the show with her grandfather and her other relatives. The neat porch was covered with an assortment of mismatched chairs and tables. The railing around the porch was covered with different kinds of plants and flowers. Mama Gracie's antique, rocking patio sofa was the centerpiece of the porch. The swing had been painted many different colors over the years and it always reminded Tara of home when she sat on it.

She enjoyed sharing the swing with her cousins Rick and Bruce. The three were close in age and grew up together. It was always nice to spend time with them, even if the occasion wasn't a happy one.

"What's been up, cousin?" Bruce asked Tara as he reached toward Granddaddy's bottle of Southern Comfort under his chair. Granddaddy grabbed the bottle, which was wrapped in a brown paper bag, and handed it to his grandson.

"Be careful, hard ankle. This here will put hair on your chest. This here is one-hundred-proof whiskey. Can you handle it?" Granddaddy questioned his grandson. Ernest was the ruler of all he surveyed. He ruled his household like the king that he was. Nothing happened without his say and input. Nothing really happened on the whole block, for that matter, without his input.

He was a proud black man who had survived the injustices of the South and the slave labor of the factory jobs up north. Ernest moved to Ohio to provide a better life for himself and his children right after World War II. Both of Tara's older uncles had served in the war and survived. Her grandfather felt a sense of entitlement to the American dream and he was determined to get his piece for his family. That drive and determination kept him preaching to his children and grandchildren. It had also turned him into a functioning alcoholic over the years.

"Now, Granddaddy, whose grandson am I? You know I can handle this and a lot more," Bruce boasted, pouring the whiskey into one of the paper cups on the table between the swing sofa and Granddaddy's favorite chair.

Relatives moved in and out of the house with ease, stopping to speak with their precious granddaddy on their way. Tara's Uncle Bubba joined the conversation on the porch. Uncle Bubba was the oldest son of Gracie and Ernest. He was the spitting image of Granddaddy. Not only did he look like him but he acted like him as well and could drink you under the table just the same.

"I've been fine, Bruce. Trying to stay out of trouble," Tara offered her cousin as she watched from the porch her younger relatives play in the yard.

"Where's that new boyfriend of yours I been hearing so much about? You know your family has to sign off on him before he can claim our cousin. I hope you told him that," Rick announced, joining the conversation on the porch.

"I know you ain't addin' your two cents, Rick. You the one that ran off and got married while you were away. And to a Mexican on top of that. Granddaddy, what you got to say about that, huh?" Tara added to the conversation, wanting to see what Granddaddy would say for selfish reasons. Her cousin Rick had flown in for the funeral with his new bride, a lovely young girl from Mexico who spoke little English. The beautiful, young girl sat on the steps at the end of the long walkway to the front porch being entertained by Tara's sister Kim and Aunt Nancy.

"Well, baby, all I got to say is that love is where you find it. I found your grandmother when she was only thirteen. I was barely a man myself. Folks didn't believe in our love way back then, in the country back in Nashville, Tennessee, but I did. That's all that matters—that you believe. It's hard out here in the world. You need a good partner by your side to get you through this life," Granddaddy taught with a faraway look in his eyes.

Life was hard. He was always glad when his babies found someone to get through it with; he just hoped they could beat the odds of life. Things were looking up for him and his family. He'd retired after working thirty years at Buckeye Steel Casting in the south end of

Columbus. His home was paid off and all his children and grandchildren were alive and grown. His only worry was this new drug thing that was taking kids way too soon, Ernest thought, taking another drink from his favorite blue tin cup.

"Come on, Tara, let's get inside and set the table. Bootsie got the cornbread done. It's time to eat and I'm starving," Aunt Nancy told her niece, walking up on the porch. Rick's new wife followed closely behind.

All the smells of Tara's favorite foods smacked her in the face when she entered the house. She could smell the spicy-sweet aroma of Mama Gracie's sweet potatoes from the door. The living room was filled with people; both couches in the living room were overflowing with people.

Tara recognized most of the people in the living room as relatives, but there were a few people in the sunroom, off from the living room, that she didn't recognize. Some of the dudes in the room were checking her out like they were at the club or something.

She didn't blame them, though. Tara was rocking her slip dress and strappy sandals; orange always was her best color and the dress hugged her body closely. However, the look was not for them. She was wearing this outfit for her Julio. So she glided effortlessly through her grandparents' house, like a princess in her palace, following behind her Aunt Nancy.

Tara was ready to eat and she hoped Julio would get there soon. Her grandparents hadn't met him yet and she hoped he got there before her Granddaddy got too drunk. You never knew who he would take his wrath out on when he was wasted. His usual suspects were the new kids on the block. Poor Julio and Rick's wife would fly low if they knew what she knew. They were guaranteed a cussing out, just to welcome them to the family. Tara knew Julio could stand the heat but she wasn't so sure about Rick's new wife.

"Whoa, Mama Gracie. I can't wait to eat," Tara said, entering the kitchen and planting a wet kiss on her grandmother's cheek.

Mama Gracie kissed Tara back while she reached for the pot holders to pull her hot buttered rolls from the oven.

M&M stood at the counter pulling drinking glasses from the wooden cabinets. "Hey, baby, I didn't know you was here," she shouted over her shoulder to her youngest daughter, glad to see her.

"Which silverware are we using, Ma? Kim said to get the good silverware out," Tara questioned her mother.

"Sister, we should use the good silverware. You know the preacher and them coming for dinner. Mama gon' want to use her good china," Tara's Aunt Bootsie replied.

Aunt Bootsie was her mom's younger sister. She was classy and refined. She was a registered nurse who ran her department at one of the finest hospitals in the city. Aunt Bootsie was the standard you measured class and style by.

"You heard what Bootsie said. Hurry up and get the table set because the dodger is done," M&M instructed her baby girl, filling the drinking glasses with sweet iced tea. Tara laughed to herself at the familiar name her mother called the hot-water cornbread Aunt Bootsie pulled from the piping-hot oil in the cast-iron black skillet. Her aunt looked like Jacqueline Kennedy standing there at the stove in her ivory-colored pencil shirt and matching blouse with her antique pearls completing her outfit.

Mama Gracie had already begun setting the table when Tara entered the dining room. Aunt Nancy and the crew were still greeting relatives back in the living room. Tara was glad to spend the alone time with her Mama Gracie.

"Mama Grace, who's that funny lady on the porch, in the blue dress, who came with Uncle Bubba from the funeral?" Tara asked curiously.

"That's your granddaddy's sister Dill, silly. Didn't you ask your granddaddy when you were out there with him, girl?" Gracie asked her young granddaughter. Young folks were always moving too fast, never slowing down to enjoy the things that really matter.

"I didn't know Granddaddy's sister was here. She's funny, Mama Gracie. Her and Granddaddy were going toe to toe when I came inside," Tara told her grandmother while they set the table together.

Mama Gracie was a God-fearing woman who lived each day trying to make it to heaven. She raised her children in the church and took her grandchildren to church every chance she got. Today had been a sad day burying her young niece—she was just a baby gone on to heaven. Gracie cherished the time with her young granddaughter as Nancy and the crew joined them around the table.

Tara was glad that she and Julio managed to get a prime seat around the main dining room table. Her boo arrived just in time to eat. He sat confidently at her side, looking sexy as ever. He had already won over the females in her family with his good looks. Her mother warned her that would happen.

"Damn, baby, can everybody in your family cook? This food is good as hell," Julio whispered in Tara's ear while he rubbed her thigh under the table.

"There ain't nothing my family can't do, baby," Tara whispered back, glancing around the table full of family members. "Here, Granddaddy, I found your favorite piece of chicken, the straw bonnet," Tara said with a smile, placing the split chicken breast on her Granddaddy's plate then passing the platter to her right.

He lifted Tara's hand from the table and planted a wet kiss on the back of it. "Who's baby?" he sang to his grandbaby from the head of the table. The deluxe dining room table held twelve people, all seated comfortably and enjoying the food. Everybody knew Ernest was crazy about his grandchildren, drunk or sober, and Tara was one of his favorites.

"Pass me the macaroni and cheese, please. I can't get enough of it," Julio told Tara, finishing up the last of the creamy pasta on his plate. He made a neat place for his seconds and waited for the dish.

"You better eat it or wear it, youngster," Granddaddy threatened Julio from his seat at the head of the table, putting the young hard

ankles feet to the fire with his words. A real man never backed down
from a challenge; he looked it square in the eye and faced whatever
came his way.

"Yes, sir, I will. You don't have to worry about that for sure,
pops," Julio told his girl's grandfather with respect. The old man was
very obviously drunk and Julio respected his place at the head of the
table.

"These collard greens sure is good, Mama. I ain't had no good
collards in a long time. They taste just like the ones Grandma Ellen
used to make down home," Uncle Bubba reminisced to Mama Gracie
while smacking his lips.

"Sister made the collard greens, Bubba," Mama Gracie answered
back, calling M&M by the name they called her as a child.

"Well, they sure is good and this ham ain't bad either." Bubba
added, piling his plate with the honey-roasted ham.

"What the damn hell you asking Mama all them damn questions for, fool? Did yo' wife cook anything? Did yo' wife cook anything!" Granddaddy shouted at Uncle Bubba from across the table.
Granddaddy didn't care much for Uncle Bubba's wife Colleen, who
sat in the living room eating, oblivious to what the shouting was
about at the main table. Tara thought the whole thing was hilarious.
She easily joined in on the laughter of her mother, Aunt Bootsie, and
Aunt Nancy. None of the women cared much for Colleen.

"Hush up, you old fool. Bob, take your old drunk daddy outside
before he ruins everybody's meal. Reverend will be here soon and I
don't want all this foolishness in the house. Take that mess outside
on the porch," Mama Gracie instructed her second oldest son. The
family continued eating throughout the house. Everyone was used to
Granddaddy's behavior.

Once they finished eating, Julio asked Tara to show him where the
bathroom was located in the large house. She was excited to get some
private time with her man.

"Right this way," Tara told him, getting up from the table with
the rest of the family. Everyone headed back to what they were doing.

Bruce told Tara to join them in his car to hit some killer weed when they were done.

Tara ran up the stairs in her grandparents' house the way she used to when she was a kid, skipping the steps as she climbed them. Julio followed behind like a horny teenager. Pictures of family members lined the stairway up to the second floor of the home. A group of relatives passed them on the stairs jumping out of the young lovers' way on their way down.

Tara pulled her Latin lover into the full bathroom at the top of the stairs and closed the door. The room was decorated in ruffles and lots of little figurines. Everything was one shade of pink or another. Once they were inside, time stood still. Julio locked the door and threw her against the wall with gentle force.

"Damn, girl, your sexy ass drives me crazy," he said, pulling up her dress and sliding his hand inside her chocolate-colored silk boxer panties. His touch made her body quiver. He held his hand there gently, as if he was handling a precious jewel.

"It feels so good when you touch me like that, baby," Tara whispered in her man's ear. As she rubbed her clit against his touch, her eyes rolled back in her head and she closed her eyes. *He is so damn fine*, she thought, enjoying his kisses on her neck.

"This belongs to me, mami. This is all mine," Julio boosted, dropping to his knees in front of her. He pulled her panties down and placed her left leg over his shoulder.

"Taste it, baby. You know you been dying to taste this all day," Tara told him while she rubbed her hand in circular motions across her clit.

Julio lifted her hips up with his hands to meet his face. He pressed his face deep between her thighs, then his tongue slide inside her with ease. Her moans of pleasure excited him, making his rock-hard dick dance inside of his pants, longing to be free.

"Turn around, baby, I got to get me some of this," he told her, getting up from the floor after licking her one last time. Tara obeyed *him, turning and placing her hands on the full-length mirror that was fixed to the back of the bathroom door.*

Julio took in the beauty of his dime piece, watching her through the full-length mirror. She looked back at him from the mirror, reaching between her legs and grabbing his dick.

Tara seductively massaged her lover's dick with her hand before sliding his weapon inside her wet walls.

Knock, knock, knock "Is anybody in there?" a voice on the other side of the door yelled.

"I'm in here," Tara yelled back at the unfamiliar voice. "I'm going to be a while. Try the one that's downstairs."

Without missing a beat, she pushed against Julio and forced him deep inside of her. He rode her like a pro. The two of them were perfectly silent as they made love in the crowded house, trying to be as quiet as they possibly could.

"I'm going to cum, baby. I'm going to cum. Cum with me, daddy," Tara moaned out loud. The sound of her voice excited him. He released his eruption deep inside of her and she was at peace.

The dorm room was eerily quiet. It was the middle of the afternoon but most of the women lay lazily on their bunks in silent protest of Rosie being sent to the hole. Tara was interrupted from her daydream by the daytime CO who was quietly passing out mail to the inmates who were in the dorm room.

Chapter Seventeen

Things were always tense when someone from the small population of women went to the hole because the women all fed off of each other. CO Means knew enough about the women doing time to know that the mail would lighten the mood around the place instantly. She would rather deal with happy inmates than angry ones anytime. As long as they didn't kill each other, she mostly went along with their program.

When Means reached Tara's bed, she jumped from the sound of the unfamiliar footsteps that woke her from her daydream. Coming toward her bed with a handful of mail was a pleasant-looking white lady who looked like some kid's mom coming to pick them up from school.

CO Means stopped in front of Tara's bunk and began placing letter after letter at the foot of her bed. The familiar writing of the people she loved looked back at her from the comforting envelopes. Tears filled her eyes; she tried her hardest to fight them back but they had a mind of their own.

"Thank you, CO Means," Tara whispered sincerely to the woman who brought the letters from the real world. As soon as Means walked away, she separated the letters carefully and placed them in neat stacks. There were five letters from Julio, two letters from her mother, one greeting card from her dad, and a letter from somebody with the last name Marshall that she didn't recognize right away.

She really didn't know which letter to read first so she decided to get the unfamiliar letter out of the way. Tara stared at the handwriting again, trying to recognize the penmanship. The institution numbers at the end of the name let Tara know that the letter was from an inmate, but she still didn't recognize the name, so she just ripped it open.

The letter was from Scott. He'd been arrested under an assumed name, the assholes at the county booked him under that name, and now he was serving time under the fake last name. It was just another way the system fucked with a motherfucker—a inmate's property and mail were always held up when you had a bunch of aliases.

He was locked up, doing time right along with her. His letter made her very sad. She had money on him making it out of the game. He played all his cards right, made all the right moves. Tara believed him when he told her that he was getting out. All signs pointed to him getting out of the game.

There were no signs of him hustling at his house when she had stayed there, Tara thought, but for real she had been high most of the time that she was there, before she got busted.

He was always preaching to her about getting out of the game and how drugs were destroying the community. Now he was serving time on a drug case. If she knew anything about her friend, niggahs better stay out his way. Tara knew him well enough to know that he was an angry black man, caged behind the walls of prison, feeling victimized by the laws of the land.

He wrote to her from a very angry place. He talked about how he felt that he was doomed to never get free from the grip of the streets; that his life was over. He told her that he didn't give a fuck and that he was going to get his by any means necessary.

Scott explained to her how he was sitting pretty up in the state pen. He was fucking on the regular, and he bragged about how he immediately established rank with the soldiers on the compound. He was in his element back in the joint and that worried Tara.

The tone of the letter reminded Tara of the old warrior she knew as a teenager; the gangster that would lay a mother-fucker down over a little bit of nothing. The one who lived each day with the motto: Kill or be killed.

Toward the end of the letter, the Scott she left behind at home made an appearance. He spoke of how much he loved her and that he thought about her every day. He told her that he knew how strong she was and that he knew she would make a believer out of anybody who stepped to her. He closed the letter by asked her if she could ever love him in a different time.

As Tara folded up the letter and slipped it back into its envelope, she whispered a prayer for her friend. He was obvi-ously so sad. She prayed that he would find peace for his rest-less soul. She prayed that they all would find it. There had to be a peace somewhere in all the madness of this life.

Tara thought for a long while about Scott's closing ques-tion. Could she love him in a different time? Of course she could and she needed him to know that she loved him. He was one of her dearest friends. She planned to write him im-mediately, just as soon as she read the rest of her mail.

She wanted to save her five letters from Julio for last. She knew they would make or break her day, so she planned on going to sleep after she read them. She knew she would either go to sleep happy or go to sleep sad over the words he wrote on the pages. Tara stared at his handwriting a moment more as her heart longed for him.

The letter from M&M cheered her up from the opening paragraph. Her mother started the letter with, *Girl, you ain't going to believe this shit.* Tara could almost hear her mother's nurturing voice in the room. She proceeded to tell her about the latest escapades of her dad with much humor.

The letter made her feel close to home. She pictured her mother sitting on her signature white couch giving her father the business with much attitude. Tara smiled to herself at the thought of M&M with her hands on her hips going at it with her dad. She could see her dad easing out the door with her mom fussing to anyone who happened to be there at the time.

Slim wasn't the one for arguing. Whenever M&M got on the warpath, he bounced. He didn't blame, though—he understood. The couple had been together for years. M&M was a pimp's dream; a moneymaker and a true queen. Her dad loved her mom, and he honestly wished he could give all the things he had promised her for years, but the streets were calling and he always answered on the first ring.

Toward the end of her mom's letter, the tone changed. M&M's words were reflective. She told her daughter how sorry she was for not shielding her from the life she chose for herself. She talked a lot about not feeling well lately and being tired of a lot of things. Tara didn't recognize the person who wrote these words. Her mother never looked back. She lived her life with no regrets.

Tara changed positions on the top bunk. She wanted to be comfortable as she read the letters from her two favorite men: her dad and her man. Inside the blue Hallmark envelope was a mahogany greeting card. Slim wasn't the letter-writing type, but he needed to stay connected to his child. He was mad as hell at losing his baby girl to crack cocaine. The poison was taking everybody out with its destructive wrath through the black community.

In his letter, he begged Tara to use her time to get the help she needed for her addiction to the shit. He told her to take full advantage of the programs that the prison offered to deal with it. It was her opportunity to free herself from the drug.

At the end of the letter, he began talking about her mom. He wrote that M&M hadn't been feeling well and sounded worried about her. He closed the letter by telling Tara how much faith he had in her coming out of all the madness on top. He wrote his loving words neatly inside of the greeting card.

By the time Tara got to the five letters from Julio her emotions were spent. She was only a rollercoaster ride of feelings. She felt mad, happy, sad, worried, nervous, anxious, fearful, proud, loved, and confused.

Tara didn't even really want to read his letters. The pressure of all of it was way more than she could handle. But her body craved him and she needed to feel close to him. She convinced herself that reading them would make her feel closer to him, so she opened them and began reading slowly.

Time just stood still for them. Julio was frozen in his anger. He blamed Tara for everything that went wrong for them. She was the cause of it all in his eyes. He wrote as if she was this invincible woman who should have been able to control all of the outside forces that pulled them apart.

He spoke as if she just abandoned their love, but she never. Their love was always with her, deep in her heart. Why couldn't he see that she had tried to keep it together for them? They both underestimated the power of their love. It consumed her every action and thoughts, and she could not function without him for a long time after he was arrested.

He never stopped for a minute to understand her in all this. He just blamed her and that drove her crazy. She was so tired of being blamed for everything. He played a role in the destruction of their relationship too. When she needed him the most, he just turned and walked away.

Tara put the letter down, then sat up on her bunk and stared out the window for a long time. She could still remember that day like it was yesterday.

"I don't want a crackhead for a wife. When you decide you love me more than that shit, you holla at me. Until then, I'm cool on the visits. I got somebody that don't mind visiting a niggah," Julio spat, *as he banged on the bars to signal the deputy he was ready to return to his cell.*

Tara watched through teary eyes as Julio walked out of the room and never looked back. She was sure he would turn around at some point, but he did not. She took a few minutes to dry her eyes and straighten herself before she prepared to leave the jail.

The coldness of his actions destroyed her that day, and to add insult to injury she had been subjected to running into his baby's mama that day on her way to visit him. That day broke her completely and she let the drugs take over afterward.

She was so tired of trying to convince him that she was just as much a victim in all this as him. This wasn't the life that she dreamed of when they stood before their friends and vowed to be together forever. That day she was foolish enough to believe they could beat the odds and that their love would stand the test of time. She believed she had found her king and they were going to live happily ever after.

Ain't reality a bitch? Tara thought, looking around the room at the endless rows of bunk beds. She sat at the edge of the bunk watching her feet dangle over the floor below. The sensation of jumping was strong and for a brief moment she thought about what would happen if she did. Hot, salty tears ran down her face and slowly dripped onto the floor.

She thought about a world without her in it. Then she thought, fuck that. She wasn't no motherfucking punk. She was Tara, daughter of street legends. The blood of conquerors ran through her veins.

"Hey, Tara, you okay?" Sherri asked, looking up at her from the floor at the side of the bed. She looked so sweet and concerned standing there with a smile on her face. Tara wiped the tears from her face with the back of her hand and abruptly jumped down from the bunk. Without hesitation, she grabbed Sherri and kissed her passionately. The kiss surprised Sherri. She knew it was a kiss that came from someplace that had nothing to do with her, but she liked this girl for real. She liked her from day one and she was just fine with the way she'd gotten her first kiss from Tara.

Chapter Eighteen

"Damn, Ray Ray, we shoulda won that fucking handball game. Damn racist-ass referee calling all those bogus-ass calls and shit," Scott complained, wiping his face with the bottom portion of his clean wife-beater T-shirt. He hated doing that shit because he liked to keep his beaters nice and white. He hadn't planned on playing handball but he couldn't pass up the chance to teach the Aryan Brothers a lesson.

"You know them A.B.'s stick together on everything," Scott added, then took a long drink from his plastic twenty-two ounce gray cup. He placed the cup on the ground quickly as the group of A.B.'s passed celebrating.

Ray Ray and Scott squared up. Soldiers from around the yard assumed their positions, ready for anything that went down. The A.B.'s passed noisily without making a move and the soldiers fell back.

"So, you want to get in another game of handball before they call us back to the block?" Scott questioned his road dog, walking back onto the court.

"Shit, fuck it. Come on, let's do this. I owe you one anyway," Ray bragged, joining him on the court.

Just as the men started the game, the COs whistle blew loudly. "Rec is over, inmates. Let's get lined up now!" the cocky CO ordered before blowing the whistle again.

"What? We still have about fifteen minutes left before rec is over. This motherfucker is on some dumb shit," Ray Ray shouted angrily. The two men stood there frozen in their spots for a long time before they moved toward the line.

"Let's go, inmates. Single file. And no talking. That goes for you too, Mitchell," the CO singled Scott out purposely.

"Yeah, whatever you say, master. Yes, sir, boss," Scott said sarcastically, getting in line reluctantly.

"You can go to the hole and talk all the shit you want, tough guy," the CO threatened the inmate.

"What's wrong with you escorting me then?" Scott shot back. His crew began making noise to throw the CO off.

"Chill out, Dirty, man. He's just trying to push your buttons. He would love nothing more than to get rid of you by sending you to isolation. Don't fall for it. You smarter than that, brother," Ray Ray calmed the warrior down as they walked. "What you up to when you get back to the block?" he questioned, taking Dirty's mind out of his anger.

"Shit, there ain't much to do but watch TV, talk shit through the chute, and jack off," Dirty told his friend as his mind drifted to thoughts of Tara.

"I'm going to take a shower and write my girl and call it a night. I'm tired of the drama in this bitch," Ray Ray shared with a wary look on his face.

The friends started out as cell mates, but that ended quickly. Dirty knew people from every set and always had other inmates hanging around his cell, so the COs finally moved him to a single-man cell to disrupt the action.

The inmates walked back to the block in a single-file line. The line snaked through the yard. Six correctional officers were assigned to the line of about one hundred hardened criminals. It was a modern-day miracle that they went home each day alive. Anything could set the men off, so the guards tried their best to control them with threats and fear. It made for an atmosphere of anger and intimidation. Nobody won in that kind of environment. It just made for a hostile breeding ground, where everyone fed on the misery of each other.

The men were escorted back to their ranges in groups of twenty-five. They were all tired from being out in the sun and they couldn't wait to get their shower and settle in for the evening.

Scott entered his tiny cell. He stripped off his sweaty beater and tossed it into the steel sink to wash out later. The rusty iron door slammed loudly behind him. The cell was the size of a closet. It was really no different from being in isolation. The only real difference was that there was a small window at the back of the room that looked out onto a brick wall.

Scott heard a CO yell down the range, "Shower time, cell number twenty-four." He ran to the door immediately.

"CO, you skipped me, man. I want my shower. It's almost count time. I want my shower," Dirty yelled, waving his towel out of the chute. At the bottom of the rusty red door, his light skin turned red with rage.

"Sorry, Mitchell. You'll have to get your shower in the morning," the CO said, walking toward his cell door.

"Fuck in the morning. How the hell the inmates that didn't even go to rec get they shower before the ones who went to rec? Man, this shit is fucked up. I bet I better get my damn shower," Dirty yelled through the chute as loud as he could. His voice echoed down the range.

The CO closed Scott's chute and locked it from the outside. His muffled shouts and insults could be heard the entire time that the inmate in twenty-four went to take his shower. Fifteen minutes later, the CO walked back to the control booth to let the inmate from cell number twenty-four out of the small showers at the other end of the range.

Once the inmate from cell twenty-four was out of the shower, the CO made the horrible mistake of pushing the wrong button. Instead of opening cell twenty-four to let the inmate back in, he opened cell twenty-three and let Dirty out.

Dirty burst from the cell with his towel in his hand ready for his shower. "Lock it up, Mitchell. Lock it up," the CO yelled down the range in his best man-in-charge voice.

"Fuck that. I want my motherfuckin' shower now!" Dirty shot back, walking in the direction of the shower.

"You will get no shower tonight, inmate. Now lock down," the CO shouted back with his hand on his panic button.

"Fuck that," Dirty said, running to his cell. He quickly jammed the door with his bedsheet before the CO could get back to the booth to lock the cell door. He succeeded in jamming the door. Nearby inmates could hear the gears of the door trying to lock.

The CO pushed the button, calling in the goon squad. They arrived on the scene in force. They were ready to break some heads but they couldn't get the door unjammed.

The situation was quickly ruled a hostage situation, even though the hostage was himself. A white shirt was called in immediately to call the next move.

Lieutenant Davis arrived ten minutes after the call. He knew Mitchell well enough to know that if they weren't careful there could easily be some bloodshed that night. Davis wasn't having that on his shift. He had dealt with Do Dirty before with some success, and he hoped his Irish luck was with him.

Dirty listened patiently while Lieutenant Davis talked that soft-talk bullshit to him. He sounded like some kind of crime-scene negotiator.

"I told yo' punk ass I want my shower," Dirty yelled through the door. He quickly stripped off his clothes in the tiny cell and studied his next move closely.

"You can get your shower tomorrow, Mitchell. Now it's time to bring this disturbance to a peaceful end, " Lieutenant Davis pleaded with the inmate.

"Fuck all you bitches!" Dirty yelled back his response. Then he was done talking and prepared for war in the tiny cell.

Dirty stood naked in front of the mirror above the metal sink. He covered his entire body with baby oil and Vaseline, then he put his white socks back on. Next, he squirted baby oil all over the floor, then tied his pillow case around his nose and mouth in case they tried to mace him.

"Dirty, they comin' in on you," he could hear inmates yelling through the door. Dirty backed up to the back of the room, against the small window, and prepared for the full-on assauLieutenant As soon as they burst through the cell, Dirty ran full speed right at them. His attack caught them off guard and he knocked them down like a heavy bowling ball crashing into bowling pins in the hallway.

Dirty ran from the room like a crazed maniac. He was enjoying the entertainment. The other inmates cheered as he ran past their windows, going up and down the range, aggravating the guards with his antics.

Each time they tried to grab him, their hands instantly slipped and slid from his body because of all the baby oil and Vaseline. Eventually, Dirty grew tired from the game, plus his eyes were starting to burn from the Mace they sprayed at him. He managed to make it back to his cell with the goon squad following right behind him. They rushed the entrance, trying to pin him in his cell, but they landed in a heap at the door, slipping on the oiled floor.

The other riot officers climbed over the pile of officers on the floor and succeeded in grabbing Dirty. They aggressively wrestled him to the floor, handcuffed him, and shackled his hands and feet together. The officers proudly carried him hog style from the cell. Blood ran down his face and dripped all the way down the range as they took him to isolation.

Ray Ray watched his boy being forcibly detained by their

jailers and it burned him up. "All the man wanted was his shower. Why do they always get such a kick out of controlling a niggah on some small shit?" Ray Ray thought out loud, pacing his cell.

Correctional officers kept a niggah on some petty-ass shit all the time. He was tired of their shit. He had a plan for their asses and they weren't going to see the shit coming either. You didn't just take a soldier down and think a niggah was just going to swallow that shit.

Ray Ray was getting sick and tired of playing good niggah. He saw the same feelings in Dirty's eyes when he ran up and down the range, acting like a wild animal. They might have thought he was crazy, but Ray knew the battle cry when he heard it.

"Prepare for war, motherfuckers. Prepare for war," Ray Ray said to himself, staring at himself in the tiny mirror above the sink in his tiny cell.

Chapter Nineteen

The camp was slowly becoming Tara's home. She was settled in and beginning to play the prison game like a master. It was all about what you had and who you knew. Fortunately for her, she had a lot and she knew a lot of people.

Tara was a people person, a seasoned politician, and she campaigned constantly, winning new friends along the way. Everyone enjoyed her company. Most of the time, after a few conversations she would find out they had some person or thing in common.

Even with all the cliques, you would think she would shy away from certain groups in the prison, but not her. Tara fit right in with ease. She would hang in the yard for hours and kick it on every set. Every day was an adventure for her. Some days she would get up early and go to breakfast with the morning crew. This was usually on pancake-breakfast morning. The motherfuckers in the kitchen flipped a mean pancake, and her popularity usually got her extras.

The pill heads and coffee geekers would come back from breakfast and kick it hard on the yard. Sometimes Tara would hang with them after breakfast and listen to their crazy-ass stories. They were always mixing up crazy-ass coffee drinks and trying to get her to try them.

R&B singer R. Kelly was king throughout the compound. Everyone knew his music and his songs would rock the dorm to sleep at night. Tara shared the love for all things Robert

Kelly. Her fans loved it when she would break out in one of his songs out of nowhere. Tara would go all the way there too, singing, "'*Cause I can't sleep, baaaaaby!*" She would break out into song anytime. Her fans loved that shit. The COs loved it too. Tara was the life of the party.

The days began to run together. Each day was a game that she never wanted to stop playing. She would roll out of bed and decide which roller-coaster ride she wanted to go on that day.

The prison was notorious for starting some program or another that was promoted as being the answer to all the inmates' problems. The women would engage in the dangling banana, desperate for a lifeline, and without notice most times the lifeline would be taken away. Tara hadn't been to her GED class in weeks. In the first two weeks, she questioned the COs constantly about her classes. She was always brushed off and given some unfulfilling answer from the only people with answers. At times she felt suspended in time, as if she was in some secret world that only she knew about where her captives had lost the rule book so they made things up as they went along. It worked for them and it worked for her too.

"You tell that bitch she owe me three packs of cigarettes for my blouse. That shit was practically brand new. I shoulda known her greedy ass was gonna spill some shit on my shit when I gave it to her ass," Tara complained, sitting at one of the picnic tables in the yard enjoying her seventh game of bid whiz of the afternoon.

"Simmer down, dawg. I know you mad about yo' shit but remember I told you when you started your little rent-to-own apparel business that you was going to have to suffer some losses sometimes. You know these project hookers ain't used to shit no how," Shorty said, slapping a joker on their competition's king of spades.

"That's a motherfuckin' Boston. That's a *Motherfuckin' Boston!*" Tara and Shorty jumped up together screaming and ran around the room dancing. People around the yard stopped to see where the noise was coming from. The CO in the yard laughed at how silly they both looked dancing and yelling. She wondered how they could find such great joy in so many small things.

Tara's sundry box arrived from home with all her personnel items, including shoes and clothes from the real world. A person knew who had and who did not right away. Material things separated the haves from the have-nots in the joint. Everyone started out on the small level playing field with the same shit in admissions; no more, no less.

Admissions Center Issue for Females
a. Clothing
Quantity Item Disposition
(5) Panties retained by inmate
(5) Socks retained by inmate
(3) Bras retained by inmate
(1) Winter hat (during winter months only and if Retained by inmate no other head cover is provided)
(1) Shoes retained by inmate
(1) Shower Shoes retained by inmate
(1) Nightgowns or pajamas return
(1) Robe return
(3) Outer garments (pants and shirt or jumpers) return
(1) Sweater, sweatshirt or coat (when appropriate return
for existing weather conditions)

b. Linen
Quantity Item Disposition
(2) Towels return

(2) Washcloths return
(1) Laundry Bag return
(1) Cup retained by inmate
(2) Sheets return
(1) Pillowcase return
(1–2) Blankets return
*Mattress & pillow provided in housing unit

c. <u>Hygiene Items</u>: Each inmate shall be provided, at a minimum, the following personal hygiene articles in accordance with Administrative Rules 5120-9-25 and 5120-9-251. If requested, these items (excluding comb/pick) shall be provided weekly to those inmates who receive/earn less than $12.00 in the past 30 days. The financial status of an inmate must be confirmed prior to each issue of a hygiene kit. Items for special hygienic needs will be made available through the institution's commissary.

<u>Quantity Item Disposition</u>
(1) ADA Toothbrush retained by inmate
(1) ADA Toothpaste retained by inmate
(1) ADA dental floss retained by inmate
(1) Comb or pick-plastic only retained by inmate
(1) Razor retained by inmate
(1) Deodorant retained by inmate
(2 boxes) Sanitary Napkins

The worldly possessions of the have-nots were well-known. The class divide was alive and well in prison. Survival was a breed skill for most people from the hood. Sisters kept their hustle on, trying to come up anyway they could.

The haves flaunted their status every chance they got. When a motherfucker got their sundry box with all their new items from home, they paraded around in their new shit for weeks like it was Christmas. Tara was no different; she was decked out in her brand-new black Nike warm-up suit with her matching crisp white running shoes. She felt like a million dollars and she needed everyone to know it.

Each time she won a hand, she jumped up and did her dance. The card table was where the action was; all eyes were on them. The hangers-on were on their job. They swarmed around the picnic tables like bees to honey. Tara and Shorty's crew was the most glamorous in the compound. They stayed fly, so much so that they started renting out certain outfits to other inmates for special occasions such as visits, professional appointments with attorneys or administration, and church.

Church was the most popular occasion. The whole compound went to church. It was one of the rare times that the camp was allowed to go back through the fence, onto the farm with the rest of the population. The women lived for this outing. It was like the players' ball up in the church.

"Hey, sexy, you look cute in your new outfit," Sherri purred, sliding up next to Tara at the picnic table. Sherri was dressed in her state uniform, sipping from her red and white twenty ounce coffee cup anxiously wanting to spend time with Tara before she was due to report to her shift at CFS. She thought about faking sick so she could hang out with Tara the rest of the afternoon but she was already in trouble for not going to work the day before. The CFS CO was known for giving out extra duty tickets. She didn't need another one.

"Damn, Sherri. Don't tell me you got to work today. You worked this morning," Tara questioned her, looking at her state hookup in disgust. It was her turn to deal. She dealt the cards as she talked to Sherri, questioning her. The women around the table hung onto every word that came out both of their mouths.

"I know I did. That was my regular shift. I got extra duty on the lunch shift. You know I got busted with those peppers and onions last week, remember?" Sherri reminded Tara of the six hours of extra duty she was doing so she could make summer sausage casserole for her. She fixed her hair and straightened her shirt while she answered the questions from Tara.

"That's right, I forgot all about that shit. Good looking out," Tara announced, recognizing Sherri's ride-or-die actions on purpose in front of the other hangers-on for record. You had to pay to play in Tara's circle. Everyone pulled their weight.

"What time you get off? Are we going to the movies after dinner?" Tara asked, picking up her kitty from the table. She'd bid a six no trump. She no longer heard a word Sherri was saying. The only thing on her mind was making her books.

"That's game, suckers, that's game. Who else want an ass-whipping? Step right up," Shorty asked the crowd at the table. The partners had been winning all day and the other women were tired of getting their asses whipped. Nobody sat down behind the last set of losers.

"Let's bounce, Shorty, and let the amateurs get some practice in," Tara bragged, getting up from the table. The friends and their entourage took the party inside to see what trouble they could get into before count time.

Rissa sat in the front row of chairs lined up in front of the RCA thirty-six inch TV enjoying her soaps. It was Friday. All the good stuff happened on Friday and she didn't want to miss a thing. She'd been inside all day. She had no desire to watch the happy hookers parade around in all their new shit in front of everyone.

It was common knowledge that Rissa couldn't stand Tara. She could hear her big mouth the minute she opened the door to the yard. She used her better judgment and headed back inside. Rissa was real cool with Rosie, so when she found out that her and the bitch Tara was cool she squashed her beef with the ho. She even let the shit with Sherri slide.

But Rissa was getting fed up with all her showboating. The bitch was always acting better than everyone else and Rosie was in the hole. Rissa would put money on the fact that the ho didn't have any real feelings for Sherri either. She was perpetrating a fraud; she was sure of it.

It burned her up that the bitch had just took the fuck over the joint. Between her and Shorty, they ran everything moving. Luckily, Shorty and Rissa were still cool. *Fuck, what is this shit? They just want me to catch a case or what?* Rissa thought, watching Tara and her posse enter the rec room.

The group entered the day Room and their presence filled the room. It was all eyes on them. The other inmates watched them, checking out the latest gear as they passed. The group, led by Tara, joined another group of Scrabble players at one of the tables near Rissa.

"What's the score?" Tara asked, sitting down. Her entourage found seats close to the action and watched the show.

"It's close but I'm winning. You can get next if you want, Tara," Linda Loudermilk's woman informed Tara, sliding over on the crowded bench. Linda sat obediently at her side.

"What's poppin', Linda? I ain't seen you in a minute," Tara said, glad to see the young friend from admissions again. She hadn't seen her since that day in the yard, when she was all hugged up and shit.

"She's all right ain't you, baby?" Linda's woman answered for her, kissing her on her check. Linda pulled away in disgust, looking Tara in her eyes.

The look Tara saw in Linda's eyes spoke volumes. Her expression cried out, *help!* without her ever speaking a word. The poor girl sat frightened to death at the side of a person she very obviously needed saving from.

"Damn, partner, I was hollering at my girl, Linda, not you," Tara put in the air to see the controller's response. Shorty recognized the exchange and prepared for war. Only three other sisters in their entourage peeped what was about to go down.

"Yeah, niggah, I feel you and all, but she don't breathe without getting permission from me," Linda's controller answered, stroking her prisoner's hair. Linda sat frozen in fear. Other inmates got up from the table, sensing trouble.

"Bitch, who the hell you talkin' fly to up in here? I know your wannabe-gangster ass ain't lost your mind," Tara answered back, getting up from the bench.

Linda's woman got up and knocked over the Scrabble board. Little square pieces from the game flew in the air and landed randomly around the rec room. Rissa, who was witnessing the exchange, quickly joined Linda's woman in the standoff.

"Fall back, partner. It ain't even worth it. Trust me, it ain't," Rissa told the crowd while pulling Linda's woman out of the rec room.

Battle lines were drawn right then and there, and everyone in the rec room knew it. People stood there quietly picking sides. Most of the inmates in the room would side with Tara because she was the leader of the popular crew. But some would side up with Rissa for the same reasons that Rissa hated everything Tara represented.

The count-time whistle blew, interrupting the excitement. A sigh of relief swept across the room. Nobody really wanted to fight, but you would never get them to admit it. Reputation was everything in the joint. Nobody backed down ever—not where Tara came from, that is. You came hard or stayed home every day.

"Come on, Linda, let's go," Tara called over her shoulder.

Linda smiled for the first time in a long time and joined her hero's posse. She even had a little swagger in her walk, exiting the rec room with the in-crowd.

Chapter Twenty

The inmates stood patiently at the gate that separated the camp from the main compound waiting for the call to be given from the main security booth, located high atop the brick lookout tower above the administration building. Nothing and no one got through the gate without the "All-clear" from the lookout tower.

The inmates were on their best behavior because the rare outing was a cherished event. The trips to the prison chapel were few and far between. Inmates never knew when they would allow everyone to get their hopes up for the coveted trip and then, with or without notice, cancel the adventure.

So, on that chilly Sunday morning, they all stood perfectly still at the gate, waiting obediently for the piercing sound of the ancient gate to slide open. Several of them prayed to themselves that it would open. Their faith willed it open and it did. You could feel the excitement of something going right sweep through the pack of women as they strolled through the gate.

Six COs and one captain escorted the inmates to Sunday morning service on the fall day. Because it was a little cold outside, the women were allowed to wear their sweatshirts with their state-issued uniforms to church service.

Tara strolled through the yard in all her glory. Her state pants had cresses neatly ironed into them with perfection by one of the girls she paid weekly to do her laundry. You could pretty much get a person to do just about anything in the joint if you paid them. She also wore a tan Nike zip-front sweatshirt over her green button-front shirt. She was glad she got the chance to rock her new Nike sweatshirt; it was her first time wearing it. Luck was on her side when she swooped it up from one of Shorty's friends who owed her on a card game.

Debts were settled with items purchased on commissary and items sent from home throughout the prison. The trade of goods and services allowed the have-nots to compete with the haves, leveling the playing field in the prison.

A two-man line was the rule. The coupled-off inmates marched through the farm announcing fresh meat was in town. The word spread through population fast. Fresh faces were on the grounds and everybody wanted to see the show. By the time the inmates from the camp arrived at the chapel, the place was full and the crowd at the door was being held back awaiting the inmates from the camp.

The girls pushed their shoulders back and strolled through the door like they were the star attractions and now the show could begin. The prison chapel was a one-story brick building that doubled as a lot of other things for the institution. On any given day, groups gathered in the chapel for recovery services, parenting classes, movies on Friday evenings, and college instruction.

The brick building barely resembled a place of worship. The only point of reference to a holy place was the portable altar that sat at the front of the room. A small keyboard was strategically placed to the right of the altar and eight chairs represented the choir. All eight faithful members of the vocal chorus were in their places. They even had choir robes. Although they were out of date, the robes were in good shape. You could tell some choir members had made it a point to care for their robes in a loving way.

"Tara, I know that ain't yo' ass over there, baby," Cricket shouted from her seat on the other side of the chapel.

"Live and in living color, homie," Tara yelled back, glad to see an old friend. Cricket looked fine as hell standing up to greet someone from her hood.

"I see you with your mack hand down. I heard you were here." Cricket nodded in the direction of Sherri and the rest of Tara's crew that followed close behind her. They all searched for seats in the crowded brick room. Linda followed close behind, afraid to leave Tara's side.

The room was too crowded for the group to sit together. The chapel was swarming with COs and white-shirt captains who led the women in different directions, trying to find seating for the overflowing crowd.

"Quit trying to sit with your buddies and get your asses in a seat now," a red-faced captain at the front of the room roared, getting annoyed with the whole mess. He knew most of the inmates pouring into the chapel weren't there for the right reasons. It angered him that they would use the sabbath for their sick, selfish reasons. They were all just animals in his eyes. He didn't understand why the government wasted money trying to rehabilitate the wild.

Inmates fell into seats wherever they stood. No one wanted the services to be cancelled for annoying the white shirt.

Tara turned to the nearest seat. "Anybody sitting here?" she asked no one in particular. The obedient inmates next to her shook their heads, so Tara sat and got real still. The women stared at the altar in silence and waited for the church service to start. The people with the power were never in a hurry for the underdogs. They were always kept waiting for one reason or another.

Back at the entrance to the prison, the zealous Baptist preacher and his gospel posse waited patiently for someone to find the gate pass with all of their names on it. You could not enter the prison without a gate pass and no one seemed to know where theirs was at the moment. It really concerned the Baptist pastor that no one cared that they were thirty minutes late for the church service. He wondered if they understood that he was there on spiritual business.

"Pardon me, sir. Do you think you could call your supervisor to inquire on a course of action for resolving this problem?" Rev. Dr. Victor Marco Davis of the great Trinity Baptist Church interrogated the incompetent officer at the gate. The gospel posse prayed silently to their Lord and Savior Jesus Christ to dispatch angels to unlock the steel door that separated them from the women in need of a blessing.

"We put in a call to Captain Day but we're still waiting for him to return the call. You can have a seat. None of you can be processed until we hear from the captain. I'll call you up when we're ready for you," the young officer at the front desk instructed the seasoned pastor, dismissing him from the desk.

Pastor Davis was a towering presence who was accustomed to being in charge. It was painfully clear to him who was in charge now. He slowly walked back to his seat and joined the saints who were in silent prayer. "Father, you know we have gathered in this place to be a blessing. Take control and allow us to do your will for your children. In the name of Jesus, we pray. Amen," the man of God prayed loudly in his spirit.

The black office phone on the metal desk rang, startling the young officer who was sitting at the desk reading the latest copy of *Sports Illustrated*. The ring caught him off guard; he dropped the magazine and nearly knocked over the entire phone when he reached over to answer it.

The clearance was given to allow the church group to enter the institution after much delay. Apparently, the captain had taken time out on his shift to catch up on some much-needed rest. He had been sleeping in the warden's office the whole time. The leather couch in the office was his favorite Sunday hideout. He gave the order to allow the church folks to enter the prison. He also gave the young officer at the front desk his order for dinner before he returned to his nap.

Once the church service finally got started, the atmosphere in the room became one of praise and worship. The prison choir sang to their hearts' content. Each singer was grateful for the opportunity to use their gifts and talents for the Lord.

By the time Pastor Davis got up to preach, the women were thirsty to hear what he had to say to them. The games that brought them there were long forgotten. Each face looked up at the pastor like he held the power of life and death in his hands.

One of the staff members from religious services intro- duced the man of God before he started his message. His im- pressive work in the community inspired the women. Pastor Davis was well aware he would have to play beat-the-clock, so he dove right into his message.

"Turn with me quickly in your Bibles if you have them, my sisters. We will be coming from 1 Samuel, the twenty-second chapter." He spoke softly as he removed his designer suit coat. He handed it to one of the saints sitting in the front row with a *reserved* sign taped to the back of the chair.

Tara sat mesmerized. The feeling that came over her was one that she recognized from a time gone by, when her Mama Gracie would take her to the Temple of Faith Church. The rhythm of the preacher's voice was comforting. It reminded her of home. His words penetrated her soul.

"I want to talk to you briefly about a cave experience. Say that with me, ladies. Cave experience," the man of God spoke with authority into the microphone. The inmates' voices echoed through the room as they repeated in unison, "a cave experience." The words flung up to the heavens.

"You see, I need you to leave here today understanding

that your character is revealed in your cave experiences. It is what you choose to develop in the valley experience that will mold you and lead you toward your purpose. This is merely a test. God places you in the valley to get the lesson, and I'm compelling you to get the lesson," Pastor Davis pleaded with the lost souls sitting before him.

Tara glanced around the chapel. Many of the women were listening intently to his words; meanwhile, a few others were flirting with the person they'd come to see that day. Sherri was sitting at the back of the room and Rissa was seated right beside her.

Her mind drifted just that quickly from the message. When Tara focused back on the word of God, the preacher was ending the service. He instructed the women to stand where they were. Once everyone was standing, he began to pray the arms of protection of God all around them during their time of struggle.

When church was over, the inmates from the camp were escorted out of the chapel first in order to keep the socializing down. "Let's go. Keep it moving. Single file, inmates. And *no* talking," a cocky officer barked out his direct orders, bringing everybody back to reality.

Tara and several other inmates lingered at the back of the line trying to use the last few minutes to see and be seen. Someone passed a small kite to Tara on her way out the door. She stuffed the folded note into her pocket to read later. The autumn sun shined brightly in the sky. A crisp wind blew lazily through the Ohio Reformatory for Women, bringing with it a temporary calm. The train of churchgoers bounced back to the camp with pep in their steps. Most of the women had been moved that day by the power of God.

Chapter Twenty-one

The federal detention center was comfortable, considering a brother was locked up. The feds treated their prisons with more respect than officers at the state level. State pens operate from very small budgets and have little compassion for their criminals. No one ever wants to appear soft on crime in small-town USA.

Julio sat down in the all-too familiar mahogany chair and pulled his seat close to the desk. The windows in the large dorm were closed tight, shutting out the outside world. He needed the alone time to begin to work on the things he kept closed in. This was his third attempt at starting the letter. He had tried his best not to write her but he had to. He couldn't breathe without her any longer. He craved her. Just the sight of her name on the paper connected him to her as he wrote. As always, he didn't know where to begin to explain all the things that he hoped she already understood. All he knew was that he had to release his heart.

My Dearest Tara,

I hope this letter gets to you and you are okay. I haven't heard anything from you so I can only pray that you're cool. You sure have taught a brother how to pray. Damn, girl. I don't blame you, though. Please don't get me wrong. I am starting to realize I've been doing a lot of that lately. Man, I can't blame nobody but myself for how everything ended up. Wow, for a long time I couldn't see that. All I saw was how you broke my heart. I was hurt because of all I couldn't be for you. I felt weak, like I was less than a man because I couldn't save you from the streets. It was like watching the thing you love the most slip away right before your eyes. The powerless feeling drove me crazy.

You looked so innocent that day back at the county jail when you came to see me high as hell. All I wanted to do was save you, but I couldn't, so I tried the only thing I knew to do at the time. I tried tough love. Man, that shit don't work. Well, maybe it does, but only on the person trying the tough love bullshit.

I allowed my anger to rule my decisions. I decided I was going to guard my heart from the pain of losing you. I honestly thought I could just forget about you. Well, mami, that shit sure didn't work. I have been living my life in denial, going through the motions trying to act as if my love for you is not real and not the biggest part of me.

The pain of that lie has nearly driven me crazy, to the point that I had to be ordered by medical to suicide watch for evaluation. All the fuck you do in that bitch is talk to motherfuckers all day long about your problems. Day in and day out, motherfuckers asking you how you feel and why you feel that shit. At first I thought it was a game. I'd fuck with them just to see them jump for my ass. But after a while, whenever they forced me to talk about you, that shit mattered. It would cut a brother to the core every time I was forced to face my true feelings. But you know what, baby? Letting that shit bleed out saved me.

Listen up, baby. You are all I ever wanted in my life. I realize that now. I am so sorry for not protecting our love. Know that if I could do it over I would do a lot of things differently. You deserve that. Our marriage didn't stand a chance because we started it wrong. I didn't protect you. If you allow me the chance, I promise you I will spend the rest of my life making

it up to you. All I want is to make my way back to the love
we shared. I know this change of heart comes late. I've beaten
myself up for it not coming sooner, when you needed it from
me most. All I can hope is that you are out there somewhere
and sometimes when you are alone you think of me. I can still
remember what it felt like when we were together. I can still
feel your touch on my skin and the softness of your kiss. That
is what sustains me now. I know our love was real and that
doesn't just die. It might get torn apart or separated by time
and space, but real love never dies. I believe that with all of my
being, Tara. I know that you love me. You might not be able to
feel it right now, but it's okay because I got enough love for the
both of us. My prayer is that the Tara who stood beside me vowing to love me through the good and bad times can realize that
we were just unfortunate in the fact that our bad came first.

Baby, I swear to you that I'm going to spend the rest of my
life being the kind of man you deserve, who gives you a love
you can trust in. It kills me to think about how alone you must
have felt the night I got arrested. We were so hotheaded back
then. In a lot of ways we still are today. I was so busy trying
to show you who the boss was that I refused to squash our silly
argument and just climb into bed with you that night. Do you
know that I dream about that shit almost every night? Our last
night together plays over and over again in my head like a song
stuck on repeat. I've mastered controlling the ending too. In my
perfect world, we make up before the shit gets heated. We spend
the rest of the night making our first baby. You give a brother
a son next and we live happily ever after doing all the things
we planned before shit got crazy. Do you ever wonder what we
would be doing now if that one night didn't happen in our des-
tinies? Do you think we could have stolen happiness from the
streets and drove away with it? There has to be a place where
the struggle is over and the loss ain't so everlasting.

Tara, we can beat the odds. I know we can. What we have doesn't come along often. You don't find it around every corner. Think about that after you read this letter. Ask yourself if what we shared is worth a second chance. Do you value your man and our marriage enough to fight for it? If your answer is yes, know that you aren't in it alone. I'm willing to fight right along with you. Finally, my love, I am here for you. Whatever you need from me, I am here on your terms. Take all the time you need, baby. I'm right here waiting for you.

I need you to look in your heart, past all the pain, and re-member what it felt like when we were together in each other's arms. Close your eyes and remember my touch, Tara. I know you can because I can still feel you next to me. Whatever happens, Tara, always remember that I will love you forever.

Your Husband,
Julio

Chapter Twenty-two

The walk back from the church service was freeing. The atmosphere was different. It felt like coming home after church and knowing you probably shouldn't cuss or talk about anybody for a while because God was looking.

Tara entered her sleeping area and started taking off her church clothes. She wanted to get a shower before dinner and considered trying to write a few letters afterward. She hadn't responded to any of her mail since she arrived in Marysville. It was just too hard to face it all. There were way too many questions to answer. Her drug addiction hurt so many people. She was so sorry for that fact, but it was what it was and she couldn't change the past. If only she had the answers they all needed—but she didn't. It was a challenge just getting through the days.

Drama was used to pass the hours in the joint. The inmates lived for it. Tara was somewhat ashamed that she got caught up as well. Hanging with the rough crowd came naturally to her, but lately she just felt guilty.

The guilt started that day in the rec room; the look in Linda Loudermilk's face frightened her. The fear was new to Tara. She'd grown up seeing women being controlled by pimps and players as a child, but in all the faces she'd seen in her lifetime she never saw fear. Linda's fear became a part of her. Tara felt obligated to protect her.

Prison was completely different from the life she knew

at home, before the drugs. Somewhere along the way, she'd turned into a selfish person who only took. Tara knew damn well she had no intentions of really being in a relationship with Sherri, but she was perfectly fine with letting Sherri and everyone else think she was all bought in. "Baby girl, you can never trust a perpetrator with nothing. All you got is your word. Never forgot it," Tara could hear her dad saying.

"You mean to tell me you went to church with the rest of those heathens? I didn't take you for one of those game players, Tara," Pammy said, unlocking her locker box to get a pack of ramen noodles. "Girl, I can't stand going over there and seeing all them playing church. It's a damn shame. I keep waiting for God to strike them all down over there on Sunday playing church and stuff," Pammy added as she poured her noodles into her plastic commissary bowl.

"How you so sure they're playing games? We don't know what's going on in a person's mind. Trust me, that church service was real. I was feeling what that preacher was saying," Tara explained while getting a Little Debbie oatmeal pie out of her locker box at the foot of her bed.

"I was raised not to play with church. My mother would kill me," Pammy responded with her nose in the air. Pamela Alexander came from a family of old money. She was exposed to all the finer things in life from the moment she was born. Her parents were Irish Catholic furniture makers. They owned retail stores all across the Midwest.

All of their best laid plans couldn't save their precious daughter from the destruction of crack cocaine. Pammy became addicted to crack in middle school. By the time she reached her eighteenth birthday she was strung out and running from seven felony drug cases. Her parents' money got her a lot of chances but those quickly ran out and now she was doing time.

"I know you not judging somebody else. We the last ones to be judging anybody," Tara checked her roommate real quick. She was done with the conversation. It wasn't either's place to criticize another woman's religion. "I'm going to take my shower before count time. I ain't going to dinner. I think I'm going to write a few letters and call it a day," Tara shared, changing the subject. She refused to let this place control her mood.

"We have a serious backgammon game going. We're playing for nutty bars. Look how many I won already," Pammy bragged and pointed at her open locker box.

"I see you getting your hustle on," Tara teased, putting on her Pepto-Bismol pink shower shoes. The bright-colored rubber shoes stood out like a sore thumb against the gray steel of the bunk beds and locker boxes.

Today was a lucky, lucky day. Everything worked out better than I could have even planned it. Man, who would have thought we'd get stalled out for hours on the farm. Punk-ass COs so slow; a bitch got a chance to come up on some serious shit while out shopping, Rissa thought, inspecting the items she had smuggled from the farm back to the camp. Her homies got her real straight with a pound of dro, a cell phone, and a beautifully hand-crafted pocket knife.

"It was a damn good day," Rissa said out loud to herself, putting her contraband away. She was pleased with her come up. Now motherfuckers would have to come see her. She wasn't a motherfucking punk. They needed to get ready to bow down. She was sick of watching the glamour girls parade around like they ruled the world. The underdog was on top now. Fuck Tara and the motherfucking horse she rode in on, Rissa thought, rubbing her pocket knife before she shoved it deep inside of her pants pocket.

Rissa climbed onto her bunk with her state-issued writing tablet and began doing the math on her business plan for moving her pound of weed. She wanted to take full advantage of her opportunity on a come up. A bitch was tired as hell of living on state pay alone. That shit kept her being a commissary hoe. She was always hustling for the necessities of life; shit like hair grease, deodorant, and food.

The food shit made her the maddest. It was cruel and unusual punishment to force hundreds of bitches to live on twenty dollars a month to buy items to last for the entire month. In most of the women's cases, nobody sent a sister a dime, so inmates had to go for what they knew.

Marissa "Rissa" Moore hated being hungry. The feeling took her back to her childhood. Unfortunately for her, she was born to a crackhead father and mother who gave birth to her in the back of a spot in the dead of winter. She grew up in one spot or another, always hungry and mad at the world.

She was a wise businesswoman who always managed to turn a profit. This was even sweeter because her profits did not have to be split with anyone else. This allowed her to be able to reinvestment her profits in a larger amount of product on her next trip. It was all gravy.

Thanks to the outing that day, things were beginning to look up. The glamour girls ain't going to be the only ones flossin' around this bitch, Rissa thought, smiling to herself and stretching out on her thin green state mattress. Her state sheets were at the laundry waiting for their turn in the washing machine, but the stiffness of the plastic didn't faze her one bit.

"Go on, girl, with your cute-ass shoes. You know you looking good, Tara," an inmate next to Rissa's bed acknowledged Tara. A group of inmates had gathered to see the new flat-screen television that one of the women had just got shipped into the institution.

Tara stood there laughing with her friends and enjoying
the new television set. She was wrapped in her bathrobe with
her hair pinned up into a bun. The sun shined through the
windows making her look like she was glowing. If you didn't
know better you could have sworn the group of women was
enjoying a lazy Sunday afternoon at a country club.

"I'm not fooling with y'all a minute longer. I need to get my
shower out the way before count time. I'll see everybody after
the count. Peace," Tara shared before walking away. Right
before dinner count was the best time to get your shower out
of the way. Typically, everyone waited until after dinner for
their showers. That's when all the freaky shit went down. You
could barely get a shower because all of the stalls were filled
with people getting their freak on.

Male COs weren't permitted into the stall area unless it was
a emergency, so the inmates used that to their advantage. On
any given day you could witness a live porn show just trying to
wash your ass. Tara hoped she could get in and out without
witnessing the freak show. Her first night at the camp made a
believer out of her. She walked right in on a threesome that
came with an open invitation to join in.

The showers were located at the entrance to the dorm
room. There were sixteen showers in all; eight showers apiece
on each side of the entrance. Each shower stall was covered by
heavy plastic white shower curtains. There were no windows
in the shower area; just a big rusty ceiling light.

Most of the stalls were occupied when Tara arrived. Just
when she thought she'd have to come back after count time,
the curtains to the last shower at the back of the room were
slowly pulled open. All Tara could see was someone's head
peeking out and looking around. When the inmate was satisfied and determined that it was cool to exit, she stepped out,
and following close behind her was Linda Loudermilk with a
grin on her face.

"Hi, Tara," Linda spoke like a child whose parent just caught them with their hands in the cookie jar. "This is my new girlfriend Lacy. She just got here from the county," Linda added, hoping Tara wasn't angry with her for choosing Lacy. She was hoping to be with Tara but that didn't look like it was going to happen anytime soon.

"How you doin', Tara?" Lacy said in her best thug voice, extending her wet hand to Tara. Everyone just stood there awkwardly. Tara ignored the wet hand, not sure where it had been.

Finally Tara spoke. "Let me get my shower, Linda. I'll holler at you later after count. Make sure you get at me, Linda, you hear me?" Tara yelled as they were exiting the room.

"I'll catch up with you right after count. I promise," Linda answered back, smiling on her way out the door. She wondered if Tara was a little jealous and that's why she wanted to talk to her after count. Linda was sure Tara wanted her.

How in the world is that girl ever going to make it through this hellhole without me holding her hand every step of the way? Tara thought as she entered the empty stall behind the new couple and turned the water on boiling hot to wash away their germs. The hot water caressed her body like the touch of a loving hand. It felt good to cleanse herself and wash away the dirt of the day.

Chapter Twenty-three

The shower did its job well. Tara felt refreshed and ready to conquer the world. The whole thing concerned her. Linda was a mark; it was only a matter of time before she got hurt. Part of this was her fauLieutenant Tara had been parading around like she was in a relationship with Sherri for weeks. It wasn't fair to any of them that she kept the games up. It was time for her to be honest with everyone. She really cared about Sherri. Tara knew that she would not have made it through her first few weeks at the camp without her. However, she was just using Sherri the same way everyone around the place used everyone else, leading them on.

Sherri made her feel wanted and important, like she really mattered to somebody. Plus she enjoyed being liked by the person everybody else wanted. That was all well and good, but people were getting caught up and hurt and she didn't want that on her conscience. She wasn't in the business of hurting people.

The two of them had kissed a few times, but nothing more. Sherri had starting pressuring her to have sex, but each time they planned their own trip to the showers something got in the way. Tara was curious about the whole sex-with-a-women thing, so she thought, what the hell, but things never worked out for them to have their moment together

After drying herself off, she slipped into her cute pink shower shoes and robe. The bright pink shower shoes made her smile as she tied her bathrobe closed tightly and headed for the exit.

Just as she turned the corner, she was stopped by a menacing voice. "You think you all that, don't you, bitch?" Linda Loudermilk's first girlfriend growled, then she swung a sock filled with locker box locks right at Tara's face. Everything seemed to happen in slow motion. Frozen in shock, Tara didn't move.

Suddenly, Linda appeared out of nowhere and jumped in the way of the blow. The out-of-control sock hit her dead in the face. Her nose turned black-and-blue instantly and blood gushed out, some spraying across a nearby shower curtain. All hell broke loose as a crowd gathered. Immediately, the closest inmates were yelling, "Fight! Fight!" Tara dove onto her attacker with both fists swinging. The inmates rolled around in a massive heap in the blood from Linda's nose.

Rissa heard all of the noise and decided to see what was going on. "Who's fighting?" Rissa asked, rushing to the front of the dorm with the rest of the crowd.

"Tara and another girl," somebody yelled over their shoulder to Rissa on the way to the entertainment. Rissa remembered the knife in her pocket. The timing was perfect. With so many women crowded around, she could do whatever she wanted and go undetected.

It was do-or-die for Tara and she knew it. She prayed that the women gathered around her were on her side. She was trapped in the poorly-lit shower room fighting for her life against an opponent who was twice her size. The only thing that saved her was her speed and quick thinking. She managed to pull the belt to her bathrobe from around her waist and use it to choke the shit out of her attacker.

"Kick that bitch's ass, Tara! Kick that bitch's ass!" could be heard in the distance.

Just when Rissa reached the doorway, a CO arrived and started screaming, "Break it up, inmates!" and the riot bell went off.

What happened after that was a mystery to Tara. She didn't remember how she got to her next location. All she knew was that her fists and her sides were hurting like hell. Every time she moved in the holding cell she wanted to scream.

Isolation was located in-between the camp side and the boot camp side of the compound. If it was deemed necessary, an inmate would be placed in restraints to protect them from themselves. Tara watched as Linda was led away in restraints kicking and screaming past her. The riot squad led Tara to the hole in handcuffs. They never even blinked as Linda was being dragged down the hall. "I can't go in the dark! I can't go in the dark," inmates could hear her screaming all the way down the hall.

Isolation was designed to break the best of the best. It was the divide-and-conquer method in full effect. The offender was placed inside of a tiny room with no windows until their Isolation order was lifted. The room looked just like her cell in admissions, only the room was twice as small and dark. The only light came from a small lightbulb over the sink. The bulb was covered with some kind of protective metal cover with holes in it that allowed the light to shine through.

Comfort was the last thing on the mind of whoever designed the room. Tara could barely turn around in the small room without bumping into something. The bed—if it could be called that—was a brick square that took up most of the room, and the toilet sat at the end of that brick square.

How in the hell did I get here? Tara thought, sitting down on the brick square. She could hear voices coming from the other side of the bright orange steel door. A small chute opened at the top of the door and a CO stuck his face into the opening. "Make yourself comfortable. You're going to be here a while. You picked a good day for your beat down. Tomorrow is a holiday, so it's going to be a few days before you have a hearing to determine the length of your stay at this fine hotel for your assault charges. When somebody gets time they'll bring you a mattress. I suggest you get comfortable," the CO advised her before closing the window.

What the fuck he mean, *assault charges?* That bitch assaulted me. I was merely protecting myself, Tara thought, curling up on the brick bed. She folded her arms under her head to make a pillow. Her knuckles were sore as hell; she had gotten in some pretty decent punches on the big bitch before they were separated. The big bitch wasn't no punk either. She definitely gave Tara a run for her money. Thank God the COs came when they did. And poor Linda. All that time Tara thought she was going to have to be her savior, but Linda had been hers that day. Before long she was fast asleep, curled up on the cement block. The events of the day had exhausted her.

The sounds of someone moaning woke her from her sleep. The room was pitch-black. She couldn't see anything. Tara kept waiting for her eyes to adjust to the darkness but they never did. The moaning sounds continued and were coming from somewhere in front of her in the darkness.

Getting up from the concrete slab wasn't an option. The pain in her side caused her to cripple over and slide to the floor. She laid on the floor until the pain subsided before she tried moving again. On her second attempt, she crawled along the floor toward the door and her head smacked into the steel door with a loud thump. The moaning sounds could be heard just a bit louder along the floor. The sounds were clearer this time and there was a male voice mixed with the moaning sounds.

Lying on the floor, listening to one of the COs getting his funky off with one of the inmates in the hole next to her, Tara felt as if the world had gone mad and forgotten to tell her. *"Get me the hell out of here right now!"* she began yelling at the top of her lungs, kicking the metal door with her feet while still lying on the ground. She kicked and kicked until someone finally opened the chute.

"What the hell is your problem, inmate? Settle down now," the CO said, peering through the opening in the door. He flipped the switch on the outside of the door that controlled the light and looked in. Tara was so curled up on the floor against the door that he could not see her. "Why can't I have one night of peace in this joint?" the CO complained as he unlocked the door.

"Where the hell have you been and where is my mattress? I've been in here for hours sleeping on concrete. I want to see the captain now," Tara ordered, startling the CO as she struggled to get up off the floor.

"People in hell want ice water too, but do they get it?" the CO answered back, annoyed about being interrupted from his Saturday-night date with the hot young thing down the hall.

"I know you better get me a mattress and some sheets in here before you go back to handling your business," Tara responded, giving the smart-mouth CO one good look and something to think about. She was fed up with the bullshit. What the fuck else could they do to her?

The pair had a brief stare-down contest before the CO spoke again. "Why didn't you tell someone you didn't have a mattress? That's all you needed to do was tell somebody and they would have gotten you one. Simple as that," he said, adjusting his dick in his tight-ass pants.

"Oh, it's simple as that, huh? Well, I need a mattress and

I need to get the fuck out of here too. I didn't even do anything. She attacked me," Tara pleaded her case to her jailer.

"Save it for your hearing. I don't have any control over
when you get out of here. That's up to the captain when you
have your hearing. I will get you a bedroll and a mattress and
then you better settle down in here. Got it?" Without waiting
for a response, he closed the door and locked it. The light
went back out as quickly as it came on, leaving Tara alone in
the darkness.

Chapter Twenty-four

A Fresh New Day

All hearings for isolation were conducted by a white shirt. Unfortunately for the women at the camp, a white shirt was only assigned to the camp once a week. Because of the holiday, the hearings for that week were pushed back another week. By the time Tara took her sore ass before the captain she was mad as hell at everybody.

The hearing only lasted about a minute. The captain read the charges that she was facing and then mumbled something about inmate Carla Holmes being charged with a felony assauLieutenant He never looked up from the paper he was reading. Not one time did he acknowledge the human being standing before him. She heard him say something about a separation order being put in place and then she was led away in handcuffs and taken back to the hole.

"Well, it's your lucky day. You're being shipped to the pre-release center. It's way better than this place. I hope that fight was a wake-up call for you. Do you realize she could have killed you with that weapon? You ladies need to stop with all this foolishness," CO Cradoff cautioned, shaking her head in disgust at the actions of the women. Cradoff was a God-fearing Christian who never gave up hoping that the misguided women would come to see the error of their ways and begin working on getting their lives on track while they were there.

"Pre-release? Where is this pre-release place?" Tara asked as she walked alongside Officer Cradoff with her hands cuffed behind her back.

"You're going to Franklin Pre-Release because it's the closest center to your permanent address. The re-release center is for short-timers and low-level offenders. They offer a lot of things that we don't. You will have more opportunities to get involved in some positive things instead of sitting out here at this Camp wasting away," she replied.

From the very first time Tara saw CO Cradoff she reminded her of her precious grandmother. CO Cradoff was always talking about Jesus and heaven. She ended each conversation with, "God bless you real good." Something about the way she walked always made Tara think of Mama Gracie. She walked as if she'd seen it all and knew all the answers.

"How long before they take me to Franklin? When do I get let out of the hole?" Tara questioned the friendly officer, hoping to figure out what had just happened at the hearing. Nothing that the whispering white shirt said made sense to her.

"Normally you would be released from the hole immediately because you were found not guilty of your charges, but because there was a separate order put in place you are being taken back to isolation for protective reasons while you await transport. You will probably be back here a few more days before they ride you out." CO Cradoff shared all she knew with the Tara, hoping something she said would make a difference in the young girl's life. She was such a beautiful girl, full of potential.

Once she was back in her cell, Tara was surprised to see that her personal belongings were waiting for her inside the tiny room, along with several letters from the outside and one from inside the institution.

***

Thoughts of home were neatly packed away in a box on a shelf in Tara's heart. The last thing she wanted to do was get that box out and open it. The pain of all the things inside was too much for her to bear at that moment. Just looking at the words on the bright white envelopes caused tears to slip from her eyes and slide gently down her face.

The pain was paralyzing. Tara sat at the edge of the concrete bed studying the letters for a long while. There were six letters in all; both of her parents had written her along with a letter from Julio and another from Scott. The fourth and fifth letters were unexpected surprises. One was from her longtime friend and road dog Karen, and the other one was from Sherri. It was odd receiving a letter from someone inside the joint by way of the U.S. Postal Service. Hadn't anyone heard of in-house mail? What a total waste of envelopes and postage stamps, to send a letter outside the institution just to send it right back where it originated from. The powers that be were always taking the long way around a problem. No wonder the states were going broke.

It was hard for her to remember the last time she'd heard from Karen. Once crack took control of her life, she spent less and less time with friends and family.

Karen was Tara's best friend. They'd known each other ever since Tara was in elementary school. Every important moment in Tara's life had been shared with Karen, including smoking crack. In the early stages of their addiction they spent every moment together, running up in stores and stealing everything that wasn't nailed to the floor in the best department stores. They would usually flip their day's work to the latest dope boy on the block and then get high the rest of the day together. This routine went on for a long while until they both became paranoid from the drugs and stopped trusting each other.

Karen was a dime piece in her own right. The two of them together put a hurting on whoever they set their sights on. Niggahs was always pushing up on them, and with that came the drama and mistrust, mainly because they were always high.

Crack was infamous for dividing and conquering just like the joint. It zeroed in on your weaknesses and kept them in the fore-front of your mind. It wasn't long after they started smoking that they started falling out. In all the years that the two of them were friends they never argued over anything, until crack came on the scene. All the things that drew them together began to tear them apart because of crack. Tara hoped her letter was the start of the healing process for both of them. She loved Karen to death. It felt good to let her friend out of the box on the shelf in her heart.

Pulling Karen's letter from the envelope was very emotional for Tara. Images of the two of them in all their escapades danced through Tara's head with a nice R&B beat playing in the background. Her memories of all the good times made her smile. It was hard to even remember what their falling-out was even about anymore. As soon as she read the letter all was forgiven and forgotten by the both of them. Karen started the letter by apologizing for not reaching out to her friend sooner. She told her friend that she was enrolled in a six-month drug-treatment program. Karen ranted and raved about how the program gave her the tools she needed to not only kick her addiction but it also helped her with recognizing the triggers that caused her to get high.

The things Karen wrote in the letter piqued Tara's interest. Crack had controlled her on the street. Even when she tried to stop smoking she wasn't able to on her own. Karen spoke in the letter about how controlling her reaction to certain people, places, and things could help her control the addiction. She even included pamphlets from her treatment programs for Tara to read. Karen was so much like her that people often thought they were sisters and most times they didn't correct them. Tara felt a sense of hope sweep across her soul. She thought to herself, if Karen could beat crack, just maybe she could.

Pacing around the small cell in the hole, Tara began to think about why she hadn't fought harder for her husband and their marriage. She knew the answer now: it was because she was afraid of hurting him again. The hurt in Julio's eyes that day back at the county jail crushed her. She decided that very day that walking away from him was worth the cost to spare him pain caused by her, especially while he was locked away.

She never considered that there was a way to overcome the addiction. She just assumed that once she was released from this hell-hole called prison she would go right back to what she knew, which was getting high and stealing. Karen's letter had her think that just maybe things could be different. What did a different kind of life look like or feel like? Karen's letter was so filled with hope that it had Tara wanting some of it for herself. She would have to write her friend back for all the answers. Where did she get this hope thing? Could Tara get it as easily as Karen had or was her friend made of something that she wasn't?

Tara had so many questions for Karen that she rushed back to her bed to begin writing her friend back. She'd forgotten all about the other letters just that quickly. If Karen's letter could give her this kind of inspiration, she definitely wanted to read the mail from her family and her beloved Julio. It was hard to decide which one to read first. After much thought she decided to save Julio's letter for last because she knew she would end up writing him back right away. Karen's letter helped her to believe that they could possibly find their way back to each other after all.

M&M was in rare form in her letter. Things at home were all the way live and on the streets. Crack was ruining a lot of things for a lot of people, both directly and indirectly. Her mother told her about so many people they knew that had been taken out by the drug. Its effects were crippling to the game. Very little money was moving on the streets and no one could be trusted. M&M reverted to hustling weed. She refused to get caught up in the crack game. She hated that shit; it had taken her daughter from her. She explained to Tara that she was getting too old to keep running in and out of stores and everybody smoked weed so it was an easy transition.

Plus the crack-heads had ruined all her good customs by selling the shit they ripped off for little to nothing. "Motherfuckers expect you to practically give your hard-earned pieces away for nothing. I'd rather keep my shit than just gave it away," her mother complained in her letter.

Slim's signature mahogany greeting card was more of the same. Her father complained about the effects of crack on his business, also. Hookers were wising up. Most of his best hoes were getting lost on the way to him with his money. They could easily be found at the nearest crack house. They were wising up to the fact that they could hold their own money. He cursed the day crack arrived in the hood. Things would never be the same for any of them again. Her dad begged her to get help from the system for her addiction while she was there. Slim pleaded with her to come home free from the whole crack thing. He told her he didn't understand much about it, but he did understand it was a destructive monster and that its wrath would destroy everyone in its path.

Tara understood that her parents were doing their best to reach her on the real about her addiction. She understood they were genuinely afraid for her. She was afraid too. Her parents were the two strongest people she knew. If they were afraid, the world needed to get wise on the epidemic. All this time she thought she was just weak and unable to handle the drug. She had no idea that the drug could not be handled by anyone.

Her family used drugs her whole life, in one form or another. Throughout her life she'd tried pretty much everything, but settled on mostly smoking weed for recreational purposes.

Julio introduced her to cocaine during the height of his drug-kingpin reign on the streets. They were living the lifestyles of the rich and famous, and cocaine was a major part of that life. The bottom fell out when Julio went to jail. Tara quickly graduated to crack and the rest was history.

Somewhere in the two letters she heard her parents saying to her that it wasn't her fauLieutenant Nobody had told her that this whole time. It felt so good to finally hear it. She felt like such a disappointment to her family. She was the only one of their children to go to prison. Her parents prided themselves in staying one step ahead of the law.

After reading the letters from her parents she took a break. There was always so much to think about. Her head ached from all the thinking. It was easier not to think at all about anything. Thinking was work and working involved taking the pain out the box and examining it. Her way of dealing with it was to act like it didn't matter. She perfected going through the motions of life, getting up and laying down each day, never connecting or caring about anything or anybody. The people she encountered along the way were simply there for her amusement.

Well, you can keep sitting here acting like you don't care or you can get honest and rip open the damn letter, Tara thought, staring down at the envelope from Julio.

Chapter Twenty-five

Every Day I'm Hustling, Hustling

Scott sat back in his chair enjoying the view. CO Ward was on all fours giving him a professional blow job. The laundry room was the spot; the door locked from the inside and Ward was the only officer on the shift with a key. It was good to be the king. A niggah was buried back in isolation but he was living the good life. Ward kept him sexually satisfied and she made sure he had everything he needed back in the dungeon. If it was up to him he would do all of his time back in the hole. He was having an absolute ball.

"You like the way I suck it, Daddy?" Ward questioned, practically swallowing his rock-hard dick in her mouth as he played with her forty-four double-D's. Her big-ass breasts felt like beach balls in his hands.

"Take them panties off and let me get some of that good pussy, baby," Scott ordered, getting up from his chair. He grabbed one of her breasts and sucked it aggressively before he released her to follow his order.

The laundry room wasn't very big; it was only used to do the clothes for the men in isolation. There were five washers, two dryers, and a folding table in the room. Ward added a chair a few weeks earlier for her pleasure. She loved sitting on his dick while he was sitting in the chair. Every item in the room had been broken in by them. Their favorite spot was on top of the dryer.

"This is your pussy. Is this my dick, Daddy?" Ward purred,

massaging his dick with her left hand as she played with her pussy with her right hand. Scott shoved her against the washing machine and rammed his dick up in her from behind.

"This is yo' dick if I let you have it, bitch. Don't get it twisted. This pussy belongs to me, bottom line. Say that shit, Latrice. Say, 'this is my daddy's pussy.' Say that shit," Scott ordered, calling her by her first name.

"This is my Daddy's pussy. This is my Daddy's pussy," Ward repeated what she was told with pleasure. She loved this man and she was willing to do whatever he told her to do. No one made her feel the way he did. She wanted him all the time now.

Things had gotten so bad that she started working overtime practically every day. Latrice practically lived at the prison now, never wanting to be away from him for very long. He made her feel alive and so very beautiful. She craved his touch and the way he made her feel. She could not get enough of this man. She adored him. Latrice was willing to put everything on the line to be with him. Her career would be over if they were ever found out, but she didn't care. It was worth the price to her to be with the man she loved.

Latrice was an average-looking woman; nothing stood out about her. However, she did have a nice shape, a firm, tight body with a tight pussy to go with it and she knew it. Unfortunately she'd never been married and she had no children, and being in corrections made it hard to find a man who understood the long hours. The fact that she was drawn to thugs and bad boys didn't help her situation either. Something about a brother with an attitude kept her panties wet.

"Fuck me hard, baby. I love it when you fuck me hard," Ward ordered her lover, enjoying every moment of their stolen pleasure.

"I love this good pussy, baby. Your ass gonna make me

cum," Scott announced, then he exploded inside her tight pussy. He wasn't sure if she had cum or not and he didn't care. It was all about him. She was his little plaything. Whatever he wanted from her he got. He was well-aware of her feelings for him. The last time they fucked she'd slipped and said, "I love you, Scott," while he was laying the pipe. He played the game well; he knew her weaknesses, all of them. He stroked her ego with all the things she needed to hear. She was a senior officer on her way to becoming a white shirt soon. He was banking on her pulling some strings to get his isolation sentence cut in half. Do Dirty was having a ball back in the hole with his sex slave, but the real action was in general population.

"You got yours. You still owe me mine. We need to get going before someone misses us. I'll try to pull you out later," Ward shared, putting her uniform top back on as she stood before him naked from the waist down.

"You trying to drain a brother dry, ain't you, girl," Scott teased and slapped her on her naked behind while she dressed. He was done with her for the day. If she knew like he knew she better handle her business when she got the chance because he was done. She was a freak, wanting it all the time. Latrice was wearing him out, and he was growing tired of the games. In the beginning it was easy just to imagine Tara while he was ramming his dick up in her, but now when he thought of Tara it just made him sad.

Writing wasn't something he did often but he did it for Tara. He had written her two letters now and he'd heard nothing from her in return. Didn't she understand he needed to hear from her to know that she was okay? In his first letter he put himself out there asking her questions that exposed his feelings for her. He wished he could recall that first letter. He was sure that was the reason why he hadn't heard from her.

"Let me get a kiss before I take you back to lockup. That will hold me until later.

Don't you forget you owe me and I want my pay," Ward reminded her lover. She rubbed his dick through his pants as she unlocked the laundry room door with her other hand.

"Damn, girl, quit being so greedy. You gonna get some more, just be patient," Scott told her, glad to be free from her grip as she opened the door and went instantly back in CO mode without missing a beat. He grabbed his laundry bag on the way out the door.

"Up against the wall, inmate, and no talking, you hear me?" she ordered, leading him down the empty hallway. Her show of authority was for the cameras mounted on the wall recording the comings and goings in the area.

How had he just allowed Do Dirty to show up and take over so easily? He wasn't even sure when his old self took over. Dirty was running things and he didn't like the decisions being made. Before he got popped he was well on the way to becoming the man he dreamed he could be, even if it was by living a double life. He was backing out of the game gracefully without stepping on anybody's toes on the way out. Why couldn't they just let a niggah be? It was as if they gave him just enough rope to hang himself, dangling the thought of the good life in front of him. Allowing him to believe he could find that elusive happiness. He was starting to believe it didn't exist, at least not for a brother from the hood. He knew his anger was what allowed him to say "fuck it" to everything.

For a while it felt good not to give a fuck, but he did give a fuck about a lot of things, especially trying to win Tara's heart. Laying the pipe on the regular to a woman he cared nothing about wasn't the way to becoming the man Tara needed. He vowed to himself he would work on doing that when she went to prison. He was so far from that. Now he was a joke and he knew it.

Dirty arrived on the set kicking in heads and taking names. The joint was more than willing to crown him king and let him reign; at least, that's what he thought in the beginning. Now he was starting to realize that the system was willing to sit back and let him choose his own path. Why was it so easy to always choose the wrong things? Was it something in his DNA that conditioned him to crime, jail, and bad choices? Maybe he really did not have a choice. Or did he? He tried on his own to make the right choices but he failed miserably.

CO Ward unlocked the rusty steel door to his cell. Dirty entered reluctantly and sat down on his bed. The feeling of being trapped overcame him. It was as if he was drowning and he needed a lifeline from somewhere. He jumped up and ran to the door. He started to bang on the door but something stopped him.

Somewhere deep inside him, he heard a small, still voice saying over and over again, "You are not alone. I am here. Seek my face and you will find me."

Chapter Twenty-six

It was a cold fall day. The sky was covered with thick rain clouds but the sun was shining in Tara's heart. It could have been a hurricane and it would not have altered her mood. She couldn't have been happier if she tried. Tara sat anxiously on the thick green plastic seat enjoying every sight, sound, and moment of her road trip to Franklin Pre-release. The prison bus was overcrowded as usual, but it didn't faze her one bit. She happily snuggled up between the two other inmates next to her. She'd never met the women sharing her road trip but they'd gotten acquainted along the way. Both the women were first-time offenders who were anticipating their arrival at the much talked-about Franklin Pre-release Center just as much as Tara, if not more.

FPRC was located just outside the city of Columbus, right across the street from the workhouse. It was a fairly new facility from what they were told, with a lot more to offer the women. The three women could not wait to get to their destination. Most of the other women on the bus felt the same way that they did. You could do so many more things at FPRC. The food was better and they even had a program for model inmates, which allowed them to leave the prison to work during the day. Most of them were just looking forward to getting a perm; the coveted item wasn't sold at commissary on the farm. There were a lot of nappy-headed women on the bus counting down the minutes until they could step back into the twenty-first century. Tara planned on getting her hair fried, dyed, and laid to the side the minute she got there.

What Tara didn't share with her new friends was the real reason for her exceptionally good mood. Ever since she'd gotten the letter from Julio back in the hole, she'd been on a natural high. All this time she believed he'd given up on their love, and that he didn't want to be with her anymore, but his letter changed everything. He asked her in his letter to fight for them and she planned on fighting to the end now. She made a new vow to never give up on their love ever again. He was the most important thing in the world to her, and she planned on proving that to him. She also planned on taking her parents' advice and seeking out help with her addiction while she was behind the walls. Why not? she thought. She had nothing but time to focus on all the things that had gone wrong in her life and come up with a plan to avoid putting herself in a position to let them ever happen to her again.

Being locked away in the hole in Marysville turned out to be the best thing that could have happened to her. All the time alone gave her the time to really get real with herself. She'd been blaming everyone else for all her problems and never once did she stop to look at what role she played in all the mess.

Tara was so grateful for a second chance at happiness with the man she loved; she was willing to do anything to find her way back to Julio. The road back to him began with being honest with herself. As hard as it was for her to admit, she understood that she was weak emotionally. She would have to find a way to overcome that weakness without using people and drugs.

"Can you see it? Look over there in the distance. You can see downtown," Juanita announced, looking out the window and pointing at the group of skyscrapers in the distance.

Downtown Columbus came in to view as the bus shim-
mied down the highway. The bus got completely quiet as the
women soaked in the view.

Juanita was an older black woman who looked completely
out of place on the bus with the rest of the inmates. It blew
Tara away when she shared with them that she was doing time
for theft. Her theft charges were the direct result of her addiction to crack cocaine. The soft-spoken Juanita told them that
crack had cost her everything. Those words bonded the two
of them together as friends instantly. The new friends shared
their life stories with each other all the way down the road.
By the time they reached Franklin Pre-release they both knew
everything about each other's road to prison.

When the tan school bus finally pulled off of the highway,
Tara thought she'd bust with anticipation, and FPRC did not
disappoint her. The difference between the two prisons was
like night and day. The first thing she noticed was how small
the place was; it was a third the size of the farm. The prison
was made up of six brick buildings that stood in a circle. In
the middle of the circle was a large parklike grassy area. A
fenced-in recreation court sat right next to the street and parking lot. Inmates could be seen walking leisurely around the
court while other inmates played tennis and volleyball in the
center of the court.

"All right, ladies, let's move off the bus in an orderly fashion. The quicker we get you processed in, the quicker you can
get to your housing units," a friendly CO announced standing beside the bus driver before doing a quick head count.

"Did she just call us 'ladies'?" Tara questioned Juanita, surprised by the COs choice of words. The pleasant CO chatted
with one of the ladies as she led them to the front entrance.
The entrance to the prison was small and very neat. A large
desk took up most of the room. To the right of the desk was

a bank of school lockers and waiting room chairs, and on the opposite side of the desk was a metal detector and a glass window with a CO stationed behind it.

"I didn't know you were working today, Clark," the CO behind the glass spoke to the friendly CO who led them from the bus.

"You know I don't pass up easy overtime. I'm making time and a half, buddy," Clark shot back, teasing the other officer. Clark placed her loaded weapon inside a slot under the window and then handed a paper to the other officer behind the big desk. The women were then led one at a time through the metal detector. Once the group cleared the detector, they were taken to admissions.

CO Clark stood behind a half door passing out state-issued clothing and bedrolls. Tara was surprised to see her handing out coats also. The coats seemed out of place to her and odd. It hit her in that moment that she would be here for awhile. This was her new home.

The admissions orientation was nothing like the one in Marysville. Once the women were issued their clothing they were led through the administration building to the circular yard. Just like at the farm, women were everywhere waiting to see the fresh meat arriving from Marysville.

Outside of each housing unit were trees and red picnic tables. The fronts of the housing units were covered with windows. Women could be seen in the windows checking out the new arrivals. Each housing unit had concrete seating areas on both sides of the door. Women sat chatting and staring on the seats. There were five dorms in all. Each dorm had its number brightly posted outside the door and each door was painted a different bright primary color. If you didn't know better you would think you were at summer camp.

"This place is a lot nicer than the farm, huh?" Juanita acknowledged, looking around at the campus. Things were looking up for them.

"Ahh, hell no! My girl, Tara!" Rosie shouted from the window in the dorm they were entering. Tara looked up and waved, excited to see her friend.

The women were seated in the dayroom of dorm one. Tara was surprised to see an expensive pool table in the room. The entire room was alive with movement. Women stood at a circular desk waiting to sign some sort of paper everyone signed before they left the building. A couple of women gathered around a microwave cooking something that smelled delicious. Another group of ladies played cards at a table next to the COs desk.

Above their heads in the dayroom was a balcony. Women were constantly peeking over the balcony at the new arrivals as they tried to focus on their orientation. There was so much going on in the room that Tara missed just about everything the friendly Officer Clark was saying to them.

"If I see another head peek over that balcony, I'm coming up there," Clark threatened the women disrupting her orientation. Officer Debra Clark was a kind and fair Christian woman who took no stuff. She'd worked in corrections most of her life and seen it all before. She believed in treating the women like human beings, not prisoners, and she refused to call them inmates. They were women, just like her, who made a mistake. Clark didn't believe in smacking them in the face with their mistake every day. She stood before them explaining the rules at Franklin Pre-release and passing out their housing assignments.

"Yes, CO Clark. I just wanted to say 'hi' to my cousin Tara. Can I show her where her room is, please?" Rosie whined to her favorite officer.

"Since you're in such a helpful mood, you can help show

everybody to their dorms. And take that head scarf off before you come down here," CO Clark instructed Rosie.

Both Tara and Juanita were assigned to dorm one where Rosie also lived. Either it was a lucky break for them or Rosie was able to pull some strings. Either way Tara was glad to be back with her girl Rosie.

"I'm so glad you're here, Tara. Franklin is so much better than being at the farm. Don't worry about a thing. Our girl Creeper runs this shit. Ain't nothing going down around here without her say-so. I'll bring you a perm for your hair and some other stuff after count time to hold you until you can shop at commissary," Rosie explained, walking through the yard like the official tour guide of FPRC. She was genuinely glad to see her friend. Tara was always the life of the party, and there was never a dull moment when the two of them were together. "Franklin Pre-release had better get ready. Let the games begin," Rosie laughed, wrapping up the private tour for her friend.

"How long have you been here, Rosie? Everybody said you were in the drug program on the farm. I thought that program lasted eighteen months," Tara questioned.

"I was in the Tapestry program but they put my ass out after the second week. I wasn't able to follow all the rules of the program. They ain't playing with a bitch in that program. You either have to be serious or keep it pushing," Rosie offered with a look of disappointment on her face. Rosie really wanted to complete the drug-treatment program. She valued the opportunity to learn more about her drug addiction. Her life had spun out of control years ago, but she did her best not to focus on what could have been, prison had a way of causing you to think ninety percent of the time. The question was, "What were you thinking about?"

Tapestry was a highly respected and an intensive residential drug-treatment program in Marysville. The prison program used a very restrictive approach to drug treatment. All negative behavior was frowned upon. All recovery citizens of the holistic program were required to follow all the prison rules to the letter. The philosophy of the Tapestry program was both practiced and followed by both citizens and staff religiously. Recovering citizens were encouraged to remind other citizens of the Tapestry creed often. Whenever a citizen was observed breaking even the smallest infractions, they were called on the carpet.

These reminder sessions were both public and very invasive. They were referred to as pull-ups. One's sins were read aloud before a large group of judgmental, watchful eyes. The group facilitator would read the transgressor's sins first, then the group would take turns condemning the wayward member of the precious fold, reminding them that the pull-ups were for their personal growth. Rosie was pulled-up so many times during her brief stay even she lost count.

Her expulsion came quickly. The final straw was her relationship with a friend from the streets. The unworthy transgressors were harshly judged for three grueling hours before they were removed from the program. The damaging part of the whole experience was that Rosie spent the entire three hours in tears pleading with the cruel group to let her have one more chance. Just when she was sure she had them convinced to let her stay, they flipped the script on her with no clear explanation. Rosie had been shipped to Franklin Prerelease Center shortly afterward.

"Look, you see that CO up against the wall over there with the black CO?" Rosie pointed in the direction of dorm five. Two correctional officers were leaning up against the wall near dorm five. They both had on dark sunglasses and each one of them was monitoring the yard like the Secret Service.

"Watch out for those two. They don't play. Everybody calls the white one Spiderman. That motherfucker is everywhere. He'll creep up on you before you know it. He don't miss nothing. Be careful around him," Rosie warned.

Tara studied Spiderman carefully; he looked like he didn't take no shit. He had that by-the-book look about him—that type wasn't to be fucked with. She made a mental note to stay clear of him.

"Hey, Rosie, where's Creeper? Can you take me to see her?" Tara asked, anxious to see her. She hadn't seen Creeper in a long time.

"Creeper runs central food services around here. She over there right now. You'll get a chance to see her at lunchtime. She gets off after the lunch service. Guess who else? Cricket's fine ass is here too. She's got everybody sweating her. Girl, Doretha died. Can you believe that shit?" Rosie filled Tara in on all the latest news as they walked back to dorm one.

"Shut up, Rosie, you've got to be kidding me. I just saw Doretha before I rode out to Maryville from the workhouse. How did she die?" Tara questioned sadly.

"They say she was released from the county after serving ninety days on a ho case. Her pimp picked her up at the gate and took her right back to the track. But she didn't stay there. Instead she got with her old smoking crew and got high. She was found dead in the Motel Six on Main Street. They say she had a massive heart attack during the night her first day home. Nobody knows what really happened because everybody with her disappeared," Rosie said explaining the tragic loss to Tara.

"Wow, Rosie, that shit's crazy. She was so young. I didn't know her that well but she was cool. We were in the same dorm. She loved her some Cricket, I know that," Tara said, shaking her head, thinking about the wasted life.

"Cricket took it pretty hard; they had to put her on suicide watch for a while. She was back there in the hole for about a month, but when she came out she was fine. She enrolled in the drug-treatment program here and now she leads the Narcotics Anonymous group on Thursday nights. She's now this serious change advocate and the bitches are eating that shit up. They pack her group out every Thursday night. I call her the professor," Rosie bragged, walking back into their dorm.

"I'm going to unpack and get settled in my room, but I'll catch up with you after count time. Are you going to lunch?" Tara asked before heading upstairs to her new room. She wanted some time to get familiar with her new roommates.

"Girl, I don't miss a meal around here. Everything is good. Creeper makes sure of that shit. Wait until you taste the pancakes. They're big as your head and light and fluffy. You have to get there early too. Sometimes they run out because so many people go to breakfast on pancake day," Rosie said before leaving.

"See you after count," Tara shot after her friend. She was glad to be at her new location. Her room was on the second floor; the first dorm room on the left. There were twelve rooms in all on the floor, four two-inmate rooms and sixteen four-inmate rooms. Each door was painted bright orange with brown accents. The orange door opened up to a small bathroom and shower area. There were two additional doors across the back wall that led to the sleeping area. Tara's was assigned to the one on the left. The room was a nice size; two sets of bunk beds were along the wall on the left. Two double-sided dressers with attached desks were on the right side of the room, and a large window took up the back wall. Each desk held a small TV. Four lock boxes were strategically placed near the bunk beds.

A pregnant young white girl was sleeping on the bottom bunk of the first set of beds. All pregnant women sentenced to serve time across the State of Ohio were housed at Franklin Pre-release Center until they gave birth because of its closeness to the Ohio State University Hospital, where the women were taken to give birth. The pregnant women were allowed a mere twenty-four hours with their newborns before their infants were either picked up by a family member or children services.

Tara unpacked her things and got comfortable on her bed. It was a mere process of elimination figuring out which one of the beds belonged to her. All three of the other beds in the room had bedding on them. As usual she was on the top bunk.

"Damn. Who do you have to know to get a bottom bunk?" she said to herself as she climbed up the ladder.

"The bottom bunks are reserved for pregnant girls, medical orders, and older inmates. If no one fits that category in the room then you get a bottom one. Hi, I'm Shady. What's your name?" the pregnant girl explained, rolling over on her side and looking up at Tara on the bunk.

"My name's Tara. When's your baby due?" Tara asked, looking down at her. Shady was as big as a house. She looked like she was going to give birth any minute. Her face was swollen and covered in acne, and her feet were so swollen that they didn't look real.

"I'm not due for another six weeks. They have me on bed rest until I deliver. All I do is lay up here all day eating junk and watching TV," Shady shared, tossing and turning, trying to get comfortable on the small mattress.

Just then the count whistle blew. Tara sat back and got comfortable on her own bed. She couldn't wait to see who her other roommates were going to be. First an older white lady walked in and immediately sat down on the bunk under Tara. She never acknowledged Tara or Shady. She sat down, took off her shoes, and placed them neatly against the wall by the window.

Next, a young, cute black girl with long black hair entered the room like a force.

"Hey, Tara. They told me you rode in today. Remember me? I've been to your mom's house a thousand times with my sister Tina. She's one of your mom's old work partners. Do you remember me? I'm Becky. Welcome to the jungle. I'm so glad we finally got a thoroughbred in this bitch," the cute black girl announced, climbing up on her own bunk.

"Sssssshh. There's no talking during count time," the older lady underneath Tara finally spoke to quiet her roommates.

"Well, then shut the fuck up, Ms. Lenny," Becky shot back.

Chapter Twenty-seven

When a man is never truly honest with himself and his true being, he can find himself lost in the illusion of his true self. The road to self-destruction is long and filled with disappointment, and when you live in this state for extended periods of time, your ability to operate from a place of caring and compassion becomes a distant memory. Scott had drifted to this point of no return. Prison instantly transported him to "I don't give a fuck" mode. Whenever he was in that mood, a niggah better back the fuck up for real. He wilded out from the gate. Where he came from, a niggah had to do something to survive. On his streets, it was survival of the fittest, and every house on the block had its own problems.

He learned how to get his hustle on at an early age. He had to if he was going to survive in the hood. Every single day, it was do-or-die. The joint wasn't any different. You had to get your hustle on in order to survive because that's all you knew how to do in the jungle. The prison system is a jungle of motherfuckers trying to survive on a daily basis. It is a place in which help, security, and protection are provided from an after-the-fact perspective.

Scott arrived on the set surviving and playing the game, but he was starting to realize that he was getting too old to continue to live his life like shit didn't matter. He wanted to be a bigger man. Life had to be about something more and he was starting to understand that the answers were bigger than him.

Looking back at his concrete bed and around the room, Scott did a final check of his home for the past three months. He was so glad to be free of his hellhole, he didn't know what to do. He would probably Crip walk out the door when they finally came to release him from his tomb. As he waited, his freedom was anticipated and valued.

"God. Allah. Heavenly Father. I'm still working on my praying and I need help with that. Please help me to be a better man," Scott whispered a prayer while he waited patiently by the door. He was going to need the help of something bigger than him to try to do something different. Motherfuckers would definitely gun for him if they knew he was trying to be a bigger man. He had fallen into that trip when he arrived on the set. Niggahs and the COs expected him to act a fool and he got busy living up to who the crowd wanted him to be, but he was sick of letting somebody else define him.

Scott strolled back into population with confidence and a new attitude. It was morning rec and the yard was alive with activity. The minute he exited the facility door, it was all eyes on him. Brothers immediately began welcoming him back.

"Man, Dirty, I didn't think they was ever going to let you out from back in that bitch," Ray Ray complained, greeting his boy with a hug. He was glad to see that his dude was still standing. Ray Ray knew his boy very well; it didn't take much of nothing to set Do Dirty off. The pair were roommates before Dirty went to the hole. They were also from the same set back home. Ray Ray was a lot younger than Dirty but the pair had been groomed on the same set. Game recognized game from the gate.

From the minute Dirty arrived on the set he was out of control. He started kicking his credentials from the jump. There were so many easily persuaded young niggahs in the joint; a true gangster could get a shorty to do just about anything on some follow-the-leader shit. It was disturbing to Ray Ray how the young niggahs didn't even understand the game. Little niggahs just jumped straight in before ever going to a single class. There were rules to this shit. Ray Ray wondered when these thirsty little niggahs were going to learn that fact.

"What's up?" Scott greeted his young soldier with a hug, glad to be back on the block with some familiar faces.

"Aw shit, is that you, Shaun? Aw, hell no. They got little Shaun up in here," Scott yelled, rushing over to greet one of his old friends.

Shaun walked up on Scott with his state-issued pants sagging and gave him a "what's up?" chin nod. Despite his nonchalant response, Shaun was overjoyed to see his boy Dirty, but he wasn't going to just act all starstruck and shit. Not in front of his boys.

Scott grabbed the young G in a headlock and hugged him close. "Don't even try to act like you all hard and shit. You know what it is. We family," Scott schooled his homie, both happy to see a friend and sad to see the little soldier trapped in the belly of the beast. He had watched this little niggah grow up. This little soldier had the coldest jump shot in the game. Everybody in the north end of Columbus had money on him going to the NBA.

Introductions were made all around before the men made themselves comfortable at one of the picnic tables in the yard. Groups of men were scattered around the yard engaged in different activities and enjoying the time outside. A crowd gathered in front of the weight benches next to the picnic tables where they sat and talked.

"Man, Ray, I did a lot of thinking while I was back in the hole. No, first I did a lot of playing. Shit, I was back there still hustling and using people for my own selfish needs. We've got to start being bigger than all this bullshit out here, man.

I can't keep being a part of my own selfdestruction," Scott explained, looking around the yard.

"I am so glad you said that shit, Dirty, man. I was ready to blow this bitch up when they dragged you back to the hole, man. Motherfuckers knew to give me fifty feet, you know what I'm sayin'? But just when I was about to explode, my dude Muhammad started schooling me on some positive ways of dealing with my anger over a lot of stuff, man. We got to start schooling each other on how to do some different shit. I'm going with him to Taleem on Friday. You want to go too Dirty?" Ray Ray shared his newfound knowledge. He hoped his friend would take the bait. They had to start changing. Ray Ray was convinced after listening to the Muslim brother that the destruction of them as strong, proud black men was occurring at their own hands.

"What's this Taleem stuff, Ray? When you start knowing so much about when the peacemakers meet? Oh, and please stop calling me Dirty, all right?" Scott advised. He was tired of being labeled what people thought he was, and he was not the person that they thought they knew. Do Dirty was left back in isolation. A new man stepped out of that hellhole. He was that man and he planned on living up to what a man was supposed to be in the world. He wasn't really sure what that shit looked like but he was determined to find out.

"Ray, man, I want to meet this Muhammad. We're all going to Taleem on Friday and don't you even think you can get out of it, either, Shaun," Scott said and lightheartedly punched his little homie in the arm. Shaun punched his hero back while looking around the yard to make sure everybody saw him kicking it with an original gangster.

"Man, Dirty—shit, I mean Scott. I ain't really into no church shit, man," Shaun confessed, wanting to get out of a wasted day at the church house with some busters.

"Have you ever been to the temple, Shaun? I know you haven't so how you going to form an opinion about something that you haven't even tried, man? Let's check it out before you shoot it out the water," Scott instructed, laying down the law. He could tell from the jockeying in the yard that everybody was watching to see what his next move was going to be.

Scott could either lead them to the promised land or to the point of no return. He had almost reached the point of throwing in the towel on trying to do the right thing because it cost too much time, but that's what made it that much more valuable—the price he had to pay. A niggah had to put something in to get something out, and he was always trying to get away with not investing his heart or whole self into anything. If he was going to break free from the streets, he would have to be all in. Maybe then he could start being the type of man that Tara could trust with her heart.

"I'm telling y'all, once you meet Brother Muhammad you going to want to kick it with him on some knowledge shit. He knows all his black history, man. He told me some shit about how there's some shit that sets us brothers up to end up in jail. We need to be wiser on that shit, man," Ray Ray added, looking around at all the brothers in the yard. They were everywhere, young and old, and most of them didn't have a clue how to start doing something different.

"I feel you, Ray. We got to start educating each other. We just feed off each other when we need to be our brother's keeper. Shit is crazy, man. Look over there at them against the wall. They straight marks and we know it. Now, why don't we think to school the brothers? We would rather sit back and watch dudes that look just like us fall in a hole without ever saying, 'Watch out! You about to fall!' What kind of man is that, who just goes through life not giving a fuck about his brothers? We better than that, y'all. I know I am," Scott preached to his friends and to himself simultaneously.

All three men sat reflecting on their own lives and the people they'd become. In each man was a leader; a person of great intelligence with the ability to change the world. A band of brothers committed to change was formed that day in the yard, even though one of the warriors was drafted against his will. Each man had the desire to do something different with his life.

Scott's release from the hole was the catalyst for their movement toward doing something different. When you've grown up and watched more people than you can remember get swallowed up by the streets, it gets old. The cost was getting way too high for Scott. He was sitting in the joint with one of the brightest young men he knew from his hood. They should have been sitting back kicking it on some college campus somewhere. Instead, they were getting a street degree in the belly of the beast.

Chapter Twenty-eight

Franklin Pre-release Center prided itself in being a progressive correctional institution for women in the state of Ohio. Its mission was to work with each and every woman on devising a plan for her own personal rehabilitation and release. Evidence-based programs, designed to assist with the women's successful reentry into the community, were constantly being tested at the facility. The women were allowed to decide on which programs best suited their individual needs. Everything from Alcohol Anonymous to pilot training was offered to the women.

The staff of Franklin Pre-release Center was forbidden to call the women "inmates." The logic was to start allowing the women to see themselves as citizens preparing to reenter society. All types of drug-treatment programs were offered to the women as well, led by people from outside and inside the institution. Several programs gave the women the opportunity to work outside the gates during the day and return to the facility at night. Even though they earned a salary that was well below minimum wage, these precious jobs were coveted by all. The process to be considered was based on the inmate's security status and institutional behavior record.

Family-strengthening programs and religious services played a big part in the reentry process. Restoring those bonds was essential to the process of preparing the women to return to their communities.

The best drug programs were offered during the day. Because of Tara's school requirement, she was unable to take advantage of the programs offered at that time. Drug treatment was crucial to getting her life back. Tara was convinced of that fact. But first things were first; she had to get her school requirement out the way. There were so many things to do at FPRC, she would really need to concentrate on her plan or she could easily get lost in all the excitement of her new location.

Every day was an adventure. There were so many distractions, and it didn't help that she knew just about everyone there or they knew her. Being roommates with Becky didn't make it any better. Their room became the party spot from day one. Somebody was always stopping by or hanging out.

This didn't sit too well with their other roommate, Mrs. Lenny, who was a by-the-book, no-nonsense older woman. Mrs. Lenny was serving time for conspiracy. That's all anyone knew about her case. Mrs. Lenny didn't discuss her personal life with anyone. She barely talked to anyone, for that matter. Her days were spent at the law library and on the phone.

It was a rainy Saturday afternoon. Tara decided to stay in and get caught up on a few letters. The night before had been wild. Becky's box from home arrived with all kinds of goodies and they had stayed up most of the night stuffing themselves. Tara's stomach was still full from all the Grippo's BBQ potato chips she consumed. She really needed to study for her GED test but her girl Creeper wanted her to meet in the yard before count time.

Monday was Creeper's visiting day and she wanted to borrow Tara's brown Guess blouse for her visit. At FPRC, women could just run out to the yard. The minute Tara hit the door she was pulled in a million different directions by various people she knew.

"Hey, Tara. Are you going outside anymore tonight?" Shady questioned her roommate in a soft voice. It was the first time she spoke since she returned from the hospital after giving birth to her baby. She had been perfectly still since coming back. Her roommates understood that she was in pain from being separated from her newborn baby. They couldn't even imagine what she was feeling. Even Mrs. Lenny was being nurturing to Shady.

"Yeah, I'm going outside. What you need, honey? What you need me to do for you while I'm out there?" Tara asked, glad to be included in the caregiving of Shady. Mrs. Lenny was busy folding the clean sheets she'd washed in the laundry room earlier in the day while sitting on her bunk bed. She looked up at Tara and waited for her response. One of them needed to stay in the room with Shady with the mood she was in. Mrs. Lenny had plans to attend the knitting group in dorm two if she didn't have to stay with Shady. She wasn't going to count on her roommate Becky returning to the room until the count whistle blew. Becky never came to the room a minute before that time. Her hope was that her other roommates would pitch in with watching after the young girl.

"Will you go over to dorm three and sign me up for the movie next Saturday? They're showing a T.D. Jakes movie and I want to see it real bad. When they show his movies, they fill up as soon as the list goes out." Shady perked up for a moment, explaining the urgency of the request. Then she lay against her flat state pillow, exhausted from the conversation and the day.

"Yes, Mrs. Shady. I will make sure your name is at the top of the T.D. Jakes movie list before count time. You can count on me." Tara did a bow and headed out of the room, leaving Mrs. Lenny to be the babysitter.

Dorm one was busy as always. The first-floor break room

was filled with women socializing with one another. There were three card games going on at the break tables and a group was gathered at the microwave cooking up one thing or another. A game of pool was in full effect while other women sat watching an episode of *The Simpsons* on the TV hanging from the ceiling across from the pool table. Meanwhile, the dorm CO was busy passing out supplies and information. It was mandatory for inmates to sign out before exiting their housing units each day. They were required to sign back in upon their return.

"Where you rushing off to, Tara? Get over here and get in this game," Juanita instructed, yelling over her shoulder while she dealt the cards for her tenth game of bid whist. She'd been playing and winning all day. Now she needed some competition and she knew Tara would give her a run for her money.

"I got you later on. I got to meet somebody outside. Hold it down for us, girl," Tara explained, rushing past the table and heading out the door. The front porch of dorm one was on stack. Women were everywhere you looked. You could not find a seat on the wall if you tried. Couples were hugged up, enjoying their time together. Franklin Pre-release was different from the farm; they didn't let you flaunt that relationship shit all out in the open like they did on the farm. The women did their thing just like on the farm but they did it on the down-low. The Pre-release Center was the spot. You could get a whole lot of shit off up in that bitch. You just had to know how to be discreet.

It wasn't even a question whether she was going to go sign Shady up for the movie first or go holler at Creeper. Tara knew once the two of them got started talking she would not be able to break away until the count bell rang.

"Hey, Tara, where you going?" Cricket questioned Tara, joining her on the circular side walk on her way to dorm three.

"I'm just going to have to follow you wherever you go, Tara, if I'm ever going to get some time with you. I been trying to spend some time with you since you got here but you always on the run. Where you running to now, baby?" Cricket asked, out of breath, rushing up beside Tara.

Cricket had been trying to get a minute with her for weeks. She was always on the go or with her starting lineup. The girl kept a crew with her whenever she was seen. Cricket was cool on the entourage. She had been there and done that. Playing follow-the-leader was one of the worst games a bitch could get caught up in while doing time. Independent thinkers were few and far between behind the walls. Cricket was a cutie-pie. If you didn't know better you would swear you were looking at a fine-ass man. She was tall with long, jet-black hair that she wore French braided in four neat braids straight back. The two of them knew each other from when Tara used to run in and out of the workhouse.

"I have to do a favor for my roommate. She just got back from having her baby. It was hard on her having to leave her baby and come back here," Tara explained as she entered dorm three. The minute the pair entered the dorm room it was all eyes on them. Nosy motherfuckers started sizing them up, trying to figure out if they were a couple. Cricket was the shit; all the women wanted a piece of her.

Both Tara and Cricket signed the movie list. Tara even signed herself up for the movie. She'd never been to a movie with a church message before but she was familiar with Bishop T.D. Jakes. His books touched her way back at the county jail. The workhouse seemed so long ago, like a distant memory.

"When we going to get a chance to catch up? You always on the go. I hope you spending all this valuable time on something positive. You was the prophet back at the workhouse. Don't sit on all your gifts and talents. You have a unique way of drawing people to you and that ain't just for no reason. I figured that shit out after all this time, Tara," Cricket confessed with a serious look on her face.

"I feel you, Cricket. I've been chasing my tail for a minute now. I really need to get my act together. I am enrolled in school, and I've been studying hard, working on my GED, and once I get school out the way I plan on enrolling in the drug program," Tara explained while mean mugging a girl who was giving her the evil eye on the way out the door to dorm three. Cricket held the door open to allow Tara to walk through. Every eyeball in the room was still focused on them.

"You don't have to enroll in the classes we host in the evening, Tara. You just have to show up to the meetings. It's completely peer-driven. The residents lead the group. I just took over the Wednesday-night classes. Our old leader just got released. I would love it if you came out this Wednesday, Tara. I'm telling you, if it wasn't for Narcotics Anonymous I would have lost my mind after Doretha died," she said, her voice breaking a little. The pain of losing somebody you love, coupled with not being able to say good-bye to them, is more than a person should be asked to bear. A person has to get some form of closure in life and in death.

"I'm starting to feel what you saying," Tara said nodding. "I thought we could just step over the bodies on the battlefield—just go through life like we just didn't give a fuck—but for real that shit is all game. I act out because I do care. I want to start working on me. I got somebody out there, Cricket, who loves me. For a minute I thought I would lose my mind too," Tara shared, empathizing with her friend.

"Where y'all sexy asses going?" Becky said, joining Tara and Cricket on the walkway.

"We were signing up for the movie. I'm supposed to be meeting Creeper out here. Have you seen her?" Tara asked her roommate, looking around.

"We're over on the porch at dorm two. You coming over with us, Cricket?" Becky asked, hoping Cricket would stop being such a bore. The cutie used to be the one to get the party started, but ever since Doe died she had been so serious, Becky thought, standing there with her hands on her hips waiting for an answer.

"Maybe next time, ladies. I've got some studying to do before parenting class tomorrow." Cricket excused herself, saying her good-byes before calling it a night. She really wanted to continue the conversation that she was having with Tara but it would have to wait for another time. Tara had a gift that the world needed. Cricket knew if she was able to get Tara involved in their movement, she would be a powerful force to have on their team. She would have to continue the conversation they were having when they didn't have an audience around. Her spirit told her that she needed to stay connected to Tara.

"I promise you, Cricket, I'm going to stop by one of your meetings once I get my GED test out the way. You know I can only concentrate on one thing at a time," Tara offered, waving good-bye before climbing the steps to dorm two.

It was almost count time and she was still out in the yard. Tara's plans were to just run over to dorm three, give Creeper the blouse, and get back to her studying. As always, her plans went out the window the minute she hit the yard. The yard was a social club, with a different party on each porch. Creeper's dorm was jumping; everybody from her hood hung out on Creeper's porch.

In the corner of the porch, in the best seat in the yard, sat Creeper, the G.O.A.T. or greatest of all time. Creeper was admired and respected by everybody inside and out. She was a professional bank robber who was given the name because of all the banks she'd crept up in over the years. She was a veteran in the eyes of all the other small-time hustlers and wannabe gangsters. Even the correctional officers respected Creeper. She was just a likable person. When she talked her face would light up. She always looked people in the eyes when she talked to them as if what they were saying was the most important thing in the world to her.

"Get your butt over here, Tara, baby. You ain't been outside all day. What's up with that?" Creeper questioned, motioning for an older white girl with long red hair to get up so Tara could sit down. "Jenny, make me some coffee so I can have a hot cup before the line gets too long." The business-professional-looking white girl followed the demand immediately without blinking.

"Creeper, I told you yesterday I wasn't fooling with you. I got to get my studying for my test done. If I come out here with y'all you know I won't get anything done. I've already been out here too long as it is. I just came out here for you," Tara whined, looking around the porch. It was really starting to annoy her to see people just wasting time. She had a plan for getting her life back in order. If she had learned anything while doing time, she'd learned that she had to stay focused on a plan. She owed it to her marriage to stay focused on the goals she'd set for herself.

Tara pulled the brown Guess blouse from her pants and passed it to Creeper on the low low. The women of Franklin Pre-release weren't allowed to share any personal items with one another. If you were caught sharing food or clothing, it was a rule infraction, and the penalty was usually extra duty. However, an asshole CO could be in a bad mood and have your clothes confiscated. You would have to wait until white shirt officers decided to release your property. The wait for just a hearing could take months.

"Good looking out." Creeper took the blouse and stuffed

it into her pants without missing a beat. Exchanges like theirs were going on all around the yard as the sun went down in Franklin County. Prison was an institution of higher learning. Every day someone showed up cleaned-faced and ready to be schooled. In most cases the problem was what they were learning.

Can a person study so hard that they erase the information that's stored inside their brain? Tara thought, flipping through her study guide and notes for the GED test. *There has to be a maximum amount of information that a person can store inside their brain at one time. Once a person reaches their maximum brain-storage capacity, information must get lost somehow.* Tara was on study overload. She just could not get the math equations straight in her head, but she was kind of starting to understand the sample science questions. Her class was going to start in less than an hour and she was still finishing up. Whatever her grade ended up being, that was it. She wasn't going to drive herself crazy taking the GED test for the first time. She would just have to retake the stupid thing, that's all.

Shady tossed on the bed and looked up at Tara. It was seven o'clock in the morning and Tara was fully dressed for her nine-thirty A.M. class. Shady could see her nervousness all over her face. Her poor roommate was a night owl who slept late everyday. She rarely got up for breakfast unless they were serving pancakes. Tara usually got up in just enough time to throw on her state uniform and fix her hair. She would even take her shower the night before to save herself more sleep time in the morning before she went to class. Even in her state of depression, Shady felt sorry for her roommate. The poor girl was going to go mad if she didn't get the dreaded test out of the way. Shady sat up on her bunk and spoke to her anxious roommate.

"Okay. That's enough studying already, Tara. You have done the preparation for your class. Now you get a chance to show them what you know. Go over, put it on paper and then be done with it," Shady explained, getting up from the bed.

"She's right. You have to trust that you've done all you can do at this point. Now relax and take yourself over to the cafeteria and get yourself some breakfast. You need to fuel your mind before you put it to work," Mrs. Lenny added, glad to see Shady up from her bed. The young girl was really starting to worry the wise, older woman. She'd seen women slip into a depression after childbirth that would push them to the point of no return. It was important to keep the young girl engaged in the day-to-day routines of life. Shady really seemed to like the new roommate. The girl was always singing and making jokes. Whenever she was in the room, Shady seemed to light up.

"Okay, Shady May. If you say so. I'm sick of looking at this math book anyway. I'm going to burn this thing?. If I go to breakfast I'm afraid I'll get too full and be sleepy when I'm taking my test," Tara said, responding to Mrs. Lenny's surprising decision to give her advice.

"Girl, take yo' ass over there and show them what you working with. Are you a man or a mouse, motherfucker? Man or mouse?" Becky added her two cents to the conversation while peeking out from under the covers.

"That's right, Tara. Are you a man or mouse? Man or a mouse?" Shady repeated. All of the roommates knew how important the test was to Tara, and they all wanted to be supportive in their own way. The connection that they felt in that moment was undeniable.

"I'm going to walk you over to your class and then I'm going for a walk. I need to get myself a plan like you, Tara. I've been lying up in this bed feeling sorry for myself, mad at the world because my baby had to go into foster care. It ain't anybody's fault but my own that I didn't make a different choice," Shady shared, looking sad, as she gathered her items to take a shower.

"Well, we all got to start getting ourselves some more choices that don't include loss and separation. I know that much for sure, Shady May," Tara said, grabbing Shady by the hands and dancing her around the room. Everybody was glad to see Shady up. Since everybody was already up, the roommates all decided to go to breakfast together before Tara's class. It felt good to be united around a positive cause. Mrs. Lenny offered to walk with Shady after lunch if she wanted some company. Becky offered to volunteer in the kitchen with Creeper to make sure the roommates got extra breakfast, so they would be full to start this important day.

Becky gave the other roommates hell most days with her out-of-control ways. She knew Mrs. Lenny was not used to being around black people. Poor Mrs. Lenny would lose it whenever Becky talked hard to her. The uncomfortable look on her face was funny to Becky. Most days Becky would wild out just to see Mrs. Lenny squirm. She would tell some crazy-ass stories about some scandalous shit just to gas Mrs. Lenny up. Becky gave the old lady a hard time because she didn't understand the sheltered white woman from small-town Newark, Ohio. Not one bit. But on that day, they put their differences aside and united like a family sending their siblings off on the first day of school. The love and support guided them out the door to conquer whatever lay in their paths.

Chapter Twenty-nine

The sun shined down on the bronze-colored arms of Julio. Months had passed and he was finally able to tolerate the immaturity of the young kids in the federal joint doing time alongside him. You used to be able to count on the fed joint to be a different level of incarceration. It was reserved for seasoned criminals, not your bottom-feeders, but crack cocaine was changing that now. Federal sentencing laws were making it easier for the big dogs to step on some mid-level narcotics state cases. The rookie hustlers were getting booked solid and filling the joints up across the country. They ruled the yard but respected Julio. The crazy-ass Latino scared the hell out of most of them. He just didn't give a fuck about shit.

Julio sat at a bench with only his baby on his mind. He couldn't wait to answer her last letter to him. Her letters were like a lifeline to his soul. He read her last letter over and over again before folding it neatly and placing it in the envelope on the picnic table. He couldn't wait to start his letter to her.

Dearest Tara,

Baby, I pray you are well considering where you are right now. I have been upbeat lately because of you. The last letter you wrote to me lifted me up. I was so afraid you gave up on us when you didn't write me back after my last letter. I really couldn't even be mad at you, especially after I blamed you for what happened to us. I feel like we got a shot this time, if we communicate with each other. We have to talk to each other and not be afraid to say what's on our minds. That has always been our downfall, boo. We just react without talking to each other. I used to think that shit was so cute when you would fly off the handle on some dumb-ass shit always ready to get big on a grown-ass man all the time. You never backed down. Not never. We just started taking that shit too far. We allowed that negative energy in our home and it moved in. We had our own little piece of paradise. We made the mistake of not valuing what we had, which was a once-in-a-lifetime love.

Do you remember right before I got arrested I asked you how you would feel if I had to lay it down for awhile? I could tell by the look on your face that shit frightened you. I wish I had been honest and discussed what you were feeling that morning. I was scared for us too but I didn't want to acknowledge that shit. Tara, I was having these reoccurring dreams that I was going to lose you. That shit would fuck me up every time I had the fucking dream. I think when I saw myself losing you to drugs it was like my nightmare coming true in real life.

Since the moment I first saw you, I have always felt like we were destined to be together forever. I just felt it deep inside of me. I am learning to trust that now. I used to just covet the love we shared, like it was something to be possessed and locked away for only me. Love has to be set free, baby, to live and breathe. It is healthiest when it is allowed to find its way, trusting as it goes along its journey. We locked our gift away behind close doors. It was never given a chance to grow into a mature love. I want us to have a fighting chance this second time around and we can if we work at it together.

I'm so proud of you for going to school while you're in there. You are one of the smartest people I know. It's so smart of you to use the system to your advantage. Take the time you are forced to be separated from the real world and use it for your own good. It's going to take us educating ourselves on where the bumps in the road are, so we can avoid them as we encounter them along our journey. I've been doing the same thing on my end here. I want to be a better husband for you and a better man for myself. That's important to me. I wish I had slowed down to really learn that shit better when we was together. I've been reading some relationship books in here. They kinda deep too. I'm starting to understand some of the mistakes we made as newlyweds. Start going to the library if you're not already and check out some of the books they have on relationships. They have stuff in them books that be on point with a lot of shit for real, Tara. We owe it to our ourselves to find out all we can about being married because I plan on be with you forever so we might as well learn how to be the happiest married couple ever.

I talked to my attorney last week; he told me he received some papers from immigration about me proving my citizenship in this country. I may have to go to a hearing to establish that shit. These motherfuckers don't never let up. They always trying to find a way to keep you under their thumb with some bullshit over your head. I got a daughter who's a United States citizen and I'm married to a citizen. That alone will keep me here. But if they just want to take me on a trip to the courthouse they can.

Anyway, I am so happy to know you still love me. Holding on to your love pulls me through the days in here. I am starting to feel like we're going to make it. I dream of us at the beach, on a beautiful sunny summer day, enjoying the sights and sounds of the ocean. The waves from the sea spill onto the shore, washing across our bodies in the sand, as we lay in each other's arms holding each other until the sun goes down. In my dream we both realize we have overcome great tragedy getting to our moment in the sun.

Then the camera zooms out on the shot like in the movies and the credits roll. You start hearing that happily-ever-after music as the people in the audience start getting up from their seats. They leave the theater knowing that a good man was lucky enough to find the girl of his dreams and the couple is going to be together forever.

Your love keeps me on some soft-ass shit all the time, Tara. I love your ass so much. My dreams of you keep me going. I have a few pictures of you that I stare at constantly. I have memorized every curve and feature of your body. My eyes soak you in daily from your pictures. I can close my eyes and visualize you without even looking at the picture now. I just need you to know how much you mean to me. I will never let you doubt my love for you again, darling. Never doubt that you have a man who loves and misses you. Until I can give you all the things you deserve, I send my love and my promise that we will be together.

Your Husband,
Julio

Chapter Thirty

Things were tense throughout the institution. Everybody walked around on eggshells because a gun had been found on the compound. That was a sure sign of a hit being ordered on somebody in population or in the administration. The entire population was placed on security lockdown and limited movement was allowed in the prison until a full investigation was ordered into the breach in security of the prison. It had been weeks since the inmates had been allowed out of their cells for anything other than showers and one phone call a day. All meals were served in their cells. Inmates known for being violent were either moved to isolation or separated in their cells from other prisoners. Being caged up in the tiny cells did something to the inmates. Some men couldn't stand being caged up. They would freak out and attack any and every thing.

Scott understood their rage. When a man feels hopeless, with nothing to live for and no connections to the outside world, he starts to feel like he ain't got nothing to lose, like he has lost everything already. The system has a way of creating way too many "I don't give a fuck" motherfuckers, Scott thought, pacing his cell. He was feeling anxious but he refused to let his mind slip to a dark place.

Love has a saving power that can rescue a man from the darkest of places, and his love for Tara kept him from his demons. He sat back down on his bottom bunk with a sigh. He was the only person in the two-man cell. His new roommate had been moved out the day after the lockdown. When the COs came and told the Kid Rock white boy to pack it up, they were just starting to get cool with each other. He pulled the letter from Tara out from his underneath his bunk and read it again. The letter gave him strength. The worn-out Koran that Brother Muhammad gave him before the lockdown was also starting to give him hope. The Holy Book instructed on discipline and faith. It was teaching him how to believe. He was convinced that his newfound belief gave him hope that he and Tara would be together someday. The letter from her was confirmation that she cared for him.

She told him how much he meant to her. Also, she mentioned that she was happy about school and she had plans for getting some help with her drug problem. He could tell by the tone of her letter that she had settled in to doing time and not letting the time do her. It had taken him a while to learn that lesson. They were getting too old to keep making the same hardheaded mistakes in life. Tara worried him when she took forever to write him back. He figured it was because of the crazy-ass letters he wrote her from back in the hole. He got caught up back there for a minute on some madness, but he was grateful to Allah that he didn't give up completely.

CO Ward walked past his door making her rounds on the shift. She agreed to work overtime because she knew she would be assigned to her baby's range. She completed her rounds and began working on inmate supply requests. Ward used the excuse to linger at her man's cell door. Security was tight during the lockdown. She couldn't risk being caught on camera socializing with him. She would have to steal a quick hello for now until the damn order was lifted. She missed him like crazy since he had been moved from isolation. It was taking her longer than she hoped to get moved back into general population now that he wasn't back in the hole.

"Baby, I miss my daddy so much. I can't wait until I can be with you again. My pussy misses you too, Daddy," CO Ward whispered through the door to Scott in her best sexy voice as she passed toilet paper through to him.

The sound of a woman's voice startled him at first, but then he recognized the whining voice of CO Ward at his door. He had been lucky in avoiding her up to now. He knew it wasn't going to be long before she found a way to get to sniff after him like a dog in heat. He had created a monster out of the mark CO. The pest of a woman was hooked on him desperately. Scott could not shake her. He was going to have to break her heart. He hoped she was bullshitting when she was hollering that "love" shit when they were handling their business back in the hole.

"I hear you out there, girl. You better be careful. You know they got the joint on lockdown," Scott reminded her, hoping to scare his fatal attraction away.

"I miss you so much, baby. Do you miss me? I can't wait 'til I can get some more of that good dick up inside me. Let me just look at it real quick. Pull it out and let me see it real quick before I leave," Ward begged, hoping for a cheap thrill through the door. She missed his touch so much; anything would do until she could get her hands on him the way she wanted.

"When is the lockdown going to get lifted? I can't even think, being locked in here around the clock. I need some exercise. This shit is cruel. Y'all got grown men caged up like animals. What you think happens when you put a man in a desperate environment? He does desperate things," Scott warned the officer. The look in his eyes frightened her.

"I'll try and find out what I can about when the security order is going to be lifted. They're close to finding out where the gun came from, so it shouldn't be much longer." CO Ward shared what she knew with him.

Unfortunately for her she was in love with a flip-out artist. It didn't take much for him to go the fuck off. That was part of what attracted her to him. But she couldn't risk him flipping out while the institution was on lock and she was all up in his door. There wasn't no telling what his crazy ass might say when he was flipping out if he decided to clock on her.

Ward mumbled, "I got to go. I think somebody's coming," and got as far away from that door as her legs would carry her. She needed her job, and she knew when to walk away and when to run. He wasn't going anywhere soon. She would have to be patient and wait until she could get moved back to his side of the prison. He was all hers.

Bad decisions brought consequences. It was a bad decision for him to play with a person's heart. Now he was stuck, and he damn sure wasn't going to tell her she was just something to do. There was no telling what she might do if he told her the truth. He was going to have to let her down easy. He really didn't want to hurt the poor girl, but he already had when he acted and didn't have his head on straight. That shit was fucked up.

He was used to using women and discarding them when he was done. That's what you did where he came from. But now he was trying to be a bigger man. Scott knew that he had to stop playing all the time and get serious about changing his life if he was ever going to deserve a woman like Tara. He loved her too much to let her go through the hell of prison and come out and not have a shot at being with the man who could make her happy for a lifetime. They both deserved that happiness. He believed with all of his heart that Tara was the women for him and he was the man for her. But, if by some unlucky twist of fate she was destined to be with someone else, he would be willing to accept that if it meant she could be happy.

Scott decided once and for all to sit down and write her a letter. He would finally put his true feelings on the line. He had to tell her that she was his everything, that he loved her for so long without ever telling her that it hurt him to keep the secret any longer. He needed to know if there was a chance for them to be together. He had to move his life forward. They were both stuck in a place where they were stunted in their growth as men and women. They were waking up and realizing that they had to grow into adults.

Scott reached underneath his bed and pulled out a notepad and a pencil. He flipped it open on his lap, wrote Dear Tara on the first line and then froze. It was easy to say how he felt about her in his head and to his brothers, but actually writing it out to her was a difficult task. With the smell of CO Ward's perfume still lingering in the stale air of his cell, Scott couldn't help feeling guilty. He knew that Ward wanted to hear him say all the things that he was about to write to Tara, but he never would. Ward and Tara were completely different. Ward was a "homie, lover, friend" but she wasn't the kind of woman that he could actually care about. Scott knew that he loved Tara and wanted to be with her on a deeper level. He just had to find the right words to tell her the truth.

"*Assalaamu alaykum*," Brother Muhammad said, approaching Scott's cell. He wore a kufi, thick glasses, and walked with a cane. After fifty-eight hard years, Muhammad's movements were slow but his mind was strong. He had been in and out of institutions since childhood and was serving a life sentence, but his faith had taught him to live each day as a strong leader and example for the men incarcerated with him.

Scott quickly set his notebook onto the bed, rose to his

feet, and reached out his hand to Mohammed. "*Wa `Alaykum as-Salaam*," he replied, shaking his visitor's hand.

"I didn't see you at Taleem today," Muhammad said with concern in his tone.

"Everything's cool," Scott said. "I've just been doing a lot of thinking, you know? On the outside, I had a girl that I was really starting to have feeling for. Her name is Tara. Whenever we were together, everything just felt right. It was like we were from the same place, going down the same path for a while. She understood me better than any other women I've ever known. I haven't stopped thinking about her since I got locked up. I want to put it all on paper but I don't even know where to start."

"It sounds like you just said it all," Muhammad laughed. It was rare for Scott to show his sentimental side, but Muhammad had become a father figure to him. "You've mentioned this young lady, Tara, before. It's obvious that you care for her."

"Yeah," Scott said nodding. "I just want her to be able to see it."

"You've also mentioned that she has a husband. Am I right?" Muhammad added. Scott could already tell what was coming. He trusted Muhammad and knew that he would speak the truth, even if it was hard to hear. "How do you know that your feelings are stronger than those between a husband and his wife?"

"I don't," Scott replied. "I mean, we were kickin' it before and it seemed like maybe she felt the same way, but there's no way to know for sure. I only know what I'm feelin'."

"I see," Muhammad laughed. "So, your plan is to just walk up to her, sweep her off of her feet and ride off into the sunset with her like in a fairy tale?"

"Something like that," Scott replied. "If she's still feeling me then, yeah."

"Let me ask you this, then. What can you offer her now, as you are, Brother?" Muhammad said, speaking each word with purpose. "You are growing, but you still have a lot to learn. If you truly care about Tara, you will do what is in her best interest, not yours. You cannot have an honest, committed relationship with her until you are whole and satisfied with yourself. Are you there yet?"

"I don't know," Scott said, shrugging.

"I can't tell you what to write, but I encourage you to be honest and to allow her the opportunity to grow as you are doing now," Muhammad said. He reached out and shook Scott's hand. "I hope you find the right words."

Chapter Thirty-one

Months passed at Franklin Pre-release Center. Winter settled in around the release center like a welcomed friend. The holidays were fast approaching and everything just seemed hopeful to Tara. Christmas still remained her favorite time of the year; it was a time of giving more of yourself and spending time with good friends and family. The move from the farm turned out to be just the right spark Tara needed to get her life moving in the right direction. The support of friends in a positive way allowed her to lean to that which was good. She'd started attending Narcotics Anonymous with her crew and they all were learning positive skills from each other. Tara enjoyed sharing her experiences with her peers and realizing that most of the women, despite which neighborhood they came from, shared similar experiences both as women and people living in poverty.

The NA group started a book club a few weeks after Tara joined and all the women were beginning to expand their minds with knowledge on issues important to their recovery. They chose books that dealt with women's issues, and they all agreed to add one book a month to the list that told the African American struggle. This was important to Tara because she was determined to discover her history. Her GED instructor opened up a whole new world for her when he gave her a book called *Convicted in the Womb* by Carl Upchurch. His book opened up a door to a new passion and kept Tara at the library soaking in all she could about her experience as a person living black in America.

Once Tara completed her GED test she was assigned a job. She was employed as a visiting hall porter. Her job was to set up and break down the visiting hall after the daily visits. Her work crew was also responsible for cleaning the bathrooms in the entrance area to the prison and the visitor restrooms. Four women were assigned to Tara's shift. They divided the work evenly. Their immediate supervisor was an old no-nonsense white man named Mr. Hardy. The seasoned officer was a few years shy of retirement. He'd spent the last thirty years of his life working in corrections. He'd seen it all over the years. When Hardy first began his journey, he was bright-eyed and optimistic, believing that his job was to rehabilitate the individuals sentenced to do time in the State of Ohio. He was confident that he could do that job with ease. But over the years, the job got harder and harder. Now, the old dreamer was just happy if nobody got hurt on his shift and he left the institution with his life at the end of each day.

He was a military man with a strong respect for pride and an honest day's work. The tall, silver-haired officer demanded respect the minute he opened his mouth. Tara's first day of orientation for her new job assignment convinced her on the spot that whatever a good employee looked like was a question she no longer had to ask herself. Tara hung on to every word her teacher spoke that first day. He would explain things and then allow them to practice what he'd just showed them. If they didn't get it right the first time, he would repeat the lesson, pointing out mistakes along the way. Within weeks, Tara was his star employee. She looked forward to going to work each day to learn something new from her teacher, and she always wanted him to be proud of her. Hardy wasn't one for praise, but every now and then, when she went above and beyond the call of duty, he would look over his gray army-issued glasses and say, "Nice job, young lady," and then he would go back to his task at the big important desk at the entrance to the institution. No one came or went without having to check in and out with Mr. Hardy on his shift.

He ran his post like the important assignment that it was. The security of the prison was a very important role and it needed to be treated as such. Tara rushed from dorm one fifteen minutes early for her shift because she didn't want to be late and interrupt the order of the day.

"Where are you rushing off to, Tara?" CO Clark said while walking up behind her on the walkway. Clark was proud of Tara. It was rare to see a new girl, as popular as her, get on track, doing the right things as quickly as she did. Clark heard old man Hardy bragging about her earlier in the day, when she arrived for her shift early and ready to work. If Hardy was bragging about one of the women, they deserved the compliment. CO Clark was in charge of orientation for the new arrivals at the facility. She prided herself in being able to recognize the new arrivals that might need extra attention. Clark had her money on Tara being one of those women; she just hadn't figured out what type attention the popular, friendly girl would need.

"Happy Monday, Mrs. Clark. Where you going this morning? You know you don't be back here working with the inmates. Are you going to be assigned to a dorm?" Tara questioned one of the few COs who she respected and felt cared about the well-being of the women sentenced to do time.

"No, girl, you know I don't be back here fooling with y'all knuckleheads. I just finished delivering holiday boxes to the captain's office in dorm five. I'm going back to the mail room. I'm not going to be back here all day with everybody asking me every five minutes about their boxes. I've been bringing

Christmas boxes back and forth over here all morning," Clark offered, walking in the direction of the administration building where Tara worked.

"Mr. Hardy called me over to talk about something. I don't know what he wants but it must be important. You know Mr. Hardy doesn't waste time," Tara explained while walking with Clark. The dorms were busy as always that morning. Groups of women gathered on each porch decorating the front doors of each dorm for the holiday crafts festival. Each dorm would host a holiday activity or craft fair during the week leading up to Christmas day. It was a big deal to see which dorm would win the holiday decorating contest each year. The winning dorm was first called to meal time for the rest of the year.

"Did you see my name on one of the boxes you brought over this morning?" Tara questioned Mrs. Clark on the way through the brick hall of the administration building. The building was off limits to the women in general population unless they were called to its secret halls. The women were only allowed in the building to the point where commissary was housed. The small institution store was located next to central food services, and across the hall in a one story building was the institution's library and the offices of the warden and captain. The other half of the building contained conference rooms, visiting halls, and offices. Once you passed the forbidden area, you had to have clearance to go beyond that point. Tara felt important as she strode confidently past that point.

"Well, since you mention it, I may have seen your name. You can let the other women know that the captain's office will start handing out holiday boxes after the lunch count," Clark informed Tara before turning down the hall that led to the warden's office. "You better hurry and go see what Mr. Hardy wants," she whispered over her shoulder, respecting the administration building's professional environment.

The two parted ways and Tara hurried to see why she had been summoned to see the Wizard. The long, winding hallway was lined with inspirational framed pictures. Tara knew the bold works of empowerment well. There was a picture for vision, wisdom, knowledge, and faith. Each picture displayed a scene on some unnamed body of water that brought to mind tranquility and a peace that passed all understanding. Tara wasn't sure how to obtain all the beautiful gifts of the spirit but she knew she was on a journey to finding out. Every day, when she came to work, as she cleaned the visiting hall and scrubbed the toilets, she imagined herself laying on one of the peaceful shores in the pictures, finally at peace and safe in her lover's arms.

"Good morning, Mr. Hardy, my dorm CO told me you wanted to see me." Tara announced her arrival to her supervisor once he let her through the large gray security door that separated the prison from the outside world.

"Have a seat, Tara; I will be with you shortly," Mr. Hardy instructed, checking his watch for the time. Tara quickly took her seat in the chairs positioned directly in front of his desk. The metal legs of the burgundy office chairs scraped across the floor as Tara nervously sat down. She was thrown off by him calling her by her first name because he usually called the women by their last names.

Tara glanced up at the old-fashioned clock nailed to the wall to check the time. She had rushed right over. She hoped she hadn't kept him waiting.

Mr. Leonard Hardy tided his work station. He returned his letter opener with the eagle's head to its rightful place in the right-hand corner of the top drawer on the right side of the desk. He then lined up the morning visiting passes in neat rolls of five across the counter next to the sign-in sheet. After that, he pulled five number-two pencils from the supply cabinet to the left of the desk. He had meticulously sharpened the pencils to perfection at some point in time. Tara watched in amazement at the attention to detail.

When he was finally done he acknowledged her sitting there in her chair. "We are extending visiting hours for the holidays. With the additional hours comes additional responsibility. We are all being asked to take on more job duties. With that being said, starting today, I will be increasing your responsibilities on your shift. You will now be responsible for training the additional staff assigned to the visiting hall. You will now have a staff of eight that will report directly to you. I am counting on you, Tara, to train them well, as they will be a reflection of our department. I will obtain additional responsibilities as well, so I'll need to be free to work on other important duties for the institution. Can I count on you to share the workload?" Mr. Hardy asked Tara, confident in her answer. He only waited for her response as a common courtesy.

"Yes, Mr. Hardy, you can count on me to do whatever you need me to do to make sure we operate smoothly during the added holiday hours. Thank you for trusting me with the added responsibility. I won't let you down," Tara offered, hoping she sounded intelligent in her reply. She wanted him to know that she valued the opportunity and he could trust her to do the right thing.

"That's what I wanted to hear. There's a small desk in the supply closet. You can begin using that as your work area. One last thing: the warden's office delivered these papers to me on your behalf. They are from the Department of Education." Mr. Hardy reached into the drawer where he had put the letter opener, pulled out a bright white business-sized envelope and extended it to Tara, who sat stunned in the seat before him.

The letter in his hand became the only thing in the room. Time stood still.

Finally, Tara reached for the envelope. With great care, she opened the letter and pulled the long-awaited official test scores out. She looked at the information on the piece of paper for a few seconds and then she screamed. Before she realized she had even done it, she jumped up and hugged Mr. Hardy.

"I passed my GED test, Mr. Hardy. I passed! I can't believe I passed. I really didn't think I would and I did." Tara was ecstatic. She had conquered her biggest fear, getting her education, and now there was nothing she could not accomplish, no mountain she could not climb. She had survived crack cocaine, lost love, and nearly being swallowed up in the belly of the beast. In that very moment, she obtained an unwavering faith in the impossible. In that moment she realized all things were possible to those who believe.

Tara's unexpected hug caught Mr. Hardy off guard. He was happy for her and he shared in the celebration. "There is nothing you can't accomplish with good old-fashioned hard work. Don't ever forget that the things you work hard for are what last," Mr. Hardy explained, regaining his composure.

Chapter Thirty-two

The sights and sounds of the holiday were alive and well on Kohr Street. Each house in the middle-class neighborhood was dressed up for the season. The friendly, yet highly competitive Christmas decorating competition was in full swing up and down the block. The annual three-house race to the finish line was heating up this year. Everyone on the block knew the coveted trophy would be awarded to either the Pollards, the Davises or Mama Gracie's house. In the eyes of Mama Gracie and Granddaddy, they had already won the friendly competition. The preparation for the holidays began up and down the block right after Halloween. Every Saturday in the fall, home owners could be seen on roofs and scaling the sides of their homes, adding inflatable reindeers and snowmen to their homes. This year was no different.

M&M pulled her black and silver with red stripes Pontiac, Grand Am, down the street. The neighbors had agreed a few years ago to add lights to the trees along the curb. The feeling of arriving at a red-carpet event came over M&M as she drove slowly past the beautifully decorated homes on the street. Once in front of her mother's house, she pulled her car to a stop, parked her prize Grand Am, and killed the engine. She was excited to see her parents; she couldn't get to the front door fast enough.

Walking up the stairs to the front door, it was odd not seeing her father sitting in his favorite chair on the front porch.

Something awfully important had to be keeping him from his guard post. Nothing happened on his watch unless he had a say in it. Mama Grace never locked her front door, morning, noon or night. You could count on 1520 Kohr Place being open for business at all times. You could stop by at one or two in the morning, get out of your car and find someone on the front porch or in the living room waiting to greet you.

"Hey there, sister. Happy holidays," Mrs. Davis yelled from her driveway as she pulled holiday groceries from her trunk. Then she turned toward her grandson who was sitting on her porch playing a portable video game. "Go get your brother Li'l Darrell to help with these groceries. We going to be all day fooling with you" Mrs. Davis scolded him, pulling over-stuffed Kroger bags from her trunk in the driveway next to the house.

"Happy holidays to you too, Mrs. Davis. How you doing? Your house sure does look pretty," M&M complimented her mother's longtime next-door neighbor. Mrs. Davis lived on Kohr Place almost as long as Mama Gracie and Granddaddy. The two families ran the block. Nothing went down on the block without their say-so. They kept a clean, proud block. You respected their street and their property or you didn't come down Kohr Place at all. Theirs was a neighborhood where people looked after one another.

"I'm fine, honey. Getting ready for Christmas dinner. The stores are running over with last-minute shoppers. If you haven't been to the store you need to get there soon. They're almost out of hams. You sure look nice. You going to church?" Mrs. Davis said, carrying bags up onto her porch. Her porch had so many Christmas decorations scattered around it that there was barely room for her to walk.

"Mama and I did our shopping yesterday. It was just as bad then. I'm going to a homecoming service they're having at her church. You like this suit? It's washable silk. Can you believe that?" M&M offered. It had been ages since she'd last been inside the church house and she wanted to look her best. Her mother had been worrying her for months about going to church. Whenever Mama started pressing her to go to church, she took that as a sign that she needed covering. God knows she needed prayer for a lot of reasons. M&M and the rest of her brothers and sisters were raised believing in God. It was a way of life for them growing up. Whenever M&M was feeling anxious about life or anything else, she ran to the safety of Mama's house and Mama ran all her children to the protecting arms of God.

Gospel music filled the air and rushed over M&M as she opened the front door of her parents' house. So many feelings stirred up inside her. No matter how far she roamed, there was no place like home. Everywhere she looked there was some sign of Christmas. Each doorway was covered in old Christmas cards. Garland and white lights adorned the mantle piece, and a six-foot-tall white pine Christmas tree took up the corner on the right of the fireplace with presents spilled from under it and across the floor.

"Look at how beautiful you look. Your mama done talked you into going with her over to that bootleg preacher's church, ain't she? I been telling y'all for years, you don't have to follow no man. The church is in your heart. I'm at church every day in my heart," M&M's father greeted her from his favorite chair in front of the fireplace.

"Hi, Daddy. Merry Christmas!" M&M rushed over to the chair and kissed her father on the cheek as he sat trying to get a string of old-fashioned bulb lights to turn on. The question was where in the world was he going to put the lights; you couldn't get another thing on the tree if you tried.

"Don't go rushing it. We got two more days until Christmas.

I did most of the shopping already but I ain't get nothing for them great-great grandkids. We going to have to run by the store on our way home from church," Mama Gracie said and kissed M&M on the forehead before putting some holy water by the front door. Mama was dressed in her very important white nurse uniform, complete with matching nurse's shoes and the funny-four corner hat nurses wear. She looked so official; you knew she was in charge. Mama was both mother of the church and head nurse of the missionary board. Hers was the very important job of providing fresh handkerchiefs and icecold water to the pastor during every sermon, both home and away. Gracie was a valued, upstanding member of the Temple of Faith Church of Deliverance. Her life revolved around her service to the ministry.

"Mama, I didn't plan on all that. I was just planning on going to church and maybe having dinner with y'all. Now you got me all at the store. Besides, you ain't got nowhere to put another thing under that tree," M&M teased her mother, shaking her head at the Christmas tree. Everybody they knew had a gift under the tree. It was the season to give and receive love.

"Why you think I'm sitting right here guarding the sucker? All my money is on the floor. Bet I don't move from this spot," Granddaddy grumbled, pulling his fifth of Jack Daniel's whiskey from underneath his chair. He then loosened the brown paper bag from around the bottle and took a long drink.

The parking lot at the Temple of Faith Baptist church was completely full. M&M was on it; she wasn't even getting ready to have to walk from far away. She double-parked on the grass at the entrance and dared somebody to tow her car. She was immaculately dressed in her black silk two-piece suit and wore her hair pulled back in a tight bun at the nape of her neck. Her Hanes Barely There sheer toed stockings shimmered in the sunlight and they were the perfect shade for her shoes and clutch bag. A single strand of yellow pearls completed her look. M&M didn't go to church often. She didn't have time for all the people who filled the pews and sat in judgment of everyone coming through the door. The one place created for wounded people now wanted everyone to arrive whole and live up to what they decided a person who loves God should look like. M&M refused to be defined, especially by hypocrites.

As always, the house was rocking. The Temple of Faith was worship central. The sanctuary was packed. There wasn't a seat to be found anywhere. Mama Gracie marched to the front of the church with her eldest daughter and waited for the people already seated in the first row to make room for her and her guest. Without Mama Gracie having to say a word, the two lead trustees of the church instantly rose to their feet and prepared a place for the mother of the church and her daughter.

The voices of deliverance got up and led the congregation in praise and worship. You couldn't find a dry eye in the house. The saints had forgotten about themselves; they were concentrating on Him and they danced to show it. Mama Gracie never took her seat. She immediately took the holy water to the pulpit, discreetly handed Bishop Hairston his crisp white handkerchief, and then she tiptoed away from the platform. The choir broke out into a powerful high note in unison and Mama Gracie broke out into a shout with the other saints and started dancing around the room. People danced, sang, hugged, cried, and ran around the church, each one expressing their love for God in their own way.

The lovefest and worship session lasted well over an hour. After the congregation finally finished expressing its gratitude to the Lord Jesus for making a way out of no way in their individual lives, they finally sat down and prepared to receive the message from their bishop.

M&M sat in her seat next to her mother feeling like a kid as Mama Gracie pressed a tissue in her hand to wipe her eyes. The emotions filling the room moved M&M. Church always did that to her. She never knew what to do after the service was over.

"Today, I'd like to choose a text that I think a lot of people in this room need to think about. That text is He is Well Able," Bishop Roger Hairston announced to the saints of God. The bishop was a Lionel Richie dead-on look-alike. He came from a long line of preachers who were talented beyond measure. The Temple of Faith was a congregation of about one hundred and fifty members, consisting of mostly African Americans, who had faithfully followed the ministry for years. They looked forward to worshipping together on Sundays and sharing praise reports that would bring the house to tears. Everyone sat listening to the word and applying it to their own lives. Most of them made a vow to do better and be better.

"I need you to hear me today when I tell you that every negative situation is an opportunity for you to glory God. If you get in the will of God, he will turn your negatives into positives. If you have something you need God to turn around in your life, join me here at the altar as the choir sings, *"I came for Deliverance/Deliverance I receive/You said you deliver me and that's what I believe'*. Sing it with me if you will." The bishop took his crisp white handkerchief out of his pocket and wiped the sweat from his forehead.

People began rising from their seats and joining the man of God at the altar. Family members began joining their loved ones as well. The choir hummed quietly in the background as the ministers from the pulpit prayed with people in the congregation.

"Somebody came here today because someone very close to their heart is far away this holiday season. God sent me to tell you that he has heard your cry and dispatched angels around those that you love. From this day forth, your life will never be the same," Bishop whispered into the microphone in a sincere voice.

M&M suddenly sprang from her seat and fell at the altar crying. Mama Gracie joined her daughter on her knees and prayed for her children.

Chapter Thirty-three

For every action, there is a reaction. Everything you do becomes a part of who you are and your history. The beauty of that is you have the ability to write your own ending every day. Each experience molds us in one way or another, shaping us into the person we will become. Some say a child's character is formed in the first few years of their life. We spend the rest of the child's life molding that character. In the early stages of life, many of us are given the opportunity to be loved, nurtured, and adored. Then we are coached to the adults we become. But without that love in childhood, for many others, prison can become a refuge and saving grace. Franklin Prerelease became that saving grace for Tara. After much struggle she was starting to believe she was an asset; a person with something to offer the world.

Obtaining her GED was something she did on her own. It was something that she accomplished without the help of anyone else, and being able to say that empowered her. Going to Group on a regular basis reinforced her newfound empowerment. She was preparing to lead her first group and she was extremely nervous about speaking in front of an audience. Cricket proved to be a godsend. She made it her own responsibility to make sure Tara stayed focused on her reentry plan. The NA group created individual vision boards with the women to encourage them to think about and visualize their futures. The greatest lesson Tara learned from the months she spent in the group was that there was someone bigger and greater than herself. Her life had meaning and it was connected to a bigger picture.

Tara was on a quest to find where her piece of the puzzle fit. Each time she connected with people on their own personal journey, her spirit leaped. It was the weirdest feeling for her. She began truly connecting to the people along the road of life for the first time.

She loved everybody around her and wanted to figure out how she could start making up for some of the wrongs she had done. So much work needed to be done to repair all the things she'd broken. At times she didn't know where to began, but prison was teaching her patience. Every day she was learning how to wait and trust more.

Her time at the prison was coming to a close. She had served a lot of her time behind the walls in true Tara fashion, acting a fool and enjoying the party, and a significant portion was spent on self-discovery and forming a new relationship with God. Somewhere along the journey, a woman stood where a girl once was, and that woman counted her blessings, glad to be alive. This time around, she planned to stop long enough to enjoy the view. She would never take her freedom for granted again.

Nobody knew what the future held for her and her beloved Julio. Fate dealt them yet another blow. The federal government decided to get one final blow in before they released him from his five-year sentence. He had been shipped by immigration to a federal holding facility for illegal aliens whose citizenship was being challenged. They were trying to launch a campaign to have him put out of the country. Every time Tara thought of that shit she laughed to keep from crying. This latest obstacle convinced her even more that they were meant to be together because the negative forces of life were working too hard to keep them apart.

The hopeless dreamer laid on the top bunk of her college of higher learning, staring at a picture of her and Julio, dressed to kill on a Friday night at the club. In the picture, she was sitting on his lap with his arms wrapped around her and he was planting a kiss on her left shoulder. Julio's eyes were closed and the look on his face said, "I have found the girl of my dreams."

The new believer believed in the impossible now. She would be with her man again. Tara believed that nothing would keep her from him.

"I see you up there reminiscing, girlfriend," Becky teased her roommate, looking over at her from the other top bunk bed. Tara had three days and a wake-up until her release day. She couldn't wait to see her family. She hadn't seen most of her family members in years, especially because the cost of their lifestyles kept them from showing up to places that the police frequented. Too many people they knew had been hemmed up just trying to see about a motherfucker.

"You know what it is, Becky. I'm up here missing everybody like crazy. I can feel them, see them, and smell them, girl. This is my baby," Tara shared, kissing the photo and holding it up for Becky to see. She then returned the photo to its home under her pillow. Tears filled up in her eyes as she spoke. They slid down her face and landed on the legs of her track pants.

"If anybody got a shot at making it out there, you do, Tara. You got so many things working in your favor. How many people you know with two men who are both crazy about them? Plus you have your family," Becky reminded Tara of all the things she had going for her once she left the prison.

The same hot, salty tears filled her eyes and ran down her face once more. Tara climbed down from her bunk and sat on her lock box. She didn't realize that Mrs. Lenny was lying on her bed resting. This was unusual for her because she rarely stayed in the room.

"That's just it, Becky. My family. If I am going to stay free I have to do it separate from my family. They are the biggest part of my 'people, places, and things.' The lifestyle that my parents chose isn't healthy for my recovery. If I'm going to beat my addiction, I have to give myself a fighting chance," Tara shared her decision with her two roommates. Shady was off at parenting class working on a plan to get her baby back.

"If you're not going home to your mom's house, where you going to live? It's hard out there, Tara. You been gone for three years. You need some help. Julio's not able to be there for you and what are your plans for Scott?" Becky jumping down from her bunk, questioned Tara. She sat in the chair at the metal desk and stared Tara in her face. "Most of us don't get a love story," she continued, "most of us don't have no Camelot shit happenin' in our lives. Most of us are shot through life on a horse with no name. Shit is hard where most of us come from. We didn't get the chance to have some down people show us which way is up. Most of us have never had anybody love us right. You got a shot at that shit. And you're smart. Damn, girl, you could take the fuck over." Becky spoke to her friend seriously. Somebody deserved to have a fairy tale ending.

"She's right, Tara. You are on the right track. Don't stop working on your recovery when you leave here. You have to learn all you can about your problem so you know how to fight it. I go to the library every day to learn all I can about my problems," Mrs. Lenny shared with a faraway look on her face.

"Thank you for sharing, my preacher and teacher. I am so excited to start my new life. This time I want to get it right. I know that I love my husband and I plan to be with him forever. I have been blessed to have two amazing men who love and care about me. I will love and care about Scott always, I am confident of that, but my soul belongs to Julio. He is my everything. My marriage is a gift from God, and I will fight for it forever. It took me a while but I get it. I can't be anything to anybody until I find out how to be the best me. I think I'm on my way. I've decided to go to a transitional house for six months until I can get a job and stack some cash for my own place. Then I'll sit back and wait for my king to return," Tara described her dreams to her friends who dreamed with her.

"Don't try to do too much too fast, though. Take things one day at a time. The problem with young people is you never slow down long enough to weigh all your options. Discover what you enjoy doing and use your natural abilities to find the job that works for you," Mrs. Lenny told her. She really liked Tara; the loudmouth, talkative girl had a way of growing on people. Once you were around her you wanted to be around her again. She had a gift for drawing people together.

"Yes, Mrs. Lenny. I promise I will remember all that I've learned. I never want to walk this way again. The cost was way too high a price to pay. I've learned this lesson. Did you ever feel like you had to go through a thing to get to the best part of that thing? I really feel like I've gotten to the best of me, y'all. I feel so much wiser now," Tara said, smiling.

Just at that moment Shady burst through the door with a bunch of other women following behind her. Someone rushed in with cupcakes on a large, metal tray from the kitchen.

"We'll miss you," Shady said as Tara removed a cupcake from the tray. Inmates from different dorms arrived for Tara's going home party. Saying her good-byes and reminiscing with her friends was a bittersweet feeling. Although Tara was going home, so many amazing women who she had met were not going home. She could never forget about them.

As the party died down, a CO gave Tara her mail for the last time. There was only one item: a letter from an inmate with the last name Mitchell. Tara waited until later, when she was in her dorm for the last night, to open and read Scott's letter.

Dear Tara,

I wanted to write to you sooner but I couldn't find the right words. There's so much that I want you to know and understand but it's hard for me. You know I ain't into all that emotional shit. I just want to get some things off my chest. Even though I'm writing this letter to you as a prisoner, I'm starting to see what freedom is like. I've been real cool with a Muslim brother named Muhammad. He's been like a teacher, showing me how to take all my anger and turn it into positive energy to make myself a better man. I still have a long way to go, but I feel like I'm taking the first steps toward changing.

The last time that I wrote you a letter I was in isolation. They kept me in that bitch for months. I wanted to reach out to you but I wasn't in the right state of mind. I probably said some crazy shit. You know how it is. The only thing that kept my head up was thinking about you. Every day I saw your face and heard your voice, telling me to stay strong. It was like you were with me.

I hope you're staying strong, wherever you are now. And I truly hope that you are happy and getting treated like a queen. You deserve everything. Maybe you already found someone whot can give you what you need. I understand if your heart still belongs to another man. But if things between us are supposed to grow, it will happen in time, when we are on the same path again.

Peace be upon you always, Tara.

C. Scott Mitchell

Chapter Thirty-four

On her last morning in the pre-release center, Tara woke with excitement and a little bit of anxiety. For weeks, she had daydreamed about her first moment back in the outside world. She couldn't wait to see her family again, and to catch up with her friends, including her best friend Karen. But most of all, she anticipated seeing her husband. Unfortunately, she would have to wait a while, but she was willing to wait however long it took.

As Tara took a shower and fixed her hair, she remembered how disappointing her last letter from Julio had been, and how helpless she feLieutenant After the tragedies that took place of September 11, 2001, the United States government began its "war on terror" and Julio got caught in the crossfire. At the time of the attacks, Julio was approaching the completion of his five-year sentence for a federal drug case. Before he could even stand trial, he was transported to an immigration camp on the east coast. He passed the time fantasizing about seeing Tara again and hoping that she was thinking about him too. Each minute seemed to last for a hour in the camp. Julio watched man after man get sent out of the camp and immediately returned to his homeland. With only the clothes on their backs, men were flown back to counties around the world, to Afghanistan, Cuba, Mexico; the list went on.

After eighteen months in the camp, Julio had watched fourteen men get sent back to their nations. He even started to think he had a chance of being one of the lucky ones. But he was proven wrong on the day that he was taken before immigration officers, federal agents, and judges, sworn in and put on trial. Although he had just served five years, one of the judges, who was a xenophobic white man who had lost his daughter in a drug-related incident in the late 1980s, was eager to throw the book at Julio before the hearing even started. He was an illegal alien who had taken part in the sale and possession of narcotics. He was quickly deemed a threat to national security and ordered to be returned to Monte Cristi—Julio's birthplace.

After the trial, Julio was handcuffed and escorted out of the building by two armed U.S. Marshals. As they walked to the prisoner transportation vehicle, Julio tried to remember every moment. He was afraid that he would never step foot on U.S. soil again. He had waited so long to see his girl and now he was on his way back to the Dominican Republic without being able to say good-bye. As he was locked into the vehicle, he pictured Tara's face and prayed to someday see that face again.

Julio was flown back to where he had started with nothing but the clothes on his back. Fortunately, he had made many allies in the States who would get his belongings put back in his hands in no time. As soon as he got to his old partner's place in Santo Domingo, he wrote a postcard to Tara, asking her to visit him so they could work things out together.

Tara read the postcard every day and wondered if it was possible for a person to lay down one day and then wake up the next day on the same planet, but be experiencing the planet differently, understanding for the first time the true meaning of why we are here? Tara got it; she finally got it. The things that lasted were the things she fought for through hard work and lots of concentrated effort. She said her good-byes to her friends and the staff, then walked out of the pre-release center, hoping never to have to walk inside again. Waiting at the curb in a quiet, low-riding '76 Cadillac was Slim, Tara's father, like so many times before. With a huge smile on her face, Tara rushed over, jumped into the car and embraced him. It was hard to believe that she was finally going home, but seeing Slim made it official.

Her homecoming was a major event for her family. They welcomed her home in grand fashion, but respected her desire to do something different. Whatever it took to get their daughter back, they were willing to pay the price, whatever it might be.

Tara was surprised to find her mother was experiencing some changes of her own while she'd been away. M&M was attending church regularly with Mama Gracie. The mother-and-daughter team encouraged Tara to get connected to a church home.

During the first few months, Tara had tunnel vision. Her first goal was to find a place of her own and save money to help fight for Julio.

Today was the day when all her effort and hard work would finally release her reward. It had been nine months since Tara stepped from the gates of Franklin Pre-release. And now, in the crowded terminal of Port Columbus International Airport, sat Tara. She could hardly contain herself. Everything moved way too slowly. Did anyone understand where she was headed? Within a few hours she would truly be free, finally back in the arms of the man she loved. Getting to this moment had been an adventure for her. So many things had happened to the both of them. Tara wondered if things would be the same once they were finally together again. Would his touch feel the same as before? Would his kiss be as sweet? Would the flame that fueled their passion still burn brightly?

"Hey, is anyone sitting here?" a young college student questioned, pointing at the seat next to Tara. The waiting area at Gate 5 was overflowing with passengers waiting to board a flight to JFK Airport in New York City. The only other available seat was right next to two crying blond-haired four-year-old twin brothers who were fighting over who could sit on their mommy's lap. Everyone looked on wondering where in the world the children's father might be.

"Oh, you're fine. Nobody's sitting here. Have a seat," Tara instructed, moving her carry-on bag from the chair. She was nervous as hell to be taking such a giant leap of faith. Not only was she preparing to leave the country for the very first time in her life but she was also going to see if dreams could come true.

Her stomach was in knots. Part of her wanted to run from the airport and not look back. So much time had passed. Could they find the love they had lost? Would it be the same or different? Tara was fearful and craved the answers to the questions swimming in her head.

"I sure hope the flight is on time. I have a connecting flight and I only have thirty minutes once we land at JFK to catch my flight to Cancun. A group of us are having a bachelor party for my little brother. We lucked out and got a condo for six days for two hundred dollars. I just hope the place is not a dump," the college cutie shared, checking his boarding pass and watch all at the same time. "Where you going?" he added, rolling his eyes at the crying kids running around in front of them.

"I'm connecting to Puerto Plata in the Dominican Republic. It's my first trip over there. I'm meeting my husband for kind of a second honeymoon," Tara shared nervously, hoping the trip would prove to be just that: a second honeymoon.

"Attention passengers. We will begin boarding guests for

flight thirty-one-seventy-four to John F. Kennedy International Airport at Gate 5," a bland voice flooded the area with instructions. The room sprang to life and the ticket holders filed toward gate five. Tara joined the group at the gate with her ticket in hand, anxious to end her journey as soon as possible. From the minute she learned that her man had been deported back to his birthplace, she started planning how she would get to him. Whatever the future held for them, she had to know what it was. She could not go on without trying. She had to see him again. Their love deserved one more chance. Even though she knew everything about him, she knew she would have to get to know the new man he'd become during his incarceration.

The small airport in Puerto Plata was run like a military operation. Many planes from the United States landed there hourly and a separate part of the airport was used to process U.S. citizens through Customs. The customs officers were trained to watch for drugs and illegals entering or exiting the country. The process was too familiar to Tara. She cleared customs in record time on her way to her baby. Each step in the process brought her closer to him. It was as if she could feel him in the distance.

A line of travelers waited patiently at a checkpoint that required passengers to show their passport and picture ID to a very important gentleman in a small booth at the front of the line. Once the important security worker inspected their documents, he gave the all-clear with a nod, allowing them to continue through the gate that separated the travelers from the beautiful Republic Dominica. The line moved slowly, but Tara waited, not bothered by the time taken to process the people ahead of her. She had learned how to wait; she was forced to learn it the hard way by the experts.

When Tara's time finally came, she took a deep breath

and handed her identification papers to the security officer. He took the papers without looking at her. Once he studied the documents both back and front, he looked up at Tara. She stood there allowing him to study her features before he looked back down at her ID. Then he checked her ID against a clipboard with information she could not make out. The officer pulled two forms from a drawer and instructed her to sign them. Once she'd done that, her documents were passed back to her and she was ushered through the gate.

Groups of passengers who passed through the security checkpoint were led to another area where their suitcases were waiting for them. Tara was relieved to have passed the checkpoint without difficulty. She managed to find her luggage with as much. Before heading out of the airport, she looked around for a restroom. She'd been traveling all day and wanted to freshen up before reuniting with Julio. The locals weren't allowed in the U.S. customs area, which was controlled by the United States. The locals were forced to wait outside in a designated area for loved ones arriving to and departing from the country.

Tara entered the first restroom she spotted, quickly combed her hair, and applied fresh lipstick. She looked in the mirror at her reflection. A beautiful woman stood before her in a peach-colored sundress with the back out. Her hair was bone straight and hung freely around her face. She looked good and she knew it. She only hoped that Julio would agree.

So much time had passed since he'd last seen her. Julio really did not know if he could maintain his composure when she walked through the door. Every time the door opened to release another passenger he held his breath, hoping this time it would be her. His body craved her; he could feel her on the other side of the door. He began pacing back and forth. He thought about going and waiting on the benches along the fence but he didn't want to wrinkle his pants. He wanted to look nice for his wife. Just when he thought he could wait no more, his darling sweetheart burst from the doors that kept him from her.

The couple spotted one another instantly. Tara ran into his arms as he ran to hers. Their embrace was electric. It provided the spark that restarted both their hearts in a single moment. Julio held his wife in his arms until they were the last people standing there in the arrival area. When he finally released her to look into her eyes, she leapt into his arms, wrapping her legs around his waist. She kissed him so long and so deeply that the years just dropped away and they were finally home.

ORDER FORM
URBAN BOOKS, LLC
78 E. Industry Ct
Deer Park, NY 11729

Name: (please print):_____

Address: _____

City/State: _____

Zip: _____

QTY	TITLES	PRICE
	The Cartel	$14.95
	The Cartel#2	$14.95
	The Dopeman's Wife	$14.95
	The Prada Plan	$14.95
	Gunz And Roses	$14.95
	Snow White	$14.95
	A Pimp's Life	$14.95
	Hush	$14.95
	Little Black Girl Lost 1	$14.95
	Little Black Girl Lost 2	$14.95
	Little Black Girl Lost 3	$14.95
	Little Black Girl Lost 4	$14.95

Shipping and Handling - add $3.50 for 1st book then $1.75 for each additional book.

Please send a check payable to:

Urban Books, LLC

Please allow 4 - 6 weeks for delivery

ORDER FORM
URBAN BOOKS, LLC
78 E. Industry Ct
Deer Park, NY 11729

Name: (please print): _____

Address: _____

City/State: _____

Zip: _____

QTY	TITLES	PRICE
	16 ½ On The Block	$14.95
	16 On The Block	$14.95
	Betrayal	$14.95
	Both Sides Of The Fence	$14.95
	Cheesecake And Teardrops	$14.95
	Denim Diaries	$14.95
	Happily Ever Now	$14.95
	Hell Has No Fury	$14.95
	If It Isn't love	$14.95
	Last Breath	$14.95
	Loving Dasia	$14.95
	Say It Ain't So	$14.95

Shipping and Handling - add $3.50 for 1st book then $1.75 for each additional book.

Please send a check payable to:

Urban Books, LLC

Please allow 4 - 6 weeks for delivery

ORDER FORM
URBAN BOOKS, LLC
78 E. Industry Ct
Deer Park, NY 11729

Name: (please print): _____

Address: _____

City/State: _____

Zip: _____

QTY	TITLES	PRICE
	A Man's Worth	$14.95
	Abundant Rain	$14.95
	Battle Of Jericho	$14.95
	By The Grace Of God	$14.95
	Dance Into Destiny	$14.95
	Divorcing The Devil	$14.95
	Forsaken	$14.95
	Grace And Mercy	$14.95
	Guilty & Not Guilty Of Love	$14.95
	His Woman, His Wife His Widow	$14.95
	Illusion	$14.95
	The LoveChild	$14.95

Shipping and Handling - add $3.50 for 1st book then $1.75 for each additional book.

Please send a check payable to:

Urban Books, LLC

Please allow 4 - 6 weeks for delivery

ORDER FORM
URBAN BOOKS, LLC
78 E. Industry Ct
Deer Park, NY 11729

Name: (please print):_____

Address: _____

City/State: _____

Zip: _____

QTY	TITLES	PRICE

Shipping and Handling - add $3.50 for 1st book then $1.75 for each additional book.

Please send a check payable to:

Urban Books, LLC

Please allow 4 - 6 weeks for delivery

Notes

Notes

Notes